The Chronicles of Fire and Ice

The Revealing

Dexx Peay

Dedication

Imagination is more important than knowledge

—Albert Einstein

This book is dedicated to SSG Thomas Mink and Robert Williams, for being great role models and teaching me to never give up.

For my awesome brothers who have always been there for me;

Chris G.
Kentavian R.
Doni M.
Joel W.
Matt R.

Thank You

The Beginning

Chapter 1
Dylan

I smiled the whole way home. I was never out this late on any night, much less a school night, but this night was special. I remembered to turn the headlights off before pulling into the driveway. Instead of slamming the car door closed behind me, I eased it shut until I heard the soft click of the latch. It took both my hands to steady the key going into the lock. Twisting the doorknob, I opened it. I was five inches in when I heard the hinges squeak. *Why didn't I fix that last weekend,* I thought. The infomercial of some old man selling vacuum cleaners blared from the television. Hoping it would drown out my pounding heartbeat, I headed for the stairs.

"Dylan…," yawned a low voice from a dark corner.

I jumped, instantly thinking, *Mom,* and envisioned the remainder of my senior year becoming nonexistent.

I murmured, "Crap," then turned the light on—ready to take my punishment.

Dalton, my little brother, was on the couch, squinting, knuckling the corners of his eyes. He'd been sneaking out of his room to watch horror movies and cartoons since he was seven. He looked down at his watch.

"Dylan … Dylan … it's 3:23 in the morning — what … I mean, ugh … do Mom and Dad know you're out this late?" he asked.

I sighed and released the tension in my shoulders. It would have been an ugly night had it been one of my parents on the couch instead of my brother. I walked over and took a seat next to him, patting the top of his head.

"What Mom and Dad don't know won't kill them, but you on the other hand—"

"Don't worry, Dylan, I won't say a word."

"C'mon." I extended a hand and helped him to his feet. "Let's clean up down here and get to bed. We got school in the morning."

We took a few minutes to fold the blankets, fixed the pillows, picked up the empty chip bags, and moved the table back. Dalton hit the power button and turned off the creepy guy on the T.V. I hit the light switch, and we walked upstairs.

"Night, little brother," I said. He nodded and walked to his room. "Dalton," I whispered. He turned around, and I put my finger to my lips.

"Gotcha, Dylan, not a word." He mocked my gesture and walked into his room.

I went into my room and gathered my things for a shower. I made it all the way to the bathroom door and stopped. I didn't have much experience sneaking in the house but I was sure the running water from the shower would wake my parents. I could hear Mom now, *"Dylan what are you doing showering at this hour?"* And that would be followed by a thousand other questions. I walked back to my room, stripped down to my boxers, hopped into the bed, and forced myself to sleep.

The sunlight slowly escaped through the blinds repelling the darkness in my room and replacing it with brightness and warmth. As it tickled my face and feet, the rising sun proceeded to ask me politely to wake up. I knew it was six in the morning because the annoying sound of my alarm clock went off at the same time Monday through Friday.

Hoping I was dreaming, I rolled over to confirm the time. Yep. It was six and time to get my day started. I yawned, still tired from this morning. I hit the snooze button, drifted to the window, and pulled the curtains to the side.

"Hello, New York," I joked in my radio personality voice. "That's right. It's me, Dylan Perry, checking in with you guys all the way from the eight-five-four. That's the beautiful city of Poughkeepsie for all you foreigners out there."

I took a moment to enjoy the fresh morning air. I greeted the neighbors, who were always up this early on their porch drinking coffee and reading the paper, with a smile. Wide-eyed, they flung the paper over their faces. I closed the curtains when I looked down and realized I was in nothing but underwear. Struggling to place one foot in front of the other, I walked out of my room to the bathroom. At the same time, Dalton was exiting his room headed in the same direction.

"Have fun last night?" He broke out in hysteria.

"Quiet, Dalton. You know how much trouble I would get into if Mom, *or Dad* particularly, found out I came in that late," I said under my breath, looking over my shoulder.

"Yes, I know, Dylan. You know I won't say a word. I'll let you go ahead and take a shower and get ready in here. I'll go use Mom and Dad's bathroom."

"Thanks, little brother," I said, fist bumping and shuffling his messy Mohawk as I walked by.

He was right. I knew he wouldn't say anything. We had a good brotherly bond. I've always tried my best to be an example and lead him down the right path. I remember back when I was younger and for every holiday and birthday, I would ask not for a sister, but a little brother. At the age of six, my wish was granted.

I showered, brushed my teeth, conditioned my curly locks, then went back to my room and slipped into some cargo shorts and a black fitted V-neck. After I got dressed, I went downstairs to greet my parents and took a seat at the table where my dad and brother were already seated.

"Eggs, bacon, and biscuit for you. A Strawberry smoothie, banana, and yogurt for you, Dylan, and cereal, toast with jelly, and orange juice for my little man," Mom said to us.

"Thank you," Dalton and I said in unison.

I finished my meal before Dad had a chance to realize there was food on the table. I tried to signal to Dalton to eat faster before the interrogation started.

"Pick a college yet, son?" Dad said, holding the morning paper in front of his face.

"What about a major?" Mom chimed. The very conversation I was trying to avoid. The same routine every day: we all sit, eat, and discuss Dylan's future. It was irritating every time they wanted to play twenty-one questions.

"I've decided Florida State University," I said. Mom's pale white skin glowed with joy.

"I didn't even know you applied to that school," she said, trying to hide her pearly white teeth. Her mouth was tight, itching to smile. "I'm so proud…"

Before she could finish her sentence, "Psych," rolled out of my mouth. Dalton and I laughed, hi-fiving under the table.

The look of disappointment took over her face. She picked around at her plate like she was a child avoiding her vegetables.

"Dylan." Dad crinkled his paper and peeped over the corner. "College isn't a joke. In four weeks, you'll be graduating high school and experiencing life as a young adult. You have a damn bajillion acceptance letters and your mom and I spent a lot of money to take you on all those tours. You need to pick which college you will be attending so we can prepare, and you already know what school has my vote."

I rolled my eyes and shook my head. "Yep!" I grabbed my book bag and grabbed Dalton by the back of the shirt, dropping his toast in the process of a bite. "That's my cue to leave," I said. I love my parents but sometimes they just talk too much, and this whole college thing was getting out of hand. They were more stressed about it than I was.

I went to the driveway and popped the trunk to my new jet-black Altima. My parents bought it as an early graduation gift at the start of senior year. I threw my backpack in the trunk and Dalton threw his in as well.

Every morning before I went to school, I picked up my best friend Marcus Peterson, or Macchiato as everyone at school knew him, and his little brother, Elias. I sent him a text message when I pulled up to his house.

"You look rough, Dill," Marcus said to me as he walked up and peeked in the window. His voice always sounded as if he has a sore throat, but it's just naturally dark and raspy. I'd joke, saying he sounded like he smoked a couple packs a day.

"You know the drill, Dalton," he said.

Marcus opened the door and Dalton and Elias got into the back seats. Marcus hopped in the front and slouched over. His horrible posture was uncomfortable to witness. Marcus and I are almost complete opposites but very alike in many ways. He runs track and plays golf, while I play basketball. I love sushi but he prefers his fish cooked. The biggest difference was our popularity. Despite us landing on two different social paths entering high school, he was still my best friend. Guess his nerdy personality and inability to hold a conversation with the opposite sex, gave people more than enough reasons to look past him; add in the fact he's always dressed in dingy athletic gear, the kids in school just made fun of him even more.

"Well hello to you too, Marc. If you must know, I spent my night with Jessica at the park for a romantic walk down by the lake. Didn't get home until 3:30 last night," I boasted.

"3:23 to be precise," Dalton interjected as he pushed his way up to the front seats.

"Dalton, shut up, and what did I tell you about your seat belt?" I growled at the rearview mirror.

Marcus barked at her name and rolled his eyes.

"I *still* can't understand why you two could never just get along," I said, driving off.

"Uhhh, because she hates me and is bent on making my life a living hell like half the other kids at school," Marcus said.

"You're just misunderstood that's all. Once people get to know you, they'll like you."

"PSH students base popularity on your household income. I've barely got a house. And besides, we've been in the same school for how many years now?"

Marcus was known for stressing about every situation but he had a point— money, cars, clothes, and extracurricular activities pretty much determined your social status.

Knowing the truth behind his words, I stared straight ahead and jokingly said, "Well, in a few weeks we'll be walking across that stage and before you know it, you'll be at Harvard University starting a new life."

"That's *if* I get in *and* get enough money to cover my tuition. I still don't know what is taking so long for a damn letter. I should have gotten it already. I was lucky enough to even get an interview. Have you decided yet?"

"I've gotten a few acceptance letters, but I haven't decided. As long as I get to go to college, I'll be happy."

Marcus shook his head as the right side of his mouth sank. He turned on the radio and ended the conversation.

First, we pulled up to the middle school located near our high school and dropped the boys off at the front entrance. "See ya guys later," I called out to them. We pulled up to our student parking lot next, which was always a party first thing in the morning. Homeroom was the first period of the day, and as it was assigned alphabetically, therefore, Marcus and I had the same teacher. As the 7:30 bell rang, Mrs. Sampson took roll making sure no students were tardy. The remainder of the twenty-five minutes was used for small chit-chat, latest gossip, laughter, and finishing homework people forgot from the night before.

First-period Advanced English with Mr. Green was next. He immediately resumed our discussion on *Beowulf*. The story reminded me of when I was a kid and would play with action figures. I would always make myself a superhero that had super strength and could fly like Superman. To this day, I still wished I could fly.

We separated to our next classes after—AP Chemistry and Advance Theatre for myself and Trigonometry and Latin IV for Marcus. Marcus always took advanced classes, pushing his brain past human limits. He was determined to be somebody and believed it started with Harvard. I'd been praying since we were kids that he got in with enough money to cover his expenses.

Between morning and afternoon classes, seniors had an extended lunch period. Marcus and I met up every day at that time.

"Macchiato, Dill. Over here you guys." The harsh-cool voice of Trey called out as we walked into the senior lounge.

"It's Trey," Marcus said, nodding in Trey's direction.

We walked over and took a seat at the table with him. Trey took off his letterman jacket and held a bag of chips over his mouth, lightly tapping the bottom.

"Party. Tonight. My house. Don't forget." Trey spat out potatoes with each word.

"Don't you get tired of wearing that jacket? It's not even football season," Marcus said.

"Of course we'll be there." I nudged Marcus.

"Jessica too?" Trey asked.

"I'm not sure yet, but I'll ask her. I'm sure she will."

"Umm … speaking of Jessica…" Marcus said hesitantly, fishing in his pants, then threw a folded piece of paper at me. "Here you go."

Jessica's scent—cherry blossoms—streaked through the air. Jessica and Marcus shared two classes together. At times we would send notes through Marcus since we didn't share any classes. The two of them were entertaining around each other.

Immediately I snatched the note and unfolded it. Gusts of cherry blossoms attacked my nostrils as I unfolded each crease—a constant reminder of her. She was like Poison Ivy—the girl everybody wanted, hated, and feared with unique abilities to make me lust over her.

Her silvery voice echoed in my head and spoke to me as if she read the words herself:

Dill Pickle,

So much fun with you last night. Sad to say my mom caught me trying to sneak in. I told her I was with Jenny and Marcia. I had a feeling that if she knew I was with you, she would blame you and not allow us to go to prom together. As a punishment, I was grounded and my cell phone was taken away for 2 weeks. I guess that's not too bad since we still get to go to prom together. I will meet you at your car after school. Have a great rest of the day.

Hugs and tons of kisses, Jessica

I was upset yet relieved. Upset that she got caught but relieved she didn't rat me out and ruin prom.

"Well, looks like Jessica won't be in attendance tonight, boys," I said, folding the note back. I goofed around with the boys for a little before grabbing a chicken sandwich and a bag of cookies for lunch.

The rest of my day dragged until my final class—Home Economics. It was an entertaining class and served as a break between the advanced science and math classes I took. Out of twenty-three students in the class, twenty of them were girls.

Murmurs and whispers filled the class as the guys and I walked in.

I took my seat in the back with my usual partner Amanda—the shy and quiet girl everyone loved.

"Hey, Amanda." I sat my books down on the table.

She closed her books and faced me, her wide brown eyes gleaming for the heavy lights of the kitchen. "How's it going?"

"The usual."

A shiver started in her arms and ran down her thin legs, her knees bucking under the table. She sealed her thin lips together and tightly hugged her body. Her milky skin faded to a pasty blue. I looked outside and thought to myself, *it's eighty-five degrees outside and it feels great inside.*

"You're shivering," I laughed.

"Cold. That's all." Her teeth chattered.

"What do you mean? Feels amazing."

Our teacher began class as soon as the bell rung. "Your recipes should be complete by now. Go ahead and get started."

Amanda and I were making white chocolate cupcakes. As I turned around to head to the cooking station, Diana, the most flirtatious girl in the entire senior class, was standing so close to me we were practically kissing. She had on red-fitted pants that hugged her best asset, and heels that complimented her long legs. Her full lips were moist from all the gloss, and her silky dark hair, which always poured down her back, set off her blue eyes.

"Can I help you?" I asked. Her hands began to stroke slowly up my arms. They quivered.

"I just love your body, Dylan, and your curly hair too, Dylan," she said so seductively.

This was nothing new for Diana. I wanted to tell her to stop but at the same time was interested to see where she was going with it this time. I had to admit she was quite striking. Before and during Jessica, Diana had an on-and-off crush on me. She was the kind of girl who was not afraid to express her feelings. Jessica never cared for her. I've never had a problem with her, even though she pushed the boundaries of our friendship.

"I love your golden skin next to mine," she said.

I laughed it off. Out the corner of my eye, Amanda was still shivering.

"Here she goes again," Amanda mouthed out. We were starting to gain the attention of some of the other students as they snickered and watched. Our teacher glared but never said a word.

Taking her time to toss her hair so that it rest perfectly against her back, her tone all of a sudden changed from seductive to serious, "...but I hate your blue contacts. When did you get contacts?" she asked, disgusted.

"What are you talking about, Diana? My eyes are brown and I don't wear contacts."

"Not today. But…" She gently stroked my face with the back of her hand. "That's weird … they were just…" she whispered, walking back to her seat.

I was confused. And if I did wear contacts, blue wouldn't be my color of choice.

Stomach slightly churning at her seriousness, I laughed to mask it. "Diana what are you talking about?"

"Take a seat, Mr. Perry," our teacher yelled as the class laughed at my semi-demise.

All of a sudden I felt like the chicken sandwich I had for lunch was about to crawl up my throat and jump out of my mouth. I placed my hands on my stomach and hunched over trying to catch my bearings. I could hear Amanda's voice in the background, like she was yelling from a distance, telling me to sit down and start on the cupcakes. The constant chattering of her teeth unexpectedly brought about one of my migraines.

"Can I please be excused," I asked, unable to raise a hand. I couldn't wait for an answer; I left for the bathroom.

My stomach was still doing numbers and my vision was beginning to go blurry. My hand trailed the row of lockers, as I steadily placed one foot in front of the other. The chattering sound of Amanda's teeth haunted my ear buds. Seeing the goosebumps on her arms as she shivered played over and over in my head like a bad dream. I couldn't get Diana's laugh out of my ears. The words *blue contacts* replayed over and over again.

I finally got to the bathroom and scanned the area to make sure no one else was present.

I scratched my hands as I hesitantly walked to the mirror. And as sure as the sky was blue my eyes were too. I stared in amazement, looking at myself, touching my face, widening my eyeballs, anything to give myself some explanation to the mystery.

I swallowed the bile that rose up my throat.

Turning on the faucet, I took a few seconds to let the relaxing sound of the running water calm me. My hands tightly grasped the edge of the sink and the sweat from my forehead ran down my face, hitting the counter. I splashed some cool water onto my face. I slowly lifted my head, not wanting to look in the mirror but at the same time curious to see. I looked closer and closer into the mirror staring at myself in shock. "No way ... no freaking way."

I was in awe.

I was so in awe, I didn't even see him walk in.

Chapter 2

Marcus

I glanced down at my phone, my foot constantly tapping. "Ahh—man, come on. Dad, let's go. It's 10:45," I yelled.

Dad was in the back putting away the last of the fruit. "Almost done, Marcus. Give me a few more minutes."

He knew I had a ton of homework like I did every night. Between track and golf practice and working with my dad in the evenings, schoolwork was always done late at night.

"Ok, Marcus. Let's just lock up and then we can get out of here and finally head home," he said, walking to the front.

I sighed, grabbed my book bag and the slice of chocolate cake in the to-go box and followed him out the door.

"Hear anything back from Harvard yet?" Dad said as he started up the old rusty pickup truck.

"Nope." I pulled out my phone and scrolled through my empty inbox. "Still waiting, Dad. NYU and Vassar, but no Harvard."

"No matter what, son, just know I'm proud of you for all your accomplishments. You know me and your mother couldn't give you the best life you deserve but—"

"Please, don't." I kept scrolling through my phone.

"I'm just saying, Marcus—"

"Dad, it's OK. Some people ditched me a few weeks after I was born and you and Mom had enough heart to take me in and raise me as your own. You've given me more than enough."

He left the parking lot and headed south towards home. "I just wish we could give you more and afford to send you to the college of your dreams."

There were a few minutes of silence. I wished he didn't bring up Harvard or apologize for his selfless act.

"Do you mind if I have tomorrow night off? I really would like it if I didn't have to work on a Friday night for once."

"Sure, you've earned it."

I was adopted before I could even crawl. Mom was starting a new job as a nurse and Dad was working as a cook. They really wanted a baby and had been saving up since Mom always wanted to adopt and didn't want to take time off for the pregnancy and nursing. That led to me becoming part of the Peterson family. Later on down the line, my siblings Elias and Katie were born and blessed our lives even more.

Our family owns a local restaurant here in town called *The Carrot Cake*. Just from the name, you can figure out that carrot cake is the specialty along with our real fruit smoothies.

Dad bought the place when I was in third grade after we moved from Brooklyn. I started working here a few days after my sixteenth birthday. Business didn't take off and we had to close. Years later we reopened. Although business is better the second time around, we make just enough to cover expenses and pay a bill or two.

We got home at exactly 11:20 P.M. I spent the next two hours doing homework. I was exhausted when I finished—eyes red and burning from sleep deprivation. I showered now so that I could get at least an extra half hour of sleep. I snuck around the dark room using the light from my cell phone to gather my things without waking my brother who shared a room with me. I took my clothes off, wrapped a towel around my slim waist and tiptoed to the bathroom.

I let the water heat up as I gazed at myself in the mirror, reflecting on life in general. At times I felt like Atlas—carrying the weight of the world. I remember seeing the statue when I was eight in front of the Rockefeller Center and saying to myself, *how do you do it, my friend?* I never thought that we'd be one in the same. My life has been one rocky journey from birth until now.

I continued staring at myself, striking a few poses and flexing my lack of muscles. Lately I've been in the gym and eating everything I got my eyes on.

The room became engulfed by steam. Entering the shower, the steamy water felt like a relaxing massage as it hit my body. I stayed in a few extra minutes then rinsed and dried off.

I put both hands down on the countertop and sunk my body down. With my head down, I reached for my toothbrush. My heart thudded painfully against my chest, and I popped up as I heard the sound of the toothbrush falling off the ledge of the sink. I wasn't paying attention but maybe the toothbrush was just really close to the edge?

I woke up to Elias blasting music and running around excited that it was Friday. I didn't know why he had so much energy in the mornings, but then again, all of my family members were morning people. I tossed and turned for a moment, squeezing the pillow over my head, trying to block out all the noise.

"Argh," I grunted as I continued to toss and turn in my bed. I got up and threw a pillow, knocking him off the bed.

He grunted from behind the bed.

I got up and ran over to his side of the room, jumped over his bed, and began a wrestling match.

I flipped him on his stomach and pinned his arm to his back. "I learned that move from TV," I breathed. My hold didn't last long, because for a thirteen-year-old, he was slightly larger than me. Coming in at one hundred and fifty pounds of pure beef and only two inches shorter than I, he was now winning the match.

We went at it trying to get the other to tap out until we heard the door swing open. It was Mom standing in the doorway, wearing her scrubs and shaking her head with a big grin on her face. Katie had her arms wrapped tightly around Mom's leg with her teddy bear clinched to her waist. Elias was the spitting image of Mom. They both had tan skin and dark hair. Mom's came down to her chin and Elias had a short crew cut. It was the round jaw, fat nose, and perfect teeth they both shared that really made them twins.

"Not too bad for an eighth-grader," I taunted.

"Just wanted to tell my two boys good morning before I head to the hospital," Mom said.

Mom was a nurse who worked the morning shift so she could be at home with Katie and Elias while Dad and I worked at night.

"Come on, Mom, you know we aren't boys anymore. We're men." Elias pounded his chest then rubbed it.

"You're right, I'm so sorry. Good morning, my two handsome young men."

Katie let go of Mom's leg and ran to Elias. He scooped down and picked her up, lifting her into the air. She giggled. Elias might have been Mom's twin but Katie was Dad's. Blond hair covered their heads and their pointy elf ears would make anybody think Dad birthed her alone.

"High-five, Kate?" I said.

She ignored me and buried her face into Elias's chest. Elias was her favorite. She wanted me depending on her mood and day.

"Before you leave, can you grab that chocolate cake from the kitchen and take it to Mrs. Perry? She asked for some yesterday, so she'll be expecting it," I said.

"Sure," she said, kissing me on my forehead.

"Elias, take Katie to Dad and get ready for school," I said.

We got dressed, ate, and headed out the door when Dylan, my best friend, came to pick us up.

When we got to school, I turned invisible. Dylan was a celebrity as we walked the halls, waving to his groupies along the way. Everyone made it a priority to speak to him or to give him a high-five in the morning. I guess good looks, a star basketball career, and parents with well-established careers will give you that status in high school.

When the eight o'clock bell rang, we left homeroom and went to our lockers to grab our books. Right as I was closing my locker, I felt a pair of hands around my waist slowly rising up to my chest, taking my shirt for one wild ride. My lips slowly formed a smile. I already knew who it was. Her head gently laid down on my back as if it was the perfect piece to my broken puzzle. Her perfume rushed from her body to mine like a wave crashing to shore. The hairs on my arms rose. My heart skipped a beat, maybe two, and suddenly my body went numb.

Her reserved voice whispered to me, "You're so warm."

I took a deep breath and let it out slowly only to have her arms still wrapped tightly around me. I missed this so much, but I wouldn't dare say it out loud.

"Monica," I said as I turned my head slightly to the right to try and catch a glimpse of her face before she moved away. She ran her hands back down from my chest to my waist and moved away from me.

"Mar-cus," I heard from a distance. It sounded so faint, yet so clear. I wanted to savor the moment.

"Marcus … hola, Marcus." The voice called out to me again but this time it sounded closer, clearer.

"MARCUS!"

I snapped around and there she was.

"Marcus, are you OK? I've been calling your name for like three minutes," she said.

I must have been daydreaming of her.

Again.

Monica and I dated my junior year, her sophomore. We broke up because she said she wasn't ready for a "real" relationship. Since then we remained good friends just as we were before the breakup. She walked up and interlocked her arms into mine right as Dylan walked up.

"Look at the lovebirds," he joked.

Monica laughed it off. "Whatever, Dylan." Her smile was flawless and captivated my soul every time. She walked us to our English class like she did every day. A friendly hug signaled goodbye.

I stopped by the vending machine when class let out to grab some chips before my next class started. I walked in and took my seat at the front of the class.

"Geek alert," I heard from the back of the class. By the screeching sound of her voice I knew it was Jessica — my rival, my archenemy, my ultimate contender bent on making my life hell on Earth — right away. We've never gotten along ever since I moved to Poughkeepsie. In Mrs. Gregory's third grade class, we were building gingerbread houses for Christmas. Jessica replaced my frosting with glue, and when I went to eat it, tears started to run down my face. In sixth grade as I went to take a seat, Jessica moved my chair and laughed as I hit the ground. That was on more than one occasion.

Over and over she did stupid things to torment me and the worst part of it all is that she's a girl. How embarrassing is it for a guy, at any age, to be bullied by a girl. I would rather get hung on the flagpole by the football team than be publicly humiliated by Jessica. Over time I started to build a resistance to her taunting and immature games.

I ignored her and went on with the day's lesson. When the bell rung, I gathered my things and headed towards the door, but before I could make it through, a tug at my elbow hindered me.

It was Jessica.

At that moment I felt as if a malevolent force possessed me. I had so much built up anger, anger that over the years turned into rage. I looked down and my fist clenched without me telling it to. My heart raced as if I was on ecstasy. I tried to calm myself down, but this force wouldn't hear what I had to say.

"Listen!" I snapped. "I *know* you don't like me, and if you haven't noticed, I don't like you either." With each word I took a step forward as she took one back until she backed into a desk. "And I know that as long as Dylan and you are together, I have to put up with your immature, hair twirling, gum smacking stuck up—" I stopped and froze in place. This wasn't me. I was on her level for a moment and I didn't like it. I turned around and walked towards the door. I stopped before I made it out and turned back around. "You know, I used to feel sorry for myself. Sorry that I didn't have the money or sorry that I have a family who I look nothing like. Sorry that I'm not the most popular guy in high school. I was sorry for everything including having to be associated with you. Anybody who has to make someone else feel bad about themselves is hiding some kind of insecurities of their own."

I looked around and about half the class was standing, staring at me, even the teacher had a dazed look on her face. I must have really sparked up a fire because sweat gradually rolled down from underneath her brown bangs. She pulled a note out from her book and looked at me stunned.

"Could you give this to Dylan?" Her words trembled. Then she smiled liked my reaction excited her.

I snatched the note and left everyone in the class speechless.

I met up with Trey and Dylan later on and delivered the note. I didn't want to tell Dylan about the encounter I had with Jessica right before that note was handed to me. I'm sure she would let him know later, that is, if I hadn't shaken her up too much. We grabbed some lunch and departed to our separate schedules.

I had one more class with Jessica, fifth period AP Biology. She didn't say a word or even look my way. After Biology, it was AP History for me.

I went to my locker to grab my last book. Right when I put the first number of my combination in my lock, a swarm of jocks came running down the hall. I turned around when I heard all the commotion and one pushed me into my locker. "Urgh," I fell to the ground.

I watched as they continued to run. No one even looked to see if I was injured, not even my other classmates in the hall. I got up and dusted myself off. I opened my locker right as the bell rung.

"Great, now I'm late." I slammed the locker. "Might as well use the bathroom now."

I ran down the hallway humming the tunes to a song I heard on the radio this morning. I wasn't paying any attention to where I was going when I crashed into Ava from third period and knocked her books everywhere. "Sorry," I whispered.

"What?" she yelled. "Just watch where you're going next time." She bent to gather her things.

"L-let me ha-help you?" I stuttered. It never failed.

"Ugh," she moaned. "No. I am already late, Macchiato."

"Just trying to be nice," I sighed. She glared at me and stormed off.

I went into the bathroom. Dylan was staring hypnotically at himself in the mirror right when I walked in. His face was pale and wet.

"No way ... no freaking way," he whispered to himself. I don't think he even realized I was in there with him. I feeling of uncertainty hit me in the gut.

"Uh ... Earth to Dylan," I laughed waving my hands so he could see my reflection in the mirror. I got no response, not even a look in the mirror. I calmly walked up to him and placed my hand on his shoulder, his clothes drenched in sweat. He gasped, like my touch snapped him out of a trance.

Chapter 3
Smokin' Party

Later that night I played some video games with Dalton before the party and not focus on the unexplainable event that took place earlier in school. Marcus was persistent on trying to get me to tell him what happened in the bathroom. I didn't want to sound like a lunatic, so I blamed the migraines. We've been friends for years and to top it off, I was a horrible liar. He spotted that lie before the words even left my mouth.

I continued the game before I finally got up to get ready. I was glad that Marcus had plans with Monica tonight so I wouldn't have to pick him up. They planned on going to the party afterward. Maybe I should just tell him about the whole blue-eyed freak show that happened in class? *He was my friend. He would believe me,* I thought.

I put the controller down, and patted Dalton on the head as I walked out of his room.

"I love you, kid."

I threw on some orange beach shorts and an old sleeveless basketball shirt that had Falcons on the front, our school mascot. Wearing that shirt for the first time in a year was nostalgic. I let out a huge sigh as the memories of my days on the court and hanging with my teammates quickly flooded my brain and left just as fast. I grabbed my keys and headed downstairs, telling my parents *bye* as I walked out.

The solo car ride was awkward. I couldn't even get into the music. The fact that there was tension between Marcus and I zoned me out. We argued about stupid things all the time then went back to being best friends seconds later. This time was different. I couldn't explain it because I couldn't understand what was going on with my eyes.

The music from Trey's house blasted over the music in my car before I pulled into his house. His driveway and front lawn was packed full of cars with people socializing and making out. I parked and walked around back.

"Guys," I greeted as I walked around, instantly shifting into party mode.

People were already splashing in the pool and dancing to the music. Out the corner of my eye stood Jessica's clique of friends, laughing and pointing, taunting people. It's what they did on a daily basis. Trey always threw the best parties at his place. Since his house was extremely huge and in a secluded location, we never had to worry about it being shut down. Add in the fact that his parents were never home and his sister moved away, his house was the spot for all weekend parties.

"Dylan is here. Let the party begin," I yelled at the top of my lungs, throwing my hands in the air.

Everyone cheered. I took a deep breath in to soak up all the excitement then let it out, holding on to the narcotic effects of popularity. I looked around and said to myself, *Damn, I love being me.* At that moment, a thick arm wrapped around my neck from the back and clenched my throat. I gasped and grasped at the wrist.

"Hey, guys, we got pizza and soda in the kitchen," Trey yelled to everyone as he slapped me on the chest and continued to press his bicep to my neck. "What's up, kid? 'Bout time you showed up."

"Yeah, I'm here, now, let's get, this, party started." I said. His grip was tight and me clawing at his arm didn't seem to faze him.

"Where's Macchiato?"

I didn't want to answer because it hurt to breathe let alone speak. Trey was no average seventeen-year-old. He was swollen like an infected cyst. All that football and weightlifting over the years had him bulked up. If you cut him, I'm sure he would bleed protein shakes.

"On a date, with Monica, they should, be here whenever, they get done." My fingers started to turn blue as my fist attacked his arm.

"Cool, man," he laughed as he overpowered my weak attempts at freeing myself. He unlatched, twisted me around, and threw me into the pool.

The party went bananas when I splashed into water. I couldn't even be mad. I just wanted to have a good time.

I swam to the surface. A few girls giggled at the water running down my face. Trey reached out his hand and with ease, lifted me out of the water.

"Sorry, Dylan," he laughed and slapped me once more on the chest, leaving a small red mark.

"No problem, man. I saw it coming." I never planned on actually getting into the water. I pulled my shirt over my head and it smacked the pavement.

"Let's go get some pizza." He waved for me to follow.

My stomach was rumbling long before I got to the party. I grabbed two slices, one cheese, the other pepperoni, and a soda.

"No need to rush, we got plenty," Trey said.

I replied mouth full. "I told you I was starving." Usually I'm not too fond of the crust but this time I couldn't resist.

I exhaled and patted my stomach as if I just had my last supper. I walked around the party during that time to enjoy myself and talk with some friends. Every time I stopped to talk to one person, a swarm would come. There were people in my high school that talked to me on a daily basis. Some, I couldn't tell you who they were, but for the most part, I knew everyone by name.

Everyone was having a great time here, but my mind was constantly wandering away thinking about Jessica. I wished she were here to share the fun with us. I missed the warm touch of her hands entangled in mine and sweet taste of her lips locked onto my skin.

I meandered over to the edge of the pool and took a seat, watching as a few people threw around a beach ball.

"She must be *begging* for another girl to come snatch you up," Diana said confidently. She walked up behind me wearing a white one-piece that had the sides cut out and ran her fingers through my soaked hair. "It should be a sin to have hair like this."

I didn't have a response. She sat next to me and put her feet in the water as well.

"Water is kind of cold." She moved her feet around in the water and took one out.

I gazed down at the water and shrugged. She shrugged too and continued.

"So where's Jessica tonight?"

"Home. Couldn't come out today."

"You look so much more handsome now that you took your contacts out."

I hung my head in slight embarrassment. "Umm, thanks, Diana." I was still crept out as to what was going on with my eyes.

She eyed me up and down. "Brown eyes just go better with your look."

I hesitated for a moment. "Diana, when are you *finally* going to accept that I'm with Jessica?" I couldn't look at her. Her body, her hair, even her dimple, it was all tantalizing and I was a man. I wasn't tempted, but I didn't want any reason to be either. I turned my head the other direction.

She laughed, her hand on her stomach. "It's not always about you, Dill Pickle." She flipped her hair.

"What are you talking about?" I turned back to her.

"That crush on you ended ages ago. I've moved on to new prey." We both laughed and she spoke again after a moment of silence. "Can you believe we're almost high school graduates?" Her sight got lost in the night sky.

"No, no I can't." I shot a glance up to the sky hoping to see what she saw. "Wow, we're almost done."

"What does life after Poughkeepsie Senior High hold for Mr. Perry?" She asked, eyes still staring into the sky.

"I'll be sure to let you know when I make a final decision. But I do hope it takes me on an unforgettable journey. You?"

"College. In Boston. It's been fun here but I have to explore beyond this town. My parents never left and I don't want to end up too comfortable and lacking a sense of adventure."

"I understand. So … do I know him?" I quickly segued back to the original discussion.

"Who?"

"The new *prey* for Diana." I nudged her arm.

"Well, just know he is a little more *mysterious* than Mr. Dylan Perry."

"What? Someone more *mysterious* than I? What makes him more interesting than me?"

"Well, to start off he has this husky voice that catches my attention when I hear him speak, you know, the voice of a working man." She rubbed her finger in circles around her kneecap.

"Are you telling me I'm not a man?"

"You know what they say, if you have to ask…"

"Whatever."

She chuckled as I nudged her again. "Anyway. He sort of has these dark and murky sad eyes, like they are waiting to tell a story and yearning to cry out to me. He has a smile that screams contagious but only if you can catch it. Short black hair that fades up the side, and lips that were created for only one thing. To top it off, he sort of has this grungy look like he's from the City, and you *know* how I love a City boy. So yeah, that's what makes him so mysterious. I just need a sample. Ha! Plus, he's not on Poughkeepsie's most wanted list."

"Well I wish you two a great *mysterious* future." I stood and noticed Marcus swimming on the far end. "Aye, Marc," I yelled out. He must have finished his date and crept past me. He turned around and nodded his head, then swam over to the ledge.

"What's up, Dylan?" He wiped his hand down his face.

"Just enjoying the party," I said. "Right, Diana?"

She didn't budge. She sat with her back arched, feet in the pool, still looking at the sky, completely ignoring the world. She slid her sunglasses down from her head to her eyes. "Macchiato."

"Hi," said Marcus, voice calm and smooth.

Diana ran her hands through her hair. The smile in her eyes was so intense you could feel it through the dark tint of her shades.

"How was the date?" I asked. "Do I see sparks flaring back up between you two?"

His light brown skin immediately went rosy.

"It wasn't a date, just two friends who *once* dated hanging out," he claimed.

He looked back and his eyes met with Monica's. She gave him a flirty little glare as she pulled her soaked hair away from her face and went back to entertaining her friends.

I must admit Monica was a gorgeous girl. Being kind-hearted just sort of took the cake. A whole new light revealed in Marcus when she came into his life. It was like she was an angel sent from up above, sworn to protect my best friend.

I've always approved of her, not that he needed it, but I liked them together. Their hearts and personalities made them the ideal couple. It's sad to say that I guess, well, I'm sort of envious. Not of her, just what they share. The love and chemistry they had for one another was epic. Like Romeo and Juliet minus the double suicide. I know they are meant for each other.

I just hope one day they see it.

I do have Jessica and like her a lot and all, but I do feel like we were pushed into our relationship. You have the popular girl in high school meets popular boy cursed with a fate to be *that* popular high school couple. Sort of like the traditional football jock and cheerleader but substitute basketball for football and dancer for cheerleader and well, there you have us.

"Must have been some heavy duty hanging out you two were doing. Do you see that *fire* in her eyes?" I said facetiously.

"Yeah it was great." He talked as if I didn't know how he truly felt. "I forgot how much I appreciated spending time just the two of us together."

"AHH HA!"

"Oh no. NO, NO, NO, I know that look, you're up to no good, bro."

"Whatever do you mean?"

We laughed and joked around for a few minutes to the point where I think we forgot about the whole bathroom freak show. "Brothers for life," he said. He shook my hand with his right and with his left, patted me on the back and pulled me into the water with him.

It was something about what he said that brought back so many memories of us growing up. Marcus has been by my side for everything major in my life. It was crazy to think how much we've grown.

I'm guessing this is pick on Dylan day, I thought. Marcus swam back to Monica.

"So, about your best friend," Diana asked as she ran her tongue across her upper lip, then bit her bottom.

"Who? Marc? Yeah, what about him?" I forgot she was still out here sitting on the edge of the pool. She smirked, gawking at him.

"No way." I gazed out to Marcus splashing Monica as she giggled.

"Way." Her steamy voice would make anybody lust over her.

"I can't believe this."

"What are you trying to say?"

"Nothing it's just that…"

"What you mean is how can a girl like me go for a guy like Macchiato?"

"No, no that's not it. It was just, unexpected, that's all."

I wasn't expecting Marcus to be the guy she was going to name. They've been classmates for years and she's never even held a conversation with him. As she got up, she swung her hair then sashayed off making sure everyone noticed. "Looks like I have some planning of my own to do."

I shook my head.

"Let's get a game of chicken started!" Someone called out.

Seven couples agreed to play. Marcus, Trey and I, of course wanted in. The competitive spirit was always extreme between us no matter what we were doing. Monica agreed to play and partner with Marcus. All he had to do was ask once and she was down. Camille grabbed me and nodded. I nodded back.

Diana walked up and tapped Trey on the shoulder. "Mind if I play?"

He ignored her presence. "Sure, find a partner."

"With you, idiot!"

Sometimes Trey's thoughts wandered off.

Everyone gathered their partners and took a few moments to strategize. Our strategy: conserve our energy and let everyone else attack one another. By the time the game was ready to start, the pool was cleared of all partygoers.

"Are you guys ready for a game of chicken?" Brian, from the junior class, announced. Everyone went wild, gathered around, and watched. All the guys submerged and when they resurfaced, their partners were on their shoulders. Trey and Diana towered everyone.

"Get ready, get set, CHICKEN!" Brian yelled.

The game started and we went with the plan to be incognito. It was like a war after that. Everyone grappled and attacked one another without any remorse. Monica and Marcus took down one couple no sweat. With six teams left, my plan to remain unspotted was thwarted. There was a couple Camille saw coming in our direction from the back. I braced myself and fought against the resistance of the water as I tried to turn around to defend the attack.

"Brace yourself," I said.

A force pushed Camille and my left foot tripped over the right. We were out. With five teams left, Marcus and Trey both knocked out one team each. Three teams remained. They all stared at each other, catching their breaths' and regaining energy.

Once the battle continued, Trey gestured to Marcus. They were going to double-team the other couple so that they could be the last ones standing and dish it out. They slowly walked up to the competition. They both took a side. Monica and Diana both grabbed an arm and pushed her over.

"So who will be the last man standing?" Brian screamed. The crowd was still going wild like drunks at a bar.

They approached each other with caution. I knew when it came down to it Monica would make the first move on Diana. Monica reached out to grab for Diana but she rolled her arms and they became locked onto one another. The guys were trying to balance the girls, forcing their strength forward for stability.

I stood on the edge cheering both teams when I noticed an increased amount of sweat dripping from Trey's forehead as their faces tensed with wrinkles. I could have been wrong since they were in the water. Their concentration was like static in the air as they stared into each other eyes.

"Do you feel that?" Trey looked down at the water.

"Distractions … won't work." Marcus never took his eyes off of Trey.

"Dude, I'm not. My feet are getting hot." He panicked, trying to jump around, the water preventing him.

Marcus dismissed Trey and remained focused on winning the game.

"Why is the water starting to bubble?" Trey said.

"Be still, Trey," Diana screamed. Trey was panicking and Marcus was now zoned out, just standing there, not even blinking.

Trey's voiced cracked as he struggled to get out a few words. "What's going on?"

Tiny bubbles the size of fish eggs rose from the space between them creating a Jacuzzi effect. The bubbles then doubled in size and stayed centered in that general area. People soon realized something wasn't normal, gossiping and pointing at the pool.

"This water is getting really hot," Trey continued.

Everyone at the party stared and tried to make sense of what was going on with Trey. The girls were completely oblivious, not paying attention to the situation going on right underneath them. Trey looked down at the bubbles and freaked out every time while trying to get the attention of Marcus, who was frozen in place with a blank stare glued to his face. Trey looked up and something must have really spooked him. He freaked out and dropped Diana. Soon as Diana hit the water, the bubbles vanished and Marcus had life back in his face.

Monica climbed down and hugged Marcus followed by a peck on the cheek. He looked over at Trey who was practically running on water to get out of the pool.

"We won!" Monica screamed. Marcus' excitement didn't match that of Monica's. His gazed followed as Trey ran around his house.

I wondered why Trey left in such a hurry and why he freaked out. I'm sure it had something to do with the bubbles, but I needed the full story. Marcus looked over in my direction and chills hit my spine. I swear for a split-second I felt as if I didn't even recognize him. I went after Trey. I *had* to know what happened in the water.

Trey was in the front yard when I found him, pacing back and forth, ranting on and on about something. A few of his nerves migrated my way as I cautiously walked up to him.

"It can't be possible, this doesn't make sense," he ranted as I approached.

"Trey, what are you talking about," I whispered, making sure not to set him off.

"Nothing." He jumped. "You scared me, Dylan. It was, I mean, it's nothing."

He was all over the place and I couldn't make out what he was saying. He continued to ramble.

"Trey, did something happen during the game?"

His hands trembled at his sides. "We should really get back to the party, right?"

"That party can wait. What happened? Something scared you and something apparently still has you freaked."

"You wouldn't believe me."

"Try me."

"I think, I think," he said as he gathered up the nerve. "I think Marcus was making the water heat up."

He was right, that did sound crazy. How could a person generate enough heat from their body to heat up a pool?

But who was I not to believe?

Was it not I who had their eyes change from brown to blue and back to brown instantaneously? What was going on today?

"Come on, man, that does sound a little far-fetched," I said. To be honest I don't think that Marcus understood what was going on in the pool.

"I know it does, but..." He stopped mid-sentence and walked off grunting.

I walked around to the back to find that the party was ending. Marcus was staying at my place tonight so he was leaving with me. I didn't want to rush him and his conversation with Monica, but I was ready to leave. I grabbed my shirt off the ground, wrung it, and walked past Marcus on my way back to the front of the house.

"I'll be in the car, Marc," I said.

When he finished, he took his time walking to my car and got in. "I'm ready," he said.

I sat there for a few minutes in silence staring at nothing. I desperately wanted to ask him about the water. I contemplated real hard and decided to let it go. I started the silent engine and the drive home was the same. We pulled up to my house a little after midnight. Marcus opened his door and got one foot out. I didn't care anymore I had to know.

"How did you do it?" I said. My hands tightly gripped the steering wheel for his protection.

"What are you talking about?" He got back in and closed the door.

"I saw the water bubbling and Trey said he felt it heat up. Did you feel it too? I mean, Trey looked like he saw a ghost when he looked at your face."

"What happened in the bathroom today?" he snapped back.

"Really? Really?" My hands gripped tighter, taking my frustration out on the steering wheel.

"So it's fine for you to interrogate my life, but when it comes to yours, it becomes an issue?"

"Just tell me."

"You sound real crazy at the moment. How do you expect to believe that *I* made water heat up and boil?" He got out of the car and my shoulders shuddered as the door slammed.

Once he said it out loud, it sounded insane but my eyes didn't lie. I didn't want to dwell on it. I dismissed it and followed him into the house.

"You hungry?" I offered as a truce.

With me following him towards the stairs, he said, "Bro, am I not always hungry?"

I rerouted to the kitchen and grabbed some munchies then headed up to my room. As I walked through the door, Marcus was bent over picking up papers and books from the floor.

"Looks like you left your window open. Wind must have knocked some things over," he said.

Dazed, I stared at the window. "My window wasn't open." I went half-crazy for a moment because I was positive I closed my window this morning. I walked over to the window and looked out. I'm on the second floor so it wasn't like someone from outside could open it.

"No wind." I stuck my hand out the window for a second.

"What's that?"

"Marc, there's no wind tonight and hasn't been any all day."

"Yeah, you're right." He looked at me with one eyebrow raised.

I closed the window and Marcus headed to the guest room. I turned the lights off and hopped in the bed. I closed my eyes.

What a weird day, I thought to myself.

Chapter 4
Decisions

The following Monday when we returned to school, everybody gave us funny glares like we had spinach in our teeth as we walked through the crowded halls, more so focused towards Marcus than me. It felt as if we were a caged freak show at a circus, and people were waiting for us to do something weird and unexplainable: *Meet Marcus, the kid who can increase his body temperature at will, and Dylan, the kid who can randomly change eye colors.*

I laughed at the scenario as it ran through my head.

Walking over with her posse of brainwashed blondes, Jessica said, "Hey, freak."

Marcus killed her smile with one look. She turned and reached for a hug, but I threw a hand up. I was exhausted from telling her about her unwelcoming behavior.

"Apologize," I calmly said to her.

She barked, "Sorry, Marc," like he was a disobedient dog.

My body went numb, temper rising.

"It's Marcus," he whispered, eyes focused on the books in his hands. He always said she had a deadly stare like Medusa. She looked at me wide-eyed for instant approval and shrugged. I crossed my arms and squinted my eyes with a stare so cold it could freeze the sun over. She let out an aggravated sigh and turned back around to Marcus.

"Marc, Macchiato, it's all the same." She glanced at me, my expression unchanged. "Sorry, Marcus." She threw her hands into the air as she forced the two words from her lips.

"Forget about it," Marcus said. She turned back to me and walked over slowly.

"Now, hug?" She shrugged with an accomplished grin.

She gave me the sad puppy-dog face. Like the *Poison Ivy* she was, I gave in. I cracked a smile and slowly opened my arms. She crashed into my chest and snuck a peck on my cheek. She pulled away slightly and caressed my face, gently making circles on my cheeks with her thumbs. Her smooth skin caused me to vibrate whenever she touched me. She reached and gave me a kiss on the lips. I could taste the strawberry flavored Chapstick as her lips pressed lightly against mine. A tingly sensation ran through the inside of my body as my ankles got weaker and weaker. Her kisses had me under a spell once again.

"Catch you in class." I heard Marcus say as he and Jessica's friends walked off in opposite directions.

She continued to kiss me as she ran her fingers through the hair on the back of my head.

"I love you," she whispered slowly in my ear.

She leaned away from me leaving one hand on my chest while the other rested on my back. I knew she wanted me to say it back, but my feelings paralyzed my lips. She leaned back a little more and cocked her head slightly to the side. She gradually approached my face.

"Jessica," I said. Her face was hypnotized. I'd seen that look before.

"How'd your eyes get blue?" Jessica asked.

She reached in for my face. I swiftly turned away from her. I buried my face into my hands. I wanted to cry. *I can't believe this was happening to me again,* I thought. I had no answer for my eyes changing colors. I didn't know where to even begin to search for the answers or why this was even a question.

She repeatedly cried my name and tugged on my shirt. I snapped backed around once I heard the sound of metal clinging together. Jessica stood there facing me, silent, looking right through me.

"What was that?" I asked.

"It—it was the lock—locker," she stuttered.

"Why did you slam the locker?" I demanded.

"I didn't." Her voice shuddered. We both stared at the locker. Confused by everything, I just kept repeating *how*.

"Dylan," Jessica called out, pulling me back into reality. She gave me this look of fear and remorse, as if she wanted to save me from whatever.

"I have to go, Jessica. I'm going to be late for class." I started to sprint off but was stopped when her hand interlocked with mine.

"Let me walk with you," she cried.

She walked me to class and hugged me tightly at the door like she would never see me again.

"Dylan," she smiled. "Your eyes are brown."

I turned around and walked into class right as the bell rung.

Marcus snorted when I took my seat. He leaned over the side of his desk and whispered, "We're in for a long day."

I opened my book and zoned out, focusing on the dirty chalkboard. "I think I want to break up with Jessica?" I didn't know what possessed me to say those words, but I said them like I needed his approval. I faced him, his dark eyes expanded and he was quick to respond.

"I support you one hundred percent. This is one subject I'm not going to argue with you about. But can I ask why? Why now? Why not, oh I don't know, three years ago?"

"I think we're just growing apart. She plans on going to school in Ohio and me, well, I have no clue where I'm going."

I smirked because he was right. Why not three years ago? A part of me does like her and wants to be with her, but the other side is telling me that she's just a little girl with a nasty, spoiled personality.

"I've been putting some thought into it and to be honest, she just isn't doing anything to better me like Monica is for you."

"Whoa, time out." His hands formed a "T" across his chest. "What does Monica have to do with this? We're just friends," Marcus said firmly.

We must have forgotten where we were because the teacher stopped and stared at us, as well as the class. We straightened up for a moment and then went back at it.

"Well you two being friends is a better relationship than Jessica and I as a couple. I guess you can say that I wish we had whatever *it* is you two have," I said.

I guessed my comment triggered something in him because he buried his eyes in his book. I did the same and tried to follow along with the lesson but my mind was scattered on Jessica, college, and being a freak.

"Wait until after prom," Marcus whispered as he wrote in a notebook.

I turned to him. "What?"

"Don't dump her until after prom. You won't have time to find a new date and coordinate everything together."

I couldn't help but laugh at his thoughtful suggestion. Here he was telling me to practically save his archenemy from embarrassment. Although I really didn't care at that moment, I understood where he was coming from. Class was over and we rushed into the non-stop traffic in the hallways.

"It's a good decision," Marcus said over all the noise.

"Which one? The decision to break up with her or the decision to do it after prom?"

"Well, both," he laughed.

"Move it, shrimp," Big Mike yelled as he walked by and slammed his shoulder into Marcus. He caught himself before he face planted on the floor.

"Big Mike!" I turned around and yelled, throwing both my arms into the air.

"Dylan, Aye, I'll catch you later." Big Mike ran off.

"You OK?" I asked Marcus.

"I'm fine."

We got to our lockers to exchange books.

"Catch you at lunch," I said as I headed to my next class.

I took a seat and got settled before the bell rang. The class size was small compared to my others. People only took this class for one of two reasons: they really love chemistry, like myself, or were proactive about their college credits. I threw on my lab coat and goggles and went to the table with my lab partner. I felt like a professional superhero every time I wore them.

Time flew and before I knew it, class was dismissed. As I walked out the door, I spotted Trey from a distance. I hadn't spoken to him since Friday night.

"Trey," I yelled out. "Trey!"

He turned around, caught glimpse of me, and sped off. I shuffled my way through, bumping into everyone as I raced to catch him.

"We need to talk." I grabbed his bag slung over his shoulder.

"I have to get to class." Trey resisted.

"Not until you talk to me." I grabbed his shoulders and spun him around.

"Fine, just not now," he said, avoiding eye contact.

"When?"

"Free period. Meet me at the outside eating area." He walked off and didn't look back. I've never seen a big jock like Trey so terrified.

"Hey, is everything OK, Dylan," Monica asked. She startled me a bit. "When did you start wearing contacts?"

My hands flew to my temples like a magnetic attraction. "Ahh! Stupid migraines."

"Do you have your migraine medicine? I can walk you to the nurse if you like."

"No and no thanks."

She pulled out a half empty bottle of water and some Tylenol from her purse. "Here, take this and take it easy."

"Thanks, Monica."

"I'll walk with you to class. Where you headed?"

"To the theater."

My head felt like a jackhammer going to work. The pain was excruciating and it felt like my temples were about to burst. I walked the whole way with my eyes closed to avoid any light. We walked into the theater and she sat me down in the audience. Heading towards the stage, Monica called out the theater teacher, Mr. Felt.

"Dylan's not feeling well, Mr. Felt. He just needs a little rest and he will be fine," she reassured him.

"Mr. Perry should be in an infirmary, not my theater," Mr. Felt shouted. His thick British accent flooded the theater. Monica walked back towards me, gathered her things and made her way to the exit.

"Thanks," I whispered, still with my hands on my head.

The whole class was on the stage practicing some improvisations for the day. Everyone who has taken an acting class with Mr. Felt knew that improvisations were the most entertaining part of his class.

Mr. Felt was kind enough to allow me to sit in the audience and watch until I felt better. I attempted to get up but with every slight movement, my head pounded a little harder. *Might as well rest my eyes while I sit here*, I said to myself. I slumped down in my seat, closed my eyes and soon found myself struggling to stay awake. Minutes later, I fell asleep.

"Dylan … Dylan … wake up, sleepy head."

I woke up surrounded by my classmates, poking at me like I was a frog being dissected.

"You were snoring, Dylan." Someone said.

Lies. I don't snore.

"Loud." Another person added in.

OK. Maybe I did.

My eyes blinked repeatedly until my vision came into focus. "Is class over yet?"

"Yes, I'm sorry I failed to entertain you today, Mr. Perry," Mr. Felt called out, looking down at me from the stage.

I stopped at the vending machine and got a drink before heading outside. I took a seat and waited for Trey to show up. I shot him a quick text to let him know that I was waiting, but I got no response and felt I was being sent on a wild goose chase. I waited for a little while then called him.

"Trey, where are you?" I yelled through the phone.

"Something came up. I can't make it. Can we talk at a later time?"

"Sure."

I hung up. I was getting slightly aggravated. With all that took place today, I just wanted to relax and eat. I went back in the Cafe, grabbed a plate of food and took a seat alone at one of the benches. At least I thought I was going to sit alone, until someone walked up and put their tray down in front of me.

Jessica was there when I looked up from my plate.

"You look tired, Dill Pickle."

"Head is killing me. Left my pills at home," I mumbled.

"So, I was talking to the girls this morning and they were telling me how Macchiato was acting all crazy and weird and stuff at the party. I even heard him and Trey aren't even friends anymore." She smiled wide, her eyes gleaming. She leaned in waiting for me partake on the latest Poughkeepsie Senior High gossip.

She continued rambling. I tried my best to ignore her. All I could hear was *blah, blah, blah.* Before she could get another meaningless word out her mouth, I interrupted her.

"—Do me a favor."

"Yeah."

"Stop listening to your friends."

"I don't know what is going on with you lately, Dylan, but I suggest you fix it and it b*etter* be before prom."

Her eyes slit, skin wrinkled at the corners of her eyes and mouth tight all around. Our neighboring table turned to spy on us. I paid them no attention. She got her tray and stormed off. I picked at my food for a little bit and got up.

"Leaving so soon?" Diana asked. "Looks like you've seen better days. Mind if I sit with you?"

"No, go 'head," I said, putting my tray back down.

"What's on your mind, Dill Pickle? I just saw Jessica storm out of here like she was trying to catch a sale at Gucci."

"Who you going to prom with." I laughed and finally gained my appetite back.

"Sorry, Dylan, *I* already have a date. You're stuck with the Wicked Witch of Poughkeepsie."

"So with who then?"

"Well, as you know I got many offers, but I decided to let Rich take me."

"Rich. I really haven't talked to him since—"

"Since you left the basketball team."

"Yeah since then."

Her fork played around with the food on her plate. "Why'd you quit? You were great at it."

"Long story. Can we save it for a rainy day?"

"Sure. We can make it a date." She giggled as she reached out for my hand.

"Your hands are a little rough," she said.

"So why are you still holding on to them?" I asked. She quickly snatched her hand back.

"So, Monica and Marcus going to prom together?"

"From my understanding, yes."

"Well I did hear him say Friday night that they were just friends, so fair game?"

"I have to go, take it easy, Diana."

I walked back to the building. I honestly didn't know what her sudden interest in Marcus was or what her plans would be if she actually got him.

At the end of the day I met Marcus at my car and we picked up our little brothers.

"How was school, guys?" I asked as they hopped in the back seat.

"Boring," Elias said.

"OK," Dalton chimed.

"What are you two, robots?" Marcus asked. "Can we get more than a one word answer? Don't forget to drop me off at work, Dylan."

"You boys want to stop by and grab a snack?" I asked.

They both agreed as their faces lit up like Christmas morning.

We walked inside the restaurant. Business was just about dead besides the older couple in the corner sharing a bowl of soup and a sandwich.

"Hey, Dad," Marcus and Elias said as we walked inside.

"Hey, Mr. Peterson," Dalton and I greeted.

"What brings the whole crew in here today?" Mr. Peterson asked.

"I just wanted to bring the boys in to grab a snack while we dropped Marcus off," I said.

"What are you guys having?" Mr. Peterson asked everyone. I ordered a smoothie as usual.

"Carrot cake please," Dalton requested.

"I'll take a slice of red velvet, Dad," Elias said.

"You know, in the summertime we could *really* use some extra help around here, Dylan. If you ever want to make a few extra bucks outside of what your parents give you, there is always a job for you here at the *Carrot Cake*," Mr. Peterson said.

"I'll keep that in mind, Mr. Peterson."

We all took a seat at the stools and indulged in our snacks.

"I'm thinking about taking Dalton to the mall with me when I leave here. Mind if Elias comes with us?" I asked Mr. Peterson.

"Not a problem. I'll call and let his mother know."

"Sweet. Mom's birthday is coming up, and Dalton and I wanted to go pick her out something."

"And I want a new game for my system," Dalton said.

"All right then, boys, finish up and let's go see what we can spend our money on," I said.

"Here, Elias." Marcus gestured. He pulled Elias to the side, put his arm around his shoulder, and handed him ten dollars. "It's all I have right now, use it wisely," he whispered.

"Thanks, Marcus," Elias smiled.

We got to the mall and the boys ran straight to the gaming store.

"Stay in there. I'll be right back," I said from outside the store. I moseyed my way to a few stores and got myself some new tanks for the summer. I lost track of what I really came to the mall for — Mom.

"So who's the lucky lady?" One of the jewelry associates asked.

"It's my mom. Her birthday is next week. I want to get something nice for her." I looked down to catch the name on her badge only to notice she was checking me out. I can understand her reasons. I smirked inside but was straight-faced on the out. She had to be my mother's age.

"Ashley, is it?" I asked.

"Why yes, it is," she purred. Her right shoulder shrugged up and body followed, leaning across the glass barrier.

"So can I ask you a question?"

"Sure thing."

"Let's say you're *seventeen*-year-old son was shopping for your forty-fifth birthday gift. What do you think he would get you?"

She cleared her throat abruptly, took a step back from the counter and suddenly went into professional mode — standing tall and straightening her hair.

"Well, you should check out these diamond earrings, but then again my *seventeen*-year-old son wouldn't be able to afford a gift like this."

"Can I take a look?" I asked. She removed them from behind the glass and handed them to me. I admired them for a moment. "They're pretty nice. I'll take them. Looks like something Mom would wear."

"Really. Don't you want to at least know the price?"

"Humor me."

"Two ninety-nine."

I handed her my card. "Can you wrap that up for me as well?"

She rolled her eyes and almost snatched the card from my hands. She probably thought I was some spoiled little rich kid.

"Thank you again, *Miss* Ashley."

I walked back to the gaming store and looked around for my brother and Elias. As I looked around, my pulse sped when there was no sign of them. I called their names out and got no response. My breaths became shallow and my heart was on one wild ride.

Graduation

Chapter 5
My brother and Me

How could I be so careless?

I wasn't even gone for more than twenty minutes and I already lost them.

Great job Dylan.

Everything horrible that could happen to them, I thought of. I got dizzy as the colors of people's shirts started to blend and the sound of pointless chitchat fuzzed like a static radio station. I walked around asking people if they saw either of the boys. I described them using hand gestures to mark their height compared to my own body. Nobody had a clue and some didn't care.

"Dalton! Elias!" I screamed.

Nothing.

"Excuse me." I walked up to one of the employees. "Have you seen two boys about this tall? One was wearing a red shirt and the other was in plaid. Both are wearing blue jeans."

She looked at me and nodded.

"Oh yeah, I know where those two are."

A sigh of relief came over me. I could breathe again and the knot in my stomach untied. "Could you point me in the direction?" I wiped the sweat from my forehead and followed her. She took me to a room located through one of the store doors. It wasn't huge so we were there in just a few steps. I walked in and the shelves were loaded with video games. I looked to the right and there they were, playing video games on one of the consoles.

"They're testing one of the games releasing next week. Drag Race 5," she said.

"Thanks."

She walked off still going on about the game. I went over and stood behind them. The way their bodies moved and twisted with each turn of the car was an indication of just how sucked into the game they were.

I interrupted them.

"Ahem. Thought I told you two not to leave. Thought something bad happened to you guys."

"What are you talking about, Dylan?" Dalton continued to mash buttons.

"Yeah, you said don't leave and we didn't," Elias said.

They were both technically right. I told them not to leave the store and in reality, they didn't. They dropped the controllers and followed me out the store. We dropped off Elias at the front of his house.

"Sorry that I scared you today, Dylan. I didn't mean to," Dalton said as we drove home.

"Don't worry about it." I reached my hand behind his seat and pulled out a box. "Check these out," I smiled. "What do you think?"

He opened the box and took the earrings out.

"I think Mom will like them." He closed the box with a smile.

"I think so too."

The sun was just starting to set, the sky dark and peachy. I put the box in the trunk so Mom wouldn't find it. We walked inside. The smell of dinner was at its peak. My mouth salivated at the aroma of steak and potatoes — Dad's favorite. I usually ate dinner in my room or at the table when we all sat as a family. Tonight I wanted to eat in Dalton's room, just the two of us.

I walked inside with two plates and took a seat on the beanbag chair. His room was painted blue with red and yellow race car décor. I used to have his old room until he was born. When mom had him, I told Dad to put bunk beds in my room so I could share with my little brother.

"You can sit on the bed, Dylan." Dalton nodded to the bed.

"Nope, I'm good on the beanbag. What are we watching?" I said. He hopped off the bed and took a seat next to me. "SpongeBob Circle Pants, my favorite," I said.

"Square."

I smirked. "I know what his name is."

We gave the TV our undivided attention as we sat there and grubbed out. I really wanted to chat with Dalton, so I took this time to connect with him.

"That was pretty good, huh?" I put the plate down. "Can I talk to you, Dalton? It's about me leaving for college in the fall."

"Yeah, Dad already told me."

"Dad? What exactly did *Dad* tell you?"

"That I will have my own game room pretty soon."

Thanks Dad.

Thanks technology.

Together you two have corrupted Dalton.

"I think Dad was kidding. I will still need a room for when I visit and the summer. What he was *trying* to say was that I won't be next door anymore and I won't see you every day."

"How long will you be gone for?"

"Most of the year and home during summer and holidays."

"Dylan?"

"Yeah?"

"Can I go to college too?"

"Sure, in about six years. I promise if Dad is anything how he is now, he'll be filling out applications for you." I nudged him playfully, and he returned the gesture.

Dalton and I have always had each other's back. Most of my friends can't stand to be around their younger siblings, but I look forward to it. I enjoy being a role model. I always said that if I had to be stuck on an island with one person for the rest of my life, I would undoubtedly choose Dalton.

"How far will you be from home?" he asked.

"That's a hard question. I haven't decided yet. I need to figure it out though because I'm running out of time." The conversation migrated and I found myself talking to myself. I turned to him. "I should know in about a week. I promise I'll tell you."

"Just don't go too far. I'll still need rides to the mall when Mom and Dad won't take me."

"Check this out. When you turn sixteen and get your license, I will *give* you my car."

"Really?"

"Yes, but you still have plenty of time to practice on your video games before you get behind a real wheel."

We headed down to the kitchen and cleaned up our plates. Mom and Dad were sitting in the living room on opposite couches. Dad was watching TV while Mom was on her laptop. I took out some vanilla ice cream from the freezer and some junk food out the pantry. Dalton got a bowl and loaded it with ice cream and sugary toppings. I glanced over at him and smiled. I loved my brother and my family more than the air I breathed. College will be hard, but I was ready to take my next step in life. I think.

Chapter 6
Project Prom

It was the day before prom. The prom committee was in a frenzy running around finishing the decorations in the gym, making sure tomorrow would be a night we'd all never forget. Not ironically the girls did all the work while partaking in conversations about dates, dresses, and makeup. The boys, of course, were huddled in the corner of the gym watching all the magic happen; their conversation focused more on the "after prom."

I walked into the gymnasium to Jessica barking orders, pointing in every which direction.

"That goes there, we need more balloons here, here, and there. More streamers and glitter people. Hey, Dill Pickle." Her arm connected around the small of my back. My arm gently rested on her shoulders. We walked in sync.

I was stunned at the amazing job she and the decorating committee had done. Giant balloons covered the floor, some hovered to the ceiling. The DJ booth was set and large hand-painted paper covered the walls that showed off the skilled artists of our senior class.

They transformed our sweat smelling, dull, and boring gym into something that looked like it should be featured on HGTV.

"Wow, everything really looks great, Jess," I said. She locked onto my elbow, smiling at my compliment.

"I have to make sure everything is perfect for us tomorrow night. What time are you picking up your tuxedo?" she said as if I better not forget.

"Once I leave here, Marc and I are gonna run and pick 'em up."

"Jeff, can you hang that just a smidge higher, and kick a few balloons in that corner over there, it looks a little lonely. And what about your hair?" She held a curl that dangled near my eye and stared at it like it was a smelly sock before letting it go.

"What about it?"

"Nothing. I'm just saying, how about a haircut? I think it should be something new and different."

"No, Jess, the curls stay. You know I can't let these bad boys go." I shook my curls in her face.

"What a dork." She pushed me away from her. "It was just a suggestion. You never know, you just may like it."

"But you love this dork."

"Yes, I do. OK, guys, take ten and get some coffee, we're going to be in for a long night. All right, Dill Pickle, I'm kicking you out. Are we still on for lunch tomorrow?"

"Yes, along with Marc and Monica."

"If they must, I guess they can join."

"That's the prom spirit." I hugged her and left the gym.

At the car, Marcus was leaned over the hood with his books sprawled open, a pen resting on his ear.

"Are you seriously doing work right now," I said. "School's over."

"Just reading over some things."

"Hey, your mom is picking up the boys, right?"

"She said she was."

"Cool, let's head out."

When we got to the tuxedo shop downtown, an older man with white hair and a hump in his back greeted us, different from the brunette with her stomach busting out of her shirt who took our measurements a few weeks ago. We handed him our tickets and he headed to the back. As we waited, we took a seat on an old couch that had half the stuffing missing. For a moment I thought I heard him back there wrestling with the plastic. Whatever it was, it sounded like the plastic won.

"Can you believe it?" Marcus said. "We've been friends since the third grade, best friends since the sixth, now prom and graduation next week."

"Where did the time go?" I looked over at Marcus as he reminisced, chuckling at his thoughts.

"Remember that time in fourth grade during recess when Philip tripped me and I fell into the mud puddle?" I said.

"It was classic." Marcus laughed.

"All the people that laughed at me, you were the only person to lend me a hand."

"What about when I joined the chess club in the seventh grade?" Marcus asked.

"Do I? I was embarrassed to be seen hanging around you."

"Yeah, but the next week you joined too, even though you didn't know how to play chess."

"Oh yeah. I tried blocking that memory out. Thanks, bro."

"We do have a lot of memories, man. I'm ready to see how things play out during these next couple of years."

"Our college years will be the best journey of our lives." I guaranteed him. Having the chance to reminisce on some of the memories we both shared reinforced the real value of friendship. I wasn't sure how many people I would keep in contact with after this summer, but Marcus was no doubt my best friend and brother for life.

"OK, one tux for Mr. Peterson and ... one for Mr. Perry." The clerk said. We paid him, grabbed our tuxes and headed home.

Marcus greeted his mother and brother when we walked in his house then ran off to the bathroom.

I took a seat on the squeaky leather couch that sounded off with every movement and gave my best effort to get comfortable. I grabbed the photo album underneath the coffee table. The first page had an old Polaroid that was discolored around the edges. The bottom portion read in red cursive ink: "Peterson Family."

"Funny, isn't it?" Mrs. Peterson said, staring from behind me. "That picture was taken right outside the adoption agency the day we took Marcus home. He wasn't even old enough to walk or talk," she giggled. "Ryan's parents weren't too crazy about the idea of us adopting a kid of a different race. They said it would only be trouble for him in the long run. The moment we first held him, we knew he was something special."

"He's lucky to have great supporting parents like you and Mr. Ryan," I said. She reached for the book, and I handed it to her. I sat quietly. I didn't want to interrupt the nostalgic moment she appeared to be having.

"Thank you, Dylan. We're glad that he has found a friend in you."

"Well, I guess that just makes me *quite* the lucky guy then," Marcus said, standing in the doorway.

"Well." She wiped her eyes. "I'll let you two get to whatever it is you have planned." She left the room.

"OK, so what's the agenda for tomorrow?" Marcus walked over and took a seat next to me. The couch squeaked.

"Here it goes." I pulled out my phone and opened the calendar. "Lunch at noon, Jessica will be at my house so I'll pick you and Monica up from here. After that, we're going to Walkway Over the Hudson for some good old Poughkeepsie town fun. Once we head back, the girls will need the remainder of the night to get ready. You know how they are with their hair, make-up, clothes and..." I was interrupted.

"Yeah, I got it, girls take a long time."

"Chill." I threw a hand up. "Now, are you ready for the big finale?"

"Wait, there's more? I feel like I should be taking notes or something." He rolled his eyes.

I knew he wasn't in the spirit of prom like I was. "There's the limo," I said. "And *you* rented it."

"Where on earth am *I* going to get the money for a limousine rental?"

"My parents rented it for me, but we're telling everyone that all your hard work slaving at the *Carrot Cake* paid for it."

"I feel like you're up to something."

"Me? Never."

Marcus had a slight glow to his skin. I believed he was secretly excited just as much as everybody else was for prom. It was cool if he didn't want to admit it.

"So seven-thirty I'll pick you up and then we'll go get the girls. The best night of our senior year will take place tomorrow. How does that sound?" I wrapped my arm around him and hugged him in closer to me.

"Well, sounds like you have the whole itinerary for the day. I'll just tag along for the ride like I always do." He shrugged.

"Cheer up, party pooper, it's prom."

I gathered my things, told his family goodbye, and headed home.

The next morning I was the first to awaken. All the excitement and anxiety didn't allow for me to sleep very long. I did my daily hygiene routine then went outside to grab the day's issue of the *Poughkeepsie Journal*, our town's famous newspaper. The day was already perfect. The sun was peeking out, the sky a nice cool blue with a temperature to match. Walking back inside, I ran into Dad who normally got the paper himself.

"So, what's the cover story for this Saturday morning, son?" Dad asked.

"Something about 30-year mortgages down? I don't know what it means, but it sounds boring."

"Won't be so boring when you buy your first house," Dad said, taking a sip of his smoldering coffee.

"I won't have to worry about that until I am old like you." I said, pouring a glass of orange juice.

"You just called me old?" Dad exposed his fang-like teeth then snarled.

We laughed and split the paper. I took the sports and entertainment sections. Dad took the business and local news. We both split the comics. Ironically, Dad does have a comical side that tends to come out rarely.

"How about we get out for a game of ball once your brother wakes up, just shoot around and work up a sweat before your big day," Dad suggested.

"Umm ... Dad, yeah, I don't want to embarrass you."

It was more like I didn't want to be embarrassed again. I put the paper down. He put his coffee down. I knew once Dad said "to shoot around" what he really meant was a full on, him versus me, basketball game. I hardly ever beat my dad in ball.

Or never.

He was a six-foot-two beast who weighed a little over two hundred pounds. He was known as Jackson "Swiss Shot" Perry when he attended Poughkeepsie Senior High. Not to mention, he went on to play D1 basketball. I'm sure Dad could have went pro if he just pushed a little harder. Maybe that's why he practically forced the game on me.

I picked the paper back up and covered my face with it. Dad swiped his bear claw down the center of the paper and forced me to go upstairs to change.

"I'll be outside waiting. Son," he barked.

Outside past the patio was the basketball court. The goal being on the opposite end of the back door, while the luscious green trimmed bushes marked the out of bounds area along the sides. Dad was outside standing under the goal, gripping the ball with his monster hands. I walked to the side and stretched.

"First one to ten," he said.

"Thought we just came out here to shoot around?"

"One quick game won't kill you. Or will it, old man?"

"Oh OK, nice. Trying to provoke me, real mature, father." I stood up from stretching and walked under the goal.

He began to dribble, the ball weaving between his legs like magic. The repeated sound of the rubber hitting the pavement over and over again quickly put me in game mode. Dad got serious, his eyes a nasty grin. He was ready to play. He took one step back, shot and scored.

"Dad one, Dylan none," he said.

He took the ball out and began again—dribbling, but this time he rushed towards the goal. I was already sweating from the beaming sun that rose by the minutes. My blood pumped faster than normal. I guarded him in a defensive position—feet spread apart, hands out to the sides, eyes glued to the ball. I knew he was going to go for the lay-up, so I quickly snatched my hand in for a steal. I grabbed the ball, turned around, and landed a fade-away shot.

"Score," I boosted.

"So you decided to finally play I see," he snapped back.

We went on for the next half hour playing a very intense game of father-son basketball. Or in Dad's words, "shooting around."

"You fouled me," Dad whined.

"I'll be right back." I dribbled and headed for the door. "I'm gonna grab you a Band-Aid and a lollipop you big baby."

"I get my foul shot," he continued to whine.

I stood to the right underneath the goal while Dad stood at the free-throw line.

"Two shots." Dad nodded to confirm.

He looked at the pavement. He dribbled and then focused his eyes on the goal. He dribbled three more times, bent his knees and gently landed the prettiest shot I had ever seen in basketball.

The perfect witness to why—

"They didn't call me Swiss Shot for nothing." He looked at me like he always did when we played against one another, like I could *never* beat him. He took pleasure in the fact. I grabbed the ball and bounced it back to him.

He repeated the same steps he took for his first shot again, but this time, the ball circled the rim. We both stared as it circled, frozen in place, frozen in time. We both had a lot riding on the game. Dad wanted to remind me that he would always be the better player and that quitting was one of the worst mistakes to make. I, on the other hand, just wanted to prove to Dad that we don't always have to be in competition with each other.

It felt like we had been standing there for minutes waiting for the ball to make a decision when in reality, it had only been seconds. I got my hands ready to catch the ball just in case. The ball circled the rim once more then fell but not in Dad's favor. I reacted and caught it right as it fell in my direction then faked like I was going to shoot. Dad practically jumped over me going for a block. I dribbled back to the three-point line, shot, and scored.

"I believe that puts me at eight and you at seven," I said, sticking my tongue out at him.

The intensity of the game went into overdrive after that. Dad didn't like to be beaten at anything. He even put himself in competition with Mom when it came to household chores. Once I witnessed them racing to see who could fold laundry faster.

Too bad I could never get him to do mine.

He managed to tie the score at nine, his ball. He removed his shirt and showed off his vein-bulging biceps and a pointless tribal tattoo that ran up his right arm and crossed over to his chest and ended at the nipple. He took the ball out and immediately went in for the long shot so he could win the game. He shot from the halfway mark without even giving me a chance to realize what was going on. I turned around to watch the ball only to see it bounce off the backboard.

I ran in, jumped, and caught the ball before it could hit the ground. I dribbled back to the same spot where Dad took his shot, but he was rushing me right as I turned around. I eased the ball in and out between my legs, spinning around him like a dancer. I turned around to face the goal again. We now stood face-to-face with the ball in my position. Our clothes were drenched in sweat, and Dad gasped for air.

So did I.

We were both exhausted and smelled of masculinity.

"This is it, son, hit or miss," he gasped, looking for breath.

I had nothing but doubt in my mind that if I took the shot, it would end in his favor. *No time for second-guessing,* I told myself. I took the shot. The ball created the perfect arch as it flew from my hands into the net.

"Swiss Shot Dylan." I jumped up and down as the ball landed perfectly into the basket.

"Pure luck." Dad said, starting his tantrum. He threw his hands into the air and for a minute, I thought he was about to cry.

"Don't be a hater all your life, father." I cupped my hands around my ears, lunging from side to side. "Hear that, Dad? That's the crowd and they're going wild."

His ego was bruised knowing that I beat him, but I was thinking, *finally.*

"Don't worry, Dad, you win some and you lose some." I patted his back gently.

"Good game, son. Pure luck, but good game."

As we both entered back into the house, I turned around right before I got to the door, froze, dribbled just once and shot the ball one more time. It was a perfect shot. *Yeah, luck,* I whispered to myself.

"Jessica called while you and your father were taking your frustrations out on one another. She said she would be here around eleven," Mom said, poking around the newspaper scraps.

"It wasn't frustration, just a friendly game of *father-son* basketball," I joked. "Right, Dad? Or were we just *shooting around?*"

Dad grimaced and took a seat on the stool in the kitchen. I headed upstairs.

I took off my wet clothes and jumped in the shower. I threw on some clothes and started to drift off until I heard Mom.

"Dylan!" she screamed from downstairs. "Jessica is here."

I got up and tripped over my own legs as I rushed downstairs. "Hey, Jess." Our eyes connected and a few inappropriate thoughts ran through my head as I nodded towards her.

Jessica was sitting on the edge of the couch. Dad was standing there, still shirtless, and Mom greeted me at the bottom of the stairs fidgeting her fingers. I walked over and greeted her with an intimate embrace and a kiss on the check. My parents shot us that *did you not see us standing here* look.

"Umm, can I get you something to drink, Jessica?" Mom walked over, breaking up our lovey-dovey moment.

"No thank you, Mrs. Perry," Jessica replied politely.

"So what color is your dress for the dance tonight?"

"We decided to go with Dylan's favorite color—"

"Orange," Mom interjected, "nice choice."

I stood up and grabbed Jessica's hand, and made my way upstairs to avoid all this awkwardness with the four of us. It was just weird when they were around each other.

"Leave the door open, Dylan," Mom screamed.

Really Mom? I thought. I couldn't believe she just said that. Embarrassing.

"Is your brother home? I should go speak to him," Jessica said. She walked over to his door and knocked.

"Come in," Dalton said. She opened the door and we walked into him on his bed with a controller in his hands. "Hey, Jessica. I haven't seen you in forever. How you been? Want to play some video games? You can play if you want to."

"Whoa, buddy, slow down with all the questions," I laughed.

He was excited to see her. Probably the only person I was close to who could stand to be in the same room with her for more than five minutes without wanting to choke her. I laughed to myself at the thought.

"What's funny?" She turned to me.

"Nothing."

"I just wanted to come in and say hi, Dalton. Me and Dill won't be here too much longer," she said.

"Aww, OK I guess," Dalton sighed, putting his controller down.

As we walked into my room, I jumped backward onto the bed making sure I could see her when I landed. Jessica stood at the door.

"Close it," I said. I knew she wouldn't pay attention to my mom's authority. She's that kind of girl who did what she wanted and when she wanted. Closing the door, she spun around in the middle of my room, expanding her hands, her long brown hair followed. She spun until she crashed gracefully onto the red shag carpet.

"I love your room, Dill Pickle," she said, looking up and around. "It reminds me of a page out of a magazine."

"It took some time, but I had to put the *Dill spin* on it. My parents have no idea how much I actually enjoy being grounded here," I laughed.

If Extreme Home Makeover had an inspiration room, it could definitely be mine. It showed my creative side. There were various magazine articles ranging from basketball to music that were blown and converted into wallpaper, which covered the two largest walls. My bed snuggled in the corner and draped with a black and orange comforter, along with quilts my grandmother made for me. Next to the bed was the desk. I customized it just to suit my needs, and it made a cool hangout spot.

I couldn't help but admire Jessica. She was simply beautiful. Gazing off into her beauty, I immediately began to have flashbacks—reminiscing on all the times we had together, the good and bad. When we were kids, I would've never imagined us dating. It just kind of happened. We've known each other for so long, sort of seemed like the natural thing to do.

"Come. Let me show you something," I said.

"What is it, Dill pickle?"

I sat her on my lap at my desk as I pulled up photos on the computer. Dad scans every photo he finds and puts them on my computer. I had pictures pre-date time and even some from elementary school.

"OMG, I had pigtails." She pulled her hair up and made two messy pigtails on both sides of her head, imitating the picture on the screen.

"Check this outfit my mom put me in that day," I said. We both laughed so hard we almost fell off the chair.

"I can't believe how much we have all grown up." She faced back to the screen. "I will never rock pigtails again."

"Crazy, right?" I glanced down at the corner of the screen. "Oh snap, time to go, Jess."

We sprinted out the door, waving to my parents and headed to Marcus' house. I hoped things would run smoothly for all of us today. I wanted everyone to have a relaxing day, free of stress and bickering. It would be fun to see the interaction between Monica and Jessica since they have never really been around one another.

"Hey, Marc, hey Monica." I greeted them both as they got into the back seat. "How you guys feeling today?"

"Great. Hi, Jess." They both said.

"Aren't you guys just excited for today?" asked Jessica.

"Yes! I can't wait." Monica jittered like she had a caffeine rush and hugged Marcus.

We pulled up to *Café Bocca* and walked in to be welcomed by the hostess. "Table for four please," Jessica said.

The girls had never been to Café Bocca but it was a favorite of my family and the Petersons. We'd been coming here since we were kids and even knew the owner, Erik. He came out to greet us and we introduced him to Monica and Jessica. We ordered for the girls and enjoyed a drama-free lunch.

Next, we headed over to Walkway Over the Hudson. Everyone was feeling on top of the world as we cruised around our amazing city. It felt like a scene out of a romance movie, where the friends are driving down the long road with the music blasting, sun beaming down on their skin, women in the backseat, hair blowing in the wind, singing to all the tunes.

Poughkeepsie was beautiful.

The cool breeze felt refreshing as it entered in and cooled us down on the warm sunny day. The city was filled with a diverse group of people walking around enjoying the Saturday afternoon. Soon as we got to the park, we immediately ran down the bridge laughing, enjoying the scenery of the multicolored trees, the river beneath our feet. Spring was my favorite time of the year.

The walkway was filled with the most entertaining people around the city. There's one guy who always made balloon animals and another guy who drew caricatures. We took in everything the city had to offer. From the downtown area where all the people were friendly, to the dark house on the corner of Old Mill Road with the creepy old man. This place was where we all called home. We took a minute to stop and post up on one of the railings, soaking up the afternoon.

"This is just beautiful," Monica said.

"It's so relaxing," Marcus said, gazing out into nature. "I could sit out here for hours and hours and just think."

"About what?" Jessica asked.

"Life," Marcus replied with a solemn look on his face.

There were times I wished I could get inside his head and explore his thoughts and help ease his mind. "Hey, guys, let's get a smoothie from the concession stand." I suggested.

"You and your smoothies," Jessica teased. We all went over and got a smoothie from the food truck and walked up and down the bridge for the next hour to enjoy more of the festivities at the park.

We arrived at Marcus' house to drop him and Monica off.

"Monica, if you like, you can come to my house and get ready for tonight?" Jessica said then jumped back into the conversation when she realized Monica wasn't answering. "That way we can save the guys a trip."

Monica looked at Marcus and then myself. Her face was expressionless. Neither one of us knew what to say. Nobody expected Jessica to ask that.

"I, guess—I guess I can," she said.

"Awesome. Dylan will text you my address. Just meet me there in about an hour. Ciao." Jessica waved as they walked off.

We pulled up to my house and I turned to look at Jessica. "That was nice of you. Thank you for being nice to Marc."

"I did it for you," she said so cavalierly. "I told you I want this day to be perfect for you, so if that means being nice to Macchiato for a day to see you happy, then I will." She exhaled like she had been dying all day from being around him.

"Why don't you like him Jessica?"

"Are you serious? He's a freak. He's like trash around campus."

I grimaced. "Watch your mouth, Jess, that's my best friend you're talking about."

"And *that's* your problem, Dylan. You could have been much more popular if you didn't always have him lingering around everywhere you go." She said it as if I've been allowing myself to be held back because of my friendship with Marcus. It annoyed me, but also made me recognized *who* I had been dating all these years. It was a conflict that would never be resolved.

"Come," I said. We reached towards each other to share a hug.

"Eight. Be at my house," Jessica said.

We both got out of the car. She got into hers and drove off. I walked into the house.

"How was your day, Dylan?" Mom asked not even giving me enough time to get both feet through the door.

"Surprisingly, it went better than I imagined." I walked into the living room and stretched over the couch, yawning. I rested my head against her.

"I know you're not tired," Mom said as she ran her hand through my hair.

"I've had a long day, Mom. Just need a little nap before the dance."

I woke up about an hour before I had to be at Marcus' house. I showered, freshened my breath, pulled out my tux and began to get dressed. As I was piecing my suit on, I was interrupted by a knock on the door.

"Come in," I said.

My parents walked inside as I buttoned my vest in the mirror. Mom walked over and stood between the mirror and me and helped me with my bowtie. Dad walked over next and put on my cufflinks one at a time. Once he was done, I reached over and grabbed my jacket to finish it all.

Marcus and I would always talk about mirrors as kids. It was a weird fascination of ours. I told him you could always trust a mirror because it'll never lie. It always told you the truth whenever you needed it, always revealing the true you. I looked in the mirror and didn't see my parents sitting on the edge of my bed — my mom holding her hands over her mouth like she wanted to cry while Dad cuddled her. Nor did I see the stack of shoe boxes in the corner, or the black and orange tuxedo I was wearing. It wasn't because I had hair covering my face, but because the mirror was showing me the truth. I saw myself naked — all of me stripped of the possessions. I saw Dylan Perry for who and what he really is — just a simple teenager from Poughkeepsie on a journey to find true happiness.

"My son is so handsome." Mom sobbed behind me.

"Looking like a man," Dad said. "I remember my senior prom—"

"Dad, no time for memory lane. I have places to go."

I threw some conditioner in my hair and shook my head letting the curls jump around. I splashed a little cologne on to feel extra fresh.

"Don't forget the corsage and the tickets, Dylan." Mom pointed to the dresser, still wiping tears from her eyes. I shuffled around making sure I didn't forget anything. Mom suggested that I went downstairs to take pictures. She got a few solo shots and some with the family. I had to stop her because she would've had me taking pictures all night.

"OK, guys, I have to get going," I said. We all walked to the front door. I opened it and there it was, a stretch limo waiting for me in front of the house.

"Just like we promised, Dylan." Dad put his arm on my shoulder. "A limo for prom."

Marcus and I pulled up to the front of Jessica's house and walked inside after being greeted.

Jessica walked downstairs.

I waited for the slow motion button to get pressed and the romantic music to creep in from nowhere like the movies. She was stunning with her orange dress that sparkled at the hems and covered everything but her arms. The slit that ran up her right thigh put thoughts in my head that I shouldn't be thinking with her mom in the same room.

Her hair was pinned up with two curly strands that came down in front to show off that face I couldn't help stare at. As I walked closer to her, the cherry blossoms started to attack me, knocking me back and pulling me in closer at the same time. This time something was different. I had been around Jessica long enough to know her scent and this time I smelled a hint of vanilla. It was different, but I still liked it.

Chapter 7
Prom

When Dylan and I got to Jessica's house, I was a bit nervous. I had to repeatedly tell myself over and over again that this was just prom and not my wedding day and technically speaking, Monica wasn't even my girl anymore. We got out of the limo and rung the doorbell.

"Are you sweating, Marc?" Dylan asked looking over at me as we waited outside.

"OK, so, I'm just a little nervous." My teeth clattered. A little was nowhere close. It felt like I didn't put any deodorant on the way my underarms were leaking.

"Come in," a voice from the inside said.

Dylan gripped my face in his palms. "Hey, relax and calm down, OK. It's just Monica."

His touch and words were cooling. I'm not sure if I was still sweating or not, but my skin felt dry. We walked inside as Jessica was walking down the stairs. Dylan sparkled like a firecracker and for a moment, I thought I saw a tear come down his face.

He put the corsage around her wrist when she made it to the last stair and stepped back to admire her. He stroked his chin and grinned. He looked up and her eyes flashed like pearls. She stepped forward and wrapped her arms around his neck.

I coughed. "Where's Monica?"

"She's upstairs finishing her hair. She should be down in just a minute. She looks divine. Wait until you see her," Jessica said, never taking her eyes off Dylan.

It felt more like hours waiting for her. Dylan was hugged up with Jessica. I sat at the edge of the stairs, skin feeling wet again. A door slammed from upstairs and I stood up. Monica walked out and stood at the top of the stairs. It was her time to shine. As I looked up, the ends of my mouth tugged up forming a smile from ear to ear. I was seeing an angel right in front of me.

Her tan skin shined and reflected off the jewels laced with her turquoise dress that strung up the back, partially exposing it. Her dress hugged her small waist and her heels gave her extra height to her long legs making her almost my height. She wore her hair down. I loved when she wore her hair down. It curled at the ends and rested on the front of her left shoulder. I met her at the end of the staircase and placed the corsage made of blue delphiniums and orchids, held together with a rhinestone-encrusted bracelet around her wrist.

"You're gorgeous," I whispered as I took her smooth honey hands into mine. I smiled as she gazed at me, eyes so innocent.

"You should put a tux on more often," she whispered back.

"OK, guys, time for pictures," Jessica said.

Dressing up wasn't really my forte' so she better make these pictures worth it.

We all pulled out our cameras and spent the next twenty minutes snapping pictures ranging from goofy to couple shots before we left. Jessica told her mom bye, and we all walked outside.

"Wow, you got a limo, Dylan?" Jessica jumped around like a caged monkey. I just knew she was going to break one of her heels.

"Why assume it was me?" Dylan said oh so calmly.

I stood there with my head down and my hand clinging onto Monica's.

"Wait." Jessica stopped. "You mean to tell me that foster boy Macchiato over here has enough style *and* money to afford a limo?"

"He's been saving the money he earned from work to afford this, OK." Dylan got instantly annoyed and walked to the limo.

"Can we not start this tonight," Monica politely said and followed Dylan, letting my hand go. Jessica and I made our way to the limo.

Our theme for prom was "A Night in Hollywood." We got to the school and had the driver pull up to the entrance where there was a red carpet. The prom committee got some of the underclassmen to be on the sideline flashing photographs as seniors got out of their vehicles. I gazed out the window when the klieg lights roaming in the sky caught my attention.

"Guys," Dylan said, "let's end this year off right. Let's have a great time, dance like no one is watching, and be Hollywood stars tonight."

"I'm ready." Jessica had both hands glued to the window, dying to get out the limo.

"But before we get out," Dylan said. "Let's take a selfie."

"Marcus." Monica tugged my arm. I turned around and Dylan had his phone in the air pointing down at the four of us. I scooted over, and he took a picture. The driver opened the door and we felt like celebrities exiting the limo.

Well, at least I did.

As we walked down the red carpet, the flashing lights blinded me. I held my hand in front my eyes the majority of the time as we walked until we entered the doors of the gym. The school was lit up with more lights and it looked just like Hollywood, not that I have ever been but I'm sure it resembled the décor. The floor was covered with giant star-shaped gold peel-offs with each senior's names on them. There was a table that had nothing but cheap gold trophies with men holding stars and a massive printout that covered one wall of the Hollywood sign.

"I'll go find a table for us," Monica said.

I hope she didn't feel too out of place here since this wasn't her class. Last thing I wanted was for her to feel uncomfortable and neglected. "OK," I responded.

Dylan and I walked around stopping and talking to some of his friends. Jessica went over and talked with her girlfriends.

"Hey, Dylan, over here," Diana called out from behind us. We both turned around and Diana's silver designer heels kissed the ground over and over as she made her way to us.

"Hey, Dill Pickle," she said. "Macchiato."

"Hi, Diana," I said.

"Where's your better half?" she asked Dylan.

"Somewhere around here with her friends," Dylan said, looking around the crowd of people.

"That's not like her to just leave you around for other girls to hit on you. So who are you here with tonight, Mr. Marcus?"

"My friend Monica," I said.

"Friend? So that means you are single? Save me a dance tonight? I'll find you when the right song comes on. Don't leave without my dance, Macchiato."

She walked off switching her hips then glanced back at me. I couldn't figure out why she was finally talking to me after all these years of being in the same school.

"What was that all about?" I asked.

"I have no clue." Dylan smirked.

"What was Diana talking to you about?" Monica asked as she walked up behind me.

"Nothing. H—how do you know Diana?"

"Oh please, Marcus, everyone knows who Diana is. I found us a table. Let's go take a seat."

We walked over to our table. The seats were director chairs of different colors. People were still coming in as the DJ played all the latest jams. We sat with some of Jessica's friends and their dates.

"I think everyone is just about here now," Dylan said.

"Everyone is up on the dance floor. You guys can dance, can't you?" Monica asked.

"Can we? Marcus do you hear them? Let's show them how we get down," Dylan said.

The girls hopped up out of their seats, grabbed us by the hands, and dragged us to the crowded dance floor. We forced our way through all the dancing while bobbing our heads to the beat.

"Let's see some moves," Jessica and Monica screamed over the music. Dylan and I both looked at each other as we prepared ourselves. We bounced and rocked as the music crawled under our skin.

"We're just getting warmed up," Dylan said.

I grabbed Monica's hand and pulled her closer as we danced. I had one hand on the center of her back and the other interlocked with hers. My hand transitioned from her back to the side of her waist as I spun her away from me. She giggled into her free hand, and spun back until her body was pressed tightly against mine. I smiled when our eyes connected. The music had everyone feeling alive. Hands waved in the air and voices cheered. The night couldn't get any better.

"Hey, Marc." Dylan screamed over the music.

"Yeah, wassup, bro," I replied.

"Let's turn it up a notch."

"You mean Weapon Z?"

Weapon Z was a code we came up with as kids to express when we thought the same thing in any given situation. It came with being best friends and being around each other for so many years. We went with the letter Z because X was so cliché.

"Yeah, Weapon Z."

We broke away from the girls and cleared the center of the dance floor with just enough room for us to do what we needed to do. I circled around the empty space and pointed to Dylan who was circling and pointing back at me. We broke out in a dance sequence, nothing fancy, just enough to get us some attention. The crowd of classmates went wild and cheered us on. I wasn't too sure if they were cheering for just Dylan or the both us. Nonetheless, they cheered. The ladies clapped and everyone joined back in for the next hour of dancing.

We went back to our table after almost passing out of constant dancing. At the table, everyone had a ballot in front on them.

"How the *hell* did I make this damn ballot?" I screamed.

"Just accept it, Marcus, geesh," Monica said. "I'm voting for you." She checked the box next to my name.

It was just weird that I would be nominated for anything at this school. In addition to myself, the guys up for Prom King: Trey, Rich, Shawn and of course, Dylan. The nominations for Prom Queen were: Camille, Diana,

Amanda, Jessica and Ashley. I voted for Amanda and Dylan.

"Well, tonight, me and Dylan will reign as your king and queen, ladies and gentlemen," Jessica said, checking her boxes. Everyone else checked their ballots and handed them to the senior class representatives as they walked by.

"I'm going to get us some punch." Dylan got up from the table and walked off.

Monica reached out for my hand then moved in closer to clinch my arm. "You know," she said, admiring the dance. "I'm really happy you brought me here tonight."

"Cause I had all the ladies lined up waiting for me to ask them to prom," I said jokingly.

"I'm serious, Marcus. I wish you would realize how special you really are."

"Let's be honest, nobody at this school wants Macchiato on their arm in a prom picture."

"I do," she said finally giving my face some attention.

I smiled.

"It's nice to know that I can still come in and save the day," she said.

"Here you guys go. Drinks on me." Dylan came back, indirectly changing the mood.

"Guys, I love this song. We have to all dance," Monica said.

It was a slow song. Didn't know how I'd feel dancing so close and slow with her. Wish I could read her mind so I knew exactly how she felt about me in that moment. I gulped down my punch and the four of us walked slowly over to the dance floor. Dylan grabbed Jessica by the waist and spun her into him as they slow danced. I hesitated for a moment before I made a move onto Monica, but she was already wrapping her arms around my neck before I fully processed my thought.

My knees buckled, but I caught myself before I collapsed.

I put my arms around her waist but was too hesitant to move close. There was enough space separating us that a small child could easily walk between the two of us.

"Argh," I grunted as someone bumped me closer to Monica.

It was Dylan.

Her chestnut colored eyes that tightened slightly at the ends sparkled as I got closer. We both laughed awkwardly. It felt like magic in the air as we danced, our eyes enjoying a lustful conversation. Then I heard a loud voice that snapped me back into reality.

"OK, OK, OK, I don't want to interrupt you guys from all the dancing and fun, but it is time to announce your prom king and queen," Samantha, our class President announced. Everyone rushed off the floor and made their way back to their tables, all excited to see who would be crowned.

"Now, are you guys ready?" Samantha said. The room cheered.

"Your senior class prom king this year is — can I get a drum roll please...." She fumbled with the paper and looked at it with slight shock and disbelief. Then she smiled. A name slowly rolled off her tongue. "Marcus ... Peterson ... Marcus Peterson congratulations. Please come to the stage!"

This had to be a mistake.

I didn't want to get up.

It was weird.

I'd never won anything.

Ever.

"Marc, would you get up," Dylan said as he pushed me out my seat. I got up and walked cautiously to the stage. Samantha put a sash and crown on me then handed me a scepter. I smiled and people finally started to clap.

"And now for your prom queen. Well, this is no shocker," said Samantha. "Congratulations Jessica Davis! Please make your way to the stage."

How is this even possible? I asked myself. The one person in this school who I absolutely couldn't stand now shared this moment with me. Everyone had their eyes on the stage. The room was so quiet anyone could hear my heartbeat if they listened closely. I could tell everyone was just as shocked as I was.

Jessica arrogantly waltzed her way to the stage, knowing for a fact she would win. My chest pounded making it difficult to breath when I caught her eyes piercing me as she walked on the stage. Samantha crowned her, handed her flowers and announced that we would share the next dance.

What? I yelped.

Before I knew it, the lights went dim and the spotlight hit us. The crowd continued to stare as we walked to the center of the gym. The DJ played our prom song and we both started to move slowly.

Out of rhythm.

"Well this is awkward. You guys can get a little closer and, I dunno, actually touch each other," Samantha said slightly annoyed over the microphone.

I didn't want this and it was no question she didn't either. She glared at me with devilish eyes as we stood in front of each other moving in opposite directions making sure not to touch one another. My head dropped down while I moved, not wanting to look up at her or anybody for that matter.

"Thanks for ruining my night, foster boy Macchiato," she whispered. "You'll never be anything more than Dylan's—little—shadow." Her words were like poisonous gas.

I stopped moving, shot her this look of disgust and walked back to my table. By then, everyone had begun to gather on the floor to dance.

"Where's your date?" Diana asked as she took a seat next to me. "You look sad. You shouldn't be sad, you're prom king … ohh, it's because you had to dance with the wicked witch. Yeah, I would hate life too."

"I'll be fine." I looked up and saw Dylan and Monica dancing together.

"That should have been me up there as prom queen," Diana said as her eyes followed the crown across the dance floor.

"That shouldn't have been me up there as prom king," I said despondently.

"Don't say that. It should have been us."

"Would you like to dance, Diana?"

"Well, I do like this song. Yes, I would love to dance with you, Mr. Marcus." I grabbed her hand and led her to the dance floor. We laughed and talked a little as we danced over the next few songs. She was a good listener and I managed not to stutter over my words.

"These shoes have no purpose for being worn over long periods of time. Can we sit this next song out?" Diana asked.

I glanced down and her shoes looked like they could be classified as a deadly weapon. "Sure," I said. Monica and Dylan were at the table talking when we got back.

"You guys tired too?" Monica asked.

"Yes, girl," said Diana. We all sat and talked for a few minutes until *Hurricane Jessica* interrupted us.

"What did *you* think you were doing dancing with *my* boyfriend?" Jessica ran over screaming frantically, waving her finger at Monica. "You have your own *homeless boyfriend* to take care of. Dylan is off limits. And you, Diana, when are you going to get a boyfriend of your own and stop trying to steal everyone else's you whore."

"HEY WHO DO—" I yelled.

"Shut-up-Ma-key-ott-oh. You've already ruined my night once and I *won't* let you or *any* of you lames add to that. So, do us all a favor and go find mommy and daddy, maybe your real parents have enough money to send you to college."

"Who do you think you are?" Monica lashed back, taking a step towards Jessica, eyes dark with rage. Her Spanish accent started to emerge. "*Eres un cerdo egoísta. Asi ingrate.*" Monica spat her words out with fire.

"Speak English, you immigrant," Jessica snapped back. Before Monica could respond, Jessica picked up a cup of punch off the table and splashed it all over her. Monica flinched as the red juice ran down her face. Jessica grabbed Dylan by the wrist, "Come on, Dylan, we're leaving."

He snatched his arm back in disgust. "No, Jessica." Dylan slowly backed away from her. "I'm tired of this, tired of you. I'm not going anywhere."

Everyone stopped dancing and tuned into tonight's episode of the *Dylan and Jessica show*. "Stop it, Dylan, you're embarrassing me. Let's go." She looked around but failed to connect her eyes with anyone else.

"You just don't get it do you? You're mean, rude, and disrespectful to everyone, and I don't want to be a part of it anymore. We're done!"

"Dylan *you* can't dump me, not tonight, not on prom." Her voice quivered. Everyone could see the embarrassment and shame adorning her like a cloth. The whole class stood there in awe, whispering and gossiping.

"I do what I want, Jess," Dylan said. "Find your own way home." He walked over to me, Monica and Diana. "You guys all right? Sorry about all this."

We nodded.

"Come on, let's get out of here," he said. We gathered our things and left the gym to the limo.

"I'm sorry about that, Monica," I said.

"No need to worry, she just better not let me catch her outside these heels."

"No, you're not going to fight. You're better than that," I said.

"I can't believe she went crazy like that, Dylan. What were you thinking staying with her that long?" Diana asked.

He didn't respond. He sat there in silence the whole ride home. He didn't want the night to turn out like this for anyone.

None of us did.

"Well at least one good thing came out of tonight," Diana said. "Marcus winning prom king and the look on Jessica's face when you two had to dance."

Monica, Diana and I all laughed. In all honesty, that was sort of the high point of the night. We pulled up to Diana's house.

"What a night. Catch you all later," Diana said as she got out. Next was Monica's house. When we stopped, I got out and walked her to the door.

"I apologize again for the punch all over you," I said, admiring her ruined dress.

"You didn't know she was going to snap like that. It's not your fault," she said.

I walked closer to her, holding her tight and close. Her head rested on my chest, her hair ruining my tux. The moment just seemed right. I had to tell her how I felt. I believed in my heart that she felt the same way.

"Monica," I stuttered.

"What is it, Marcus?" she asked. I ran my fingers through her sticky hair.

"I can't—I can't keep these bottled-up feelings for you anymore. You're the *only* person who I've had feelings for like this. Although it crushed me when we broke up, you didn't abandon me, our friendship continued to grow. You're the only person who understands me, who makes me feel normal in a world where I feel like a Martian. Guess what I'm trying to say is that I've fallen hard for you. I think … I mean, I know for sure that I want to be with you and I don't want to go another day without you not knowing how I truly feel about you."

I was relieved that I got that off my chest.

She looked at me with a sparkling tear in her eye. She wrapped her arms around my slim back and pressed her sticky face to mine, pecking me on the cheek.

She whispered my name and took a step back. "You're about to graduate and leave for college to who knows where while I'll be here in Poughkeepsie, still in high school. I know that you've dreamed of getting away from here for the longest time, and you are destined for far more than what this city has to offer. If we get back together I feel like I'll be holding you back. In fact, I know I will. You will lose focus on your work and life and I don't want to be the blame for that. You are an amazing man who will do great things in the future. Just not with me at your side."

It was like we had broken up again. That crushed feeling I had back then reemerged, my healing scars bleeding once more.

I couldn't have felt anymore low at this point. My real parents didn't want me, my classmates didn't accept me, and now the girl of my dreams was nothing but an illusion.

What's the point? I thought.

It took every ounce of strength I had left to contain myself and stop the tears from falling.

"I'm sorry, Marcus. I have to go. I had a great time tonight." Tears running down her face, she walked into the house, closing the door behind her.

Once I got back inside the limo, I lost it. The emotion took over. I balled up my fists, trying to contain myself. I didn't want to just burst out crying, but the tears came.

"I'm sorry, bro," Dylan said, doing his best to console me.

I was dropped off at my house. I walked in and went straight to my room. I threw my tux off, hung up my sash, my crown, and scepter. I took a long hot shower to wash the rejection off me.

I slept in the living room so I wouldn't wake Elias. I turned on the television then noticed a note on the coffee table with an envelope next to it.

The note read:

I hope you had a great night at prom with your friends. A letter from Harvard University came for you a while ago, but I held onto it until after prom so whatever the decision was wouldn't affect your night. Just know that you make us proud and I know the Dean has made the right choice.
-Mom

This was the moment of truth, my one chance to forget about the last seventeen years and move on from here. I picked up the envelope and stared at it as I read the front. I couldn't believe my name was on this. I slowly opened the top and pulled out the letter. I unfolded the paper and saw the Harvard letterhead on it. This was really happening. I started to read and my excitement soon turned to anger once again and more tears shed when it said I wasn't admitted for the upcoming academic year.

My head dropped as the letter hit the floor.

My body melted off the couch.

I felt like I didn't have anything else to live for.

I pulled my phone out and sent Dylan a text, letting him know Harvard University rejected me. I dropped my phone and when it hit the floor, every candle in the living room instantly lit up the dark room. I pulled the blanket on top of me and went to sleep. Seemed like the only thing that accepted me.

Chapter 8

Fire and Ice

I finally got in the bed and relaxed when my phone buzzed with a message from Marcus.

I squeezed the phone in my palm, my face now hot.

I couldn't believe that Harvard rejected *him* of all people. His personality and spirit mixed with his brainpower would have been a great asset to that school. Another reason for me to dwell even more about the horrible night Marcus had, and to add icing to the cake, he was denied from his dream school. I walked towards my dresser and opened the first drawer and there they were, six pieces of papers all lying on top of each other.

I picked them all up.

"Stanford, NYU, Columbia, Syracuse, Brown,"—I counted off as I laid each one back into my sock drawer— "and Harvard."

I was accepted to all these colleges and thought that it would be a great surprise to tell my best friend I was accepted once he got his acceptance letter. I didn't even tell anyone that I applied outside my parents; I think it's best if I kept it that way. As I put the Harvard letter back, my eyes started to itch like a nasty irritating hair was stuck on it. I glanced up at the mirror and there it was, my eyes were blue. Seconds later the itching turned into a tingling sensation that quickly radiated down to my hands like a jolt of energy. What looked like frost emerged from my fingertips, then spread all over the paper until it froze.

I choked on the lump in my throat; my fingers went numb as the frozen paper slipped from my grip.

I was stunned.

Scared.

Confused.

Slightly horrified at the sight, I backed away from the paper so quickly I tripped over my shoes. The shock of it all wouldn't let me stop and collect my thoughts. I shuffled until I hit my head against the wall. I sat there, rubbing my head, amazed at what happened, then got up and walked towards the paper that *magically* covered itself in ice.

How did I do this? I toyed between thinking this was the coolest thing I'd ever done, and the scariest. "This is *so* cool," I laughed to myself.

Anxiety had me in and out of sleep. I just *had* to know if I could do it again, if I could freeze something. I jumped out of bed and grabbed a pen off the desk. I looked at it as if I had some clue of what I was doing or if I could even do it again. I held the pen up in front of my face with a big smile and screamed out, "OK, this is it. Freeze." The pen stared back at me, no frost. I walked to the mirror and decided to try something else. I sealed my eyes tight, counted, and on three I screamed: "Blue." I opened my eyes and two boring brown ones looked back. Maybe I was dreaming last night and didn't really freeze anything? One step to the right and my foot was in the water that had melted from the ice.

"I knew I wasn't crazy," I screamed.

"Well that's good to know, Dylan," Mom said from outside my door. "Breakfast is ready, come downstairs if you're hungry."

I went downstairs and sat at the table where the rest of the family was already seated and chowing down.

"How was your big night?" Mom asked, eyes gleaming as she leaned across the table.

"You sure you want to know," I murmured, forgetting about the magic and remembering the horror.

"Of course we do, sweetie."

"OK, here's the abridged version: Jessica threw punch onto Monica, that was after Marcus won prom king and all this was before I dumped her," I said. Mom's jaw dropped in awe and Dad's reaction... was well... normal.

"Well that was some prom night you had," said Dad.

"And last night I made up my mind on what college to attend. I will be notifying the dean tomorrow of my decision."

Mom sunk into her chair and quickly changed the subject, "Please tell me you have put some more thought into your college decision?"

"Please say Stanford ... please say Stanford," Dad whispered to himself.

"Jackson," Mom said, slapping Dad across the head. She redirected her attention back to me. "Whatever school you choose, just know we'll be happy for you," Mom chimed.

"I've decided to go with..." I hesitated.

Every part of me wanted to say Harvard University, but deep down I honestly had no idea what school I wanted to attend. My whole life I've wanted to go to Harvard and now I'm faced with the decision of a lifetime. But was it truly *me* who wanted to go to Harvard or was it a projection of Marcus' desires? My parents were on the edge of their seats, practically biting their nails waiting for me to say something.

"NYU," I blurted before my brain could finish my thoughts.

"What?" Dad yelled.

"Jackson!" Mom yelled, hitting Dad on the head once more.

"I'm just saying, Christine, all the offers he got and *NYU* is his decision?" Dad said with such disappointment.

I didn't want to be too far from my little brother and if anything went wrong, I could be home in a few hours. Of course Harvard and Stanford were my top two choices and NYU was my last but nonetheless it was still a good school and still in the best state ever — New York.

Sounds convincing, Dylan.

"So what about Marcus? Is he going to Harvard?" Dad asked.

I knew that if I told them Marcus didn't get in, they would know that I turned it down to spare his feelings and they just wouldn't understand. So I lied. "I'm not sure yet. He's still waiting on his acceptance letter, but I'm sure he did. He's a smart guy."

Dad let out a long sigh then said, "I guess we'll get all your things sent in tomorrow and get you registered for classes and payments and all that jazz." He buried his head into the paper.

"Well, little brother, looks like I won't be too far from you after all." I smiled at my parents. It was obvious they seemed a little upset.

The next day at school while walking in with Marcus, some of the girls in Jessica's clan bombarded us.

"So Jessica says she accepts your apology and you guys can like … get back together and stuff," one of them said.

Marcus and I turned to one another and laughed at the silly blondes. I pulled out a piece of notebook paper and wrote a quick note.

"Here, give this to Jessica when you see her." I handed her the paper that read:

Jessica let me spell it out for you O-V-E-R!! Signed Dylan Perry

The nosey clan member opened the note, and the rest of the clan leaned in. Their noses flared, skin flushed red in the face. She balled the paper up and threw it at me before they stormed off.

"You know that's gonna piss her off, right?" Marcus said cheerfully.

"Yep, I know," I replied with a smile on my face.

"Now, *you* know how crazy she gets when she's angry. You might want to watch your back, bro."

"She's harmless. Plus, *you're* the one who has two classes with her, not me. Remember that."

"We graduate in eleven days. I'm not too worried about her," Marcus chuckled as we walked off to class.

Walking into English, Marcus and I were greeted by a round of applause from our classmates. I walked closer to the crowd, turned, and did the same.

"Why is everyone clapping?" Marcus asked dumbfounded.

Samantha ran up to Marcus, her glasses nearly falling from her face, and grabbed his hand. "Every year some cocky jock with muscles wins prom king and the queen is always one of those butthole cheerleaders. *Well*, it's about time someone broke the barriers around here." She threw her hands to her hips and shifted her weight to one side.

"But, Jessica won prom queen?" he said.

"True. But, you winning is a start. The geeks, I mean, the socially under-classed according to the *Stereotypical Encyclopedia of American High Schools*, from here on out, have something to look forward to. You're like a hero now, Marcus."

Marcus grinned. His smile glowed, brightening his brown skin. He walked to his seat shaking the hands of his peers along the way. Those same people that shunned him congratulated him for setting a trend. The walk to his seat was so *presidential*. A light had come over him and I wasn't going to let anyone steal his joy.

Classes went smooth for us that day, the next day, and pretty much the rest of the week. I managed to steer clear of Jessica the entire week but I couldn't say the same for Marcus. At least she didn't have much to say to him.

On the last full day of school, I met up with Marcus at the lockers after class. Everyone was cleaning out all their belongings and storing trash and old unwanted photos for the bonfire.

"Hey! Wanna hit up Trey's end of the year party wit me?" I asked Marcus.

"Wait what party? You talked to Trey?"

"Yeah, you haven't?"

"No. He's been avoiding me the past few weeks."

"Well, he's having one last party tonight and you're coming, OK. I'll let him know he needs to cut the act and stop avoiding you."

"Can you believe that this is it? No more high school classes for us"

"Nah, I can't. Just finals and then we walk the stage. Hey, have you had any contact with Monica?"

He stared off for a second then turned back to me. "No not really. Don't think I can be around her without my emotions going haywire. Definitely need some space." The last thing he pulled from his locker was a picture from two years ago of her locked onto his arm in the hallway. I couldn't believe he threw it in the bonfire collection can. He stared absentmindedly at the trashcan.

"Hey," I said, placing an arm around him, guiding him down the hall, "you never told me where you going for college?"

Still walking, he looked over his shoulder at the trashcan. "NYU. I applied there a while ago as a backup plan in case I didn't get into Harvard. Good thing I did, right?"

"That's a great thing." I stopped and guided his face back to mine.

"Serious?"

"Yeah man, you get to spend another four years with your best friend."

"Quit playing."

"No lie, kid."

"Just when Poughkeepsie couldn't get enough of us, New York City better get ready."

"What dorm you staying in?"

"Goddard, you?"

"Dad said they're putting me in Founders. See if we had planned this, we could've been roommates."

"Yeah, I know, right. Well, at least I will have one friend at school."

"Hey, this is college not high school. Nobody will know who you are or where you come from. You can be anyone you want."

"I just want to be Marcus."

"Well, be Marcus then."

Later that night I stopped by Marcus' house to pick him up for the party. Before I could get slightly comfortable, his parents hit me with a heap of questions. I didn't mind it though.

"So I hear that you and Marcus will be attending school together in the fall," Mr. Peterson said.

"NYU, pretty cool, right?"

"And your major?"

"Chemical engineering. NYU offers a dual-degree program in computer science and engineering. I'll take classes at NYU for the first three years then transfer to Stevens Institute for Technology and finish out my last two years in the engineering program. When I graduate I'll have a degree in computer science and chemical engineering."

"Dylan Perry, always going where most people dare not go," Marcus yelled from the back room.

"Sounds like a solid plan you got there, Dylan. Wish you the best, son," Mr. Peterson interjected back into the conversation.

"Thanks, sir," I said and excused myself. I headed down the hall into Marcus' messy room blanketed in a mix of dirty and clean clothes, along with random clutter lying haphazardly around the room.

"You need to clean your room, Marc," I said.

"Sorry. I do share a room with my brother. It gets kinda messy in here sometimes."

"Messy? Marc I can't even see where I'm walking right now. I'm scared to sit down in here."

"Just throw all that stuff over there on Elias's bed and take a seat on the floor."

"Bro! No. When was the last time you vacuumed?"

"Dang, Dylan now you're just being overdramatic," he laughed.

"Whatever, man." I stood. "Still picking Math as you major?"

"Oh yeah that reminds me, forgot to tell you I changed it to Pre-Med. Think I want to maybe be a doctor and save some lives one day. Just not sure which kind."

"That's a noble profession, Marc."

"I want to give people a chance at life when an obstacle threatens to take it away, you know, sort of how Kathryn and Ryan gave me life when others wouldn't."

Marcus stood and paced through all the mess on the floor. He did this when he thought too much about the fact that he was adopted.

"Marc, can I tell you something? As a friend?" He faced me. "We all know the story: your parents dropped you off, you were adopted, but somehow you still feel abandoned. You *have* to stop dwelling on that and just accept the fact that you have a family. And sure it's not the family with the most financial stability but it's a family who loves you and wants nothing but the best for you. Stop letting adoption define you and just grow from it." I'd been holding that in for years.

I thought after my big spiel, Marcus would have a response, some type of rebuttal, but he gazed out the window into the darkness.

"Marc, did you hear what I just said?" He stood silent.

"Marc…" I whispered.

A chill ran down my spine and up again. He had the same look on his face from the day in the pool when the water bubbled. I took a cautions step towards him and couldn't believe what I was seeing. Were my eyes playing tricks on me again? They haven't been the most reliable part of my body these past couple of weeks. They *had* to be playing tricks on me. I almost wished I was seeing things again, but I wasn't. A flame had ignited at his fingertips and blazed up his wrist.

I couldn't breathe but what managed to escape from my last breath was, "No way…"

The color drained from his face, his skin pale in the light of the fire. Heart thumping painfully, I took another step closer as the flames continued to grow. Eerie wasn't the word. The flames grew all the way up his forearm, turning his sleeves to ashes. To top it off, his eyes were reddish-orange. I watched my best friend's hands and eyes catch on fire. A strange feeling possessed me, forced me to grab him by the wrist. Steam quickly filled the space between us. I must have somehow extinguished the flames because they were gone and so were the fiery eyes.

Fire and Ice, I thought, still holding onto his wrist, admiring the warm clouds of moisture around us.

"What are you doing?" Marcus squealed, snatching his arm away from me.

"You were on *fire* that's what just happened."

"Explain how you put it —" He slowly covered his mouth with his hand, staring at me, examining my face. I'd seen that look before. I've been examined.

He gasped, "How did your eyes get blue?"

"Is everything OK in there?" Mrs. Peterson said, banging on the door.

"Yes, Mom we're OK. No need to come in," Marcus panicked.

"How long have you been setting things on fire?"

He paused for a moment. "About two months," Marcus said, pouting and plopped on his bed.

"Wait! The pool. It *was* you heating it up. I knew it."

Mystery solved.

His eyes rushed to the door. "Shhh! Keep it down. It all started when I noticed the temperature would increase around me and sometimes things would catch on fire, but never my hands. I freaked out 'cause for the most part I wouldn't remember anything. That's why I didn't tell anyone. What about you?"

"For the past few weeks my eyes would turn blue at random, but prom night I froze—"

"What did you freeze?"

"A cup of water I was drinking—and then just now."

"So what do we do with all this?" he asked disgustedly like we just contracted a deadly disease.

I grabbed my belongings and waltzed to the door with the biggest smile on my face.

"Where are you going?" Marcus asked.

"You can stay here but I'm going to find the Professor and join the X-Men."

"What? Dylan, this is no time for games."

"Yeah. You're right — The Fantastic Four could be a better fit for us, but they already have the human torch so you may be out of a job."

"Dylan, for real! Let's be serious about this."

"Awe, man this is the coolest thing to ever happen to me."

"Why us though?"

"Whoooo caressss…" I said, spinning in circles around the room.

"Wait, can you be serious just for a split second. If we both have these…"

"Superpowers."

"Right, these superpowers, then there *has* to be others out there with different abilities, too right?"

"Well that makes sense, but how will we find them?"

"What if they don't want to be found? Dylan, I don't think we can share this with anyone."

It was amazing! What teenage boy doesn't wish that he and his best friend wake up one day with superpowers? Amazing as it was, I had to agree with him. I'd seen too many movies where people with superhuman abilities were hunted down or experimented on by government agencies.

"I agree. I don't think we can tell anyone, not even our parents. How do you think we even got these powers? I don't remember falling into any kind of toxic waste or being an alien from a distance planet," I said.

"Let's just go on with our normal everyday lives and try to not use these powers OK," Marcus urged.

"*Try* not to use these powers? What if someone said you couldn't run track because you were naturally fast? It's not everyday people wake up and realize they're different than the average human. We can be heroes, Marc! Just a minute ago you were saying how you wanted to give people second chances at life. Here it is, this is your chance."

"Relax. After graduation we'll figure this whole thing out."

"I'm so looking forward to graduation."

Chapter 9

Graduation

The tone at school with all the seniors was pretty serious due to finals. No one stopped in the halls to catch up on gossip or joke around. I don't even think people pulled their cellphones from their bags. During lunch, most of the class commented on how much fun Trey's party was. There was even a rumor that Jessica was making out with somebody in the bathroom.

I normally don't help spread rumors but if it got her off my case, I would tell a few people what I heard. I never made it to the party. Discovering you have the ability to freeze objects without using a freezer trumps a party any day.

On Tuesday Trey finally gave in and started speaking to Marcus. They talked about what happened at the first pool party and of course Marcus lied. By Wednesday the crew was back together.

The week wrapped up on Friday with graduation rehearsal.

Saturday was graduation day.

It's so ironic.

When we're younger, we look forward to riding our first bike or opening a room full of gifts on our birthday. In our teenage years we look forward to dating, driving, and our first kiss. But as a senior in high school, the countdown to graduation starts that first day of class. Today that countdown has finally ended. I've been excited all year but after my discovery last week, I was dying for this day to come.

When I woke up my room had been completely taken over by blue and white balloons, the school colors, hanging from the ceiling and across the floor. I found three cards on the dresser from Mom, Dad, and Dalton. I opened Mom's first. A hundred-dollar bill fell out. I looked to the left and read her words:

> *Dylan,*
>
> *You always strive for excellence so never stop challenging yourself. I am very proud of the young man you have become. Do great things in New York City. Do great things in life. Be great.*

A tear formed and I ran my knuckle in the corner. I read Dad's card next:

> *Sorry no money or gift cards, I bought you a car already. Congrats son.*

Dad's card didn't surprise me. At least it helped put a smile on my face. Dalton's card was next. It was homemade. On the outside he drew a picture of the world. On top of that he had a stick figure wearing a cape:

> *You are my HERO Dylan!*

That was all he wrote.

Right then, a tear fell.

It rolled down my face and froze before I could push it off. I felt more forming up in my eyes, so I put the cards up before the waterworks came. My parents told me the night before they would be gone with Dalton all day and would meet me at school for graduation. Outside the sky was grayish-blue and trickles of rain tapped lightly on the roof. Forehead glued to the window I mumbled, "Not today, rain."

I'd planned on spending the day with Marcus and his family since mine were gone. I packed my bag with some clothes and my cap and gown.

I walked right in once I got there.

"Hey, Mr. and Mrs. Peterson," I said, brushing my feet against the welcome mat then removing my shoes at the door.

"Wassup, Dylan," Elias nodded, his eyes fixated on the TV while Katie sat on his laps; his parents were on the couch looking uninterested at the cartoons playing.

"Well, someone is in a great mood today," said Mrs. Peterson, sounding like she could sense my joyous emotions.

"Come in. Take a seat," Mr. Peterson said.

I took one look at the couch and offered to stand.

"Where's Marcus?" I asked Katie in a squeaky voice who was now running around the small living room, clapping wildly. She pointed to the back room.

"He's in the shower," Mrs. Peterson replied for Katie.

"How does your room look, Elias?" I grinned.

He snorted. "Mom made me and Marcus clean it. Said she was afraid stray animals were in there." He stood and stretched his arms, an amusing smile on his face. "I mean, it would've been cool to see, but, we cleaned it anyway."

"Thank you," I whispered to myself. "Hope it stays that way while Marcus and I are off to college."

"How does it feel now that you're done with high school?" Mr. Peterson asked.

I wasn't sure if I was tired of people asking me that or just irritated at the question. Seriously, how do people think I feel knowing that I'm moving out of my parent's house and not having to put up with the drama of high school?

"It feels good, but it will feel even better when I walk across the stage with a diploma in my hands."

"I remember my high school graduation—"

"Ryan, please don't bore him with your old stories," said Mrs. Peterson in slight embarrassment.

"How do you know he doesn't want to hear my stories, Kathryn?"

"Have you guys heard Marc's speech for graduation?" I chimed in before an argument began.

Mr. Peterson sat straight. "No. He said no one can hear it until graduation."

Marcus was our Salutatorian and had to give a speech after the Valedictorian. Our senior class had 255 students graduating and I was number twelve. I missed the top ten by point seven points on my overall average, making me miss out on another picture in the yearbook. We were all looking forward to hearing his speech. Although Marcus had very little experience speaking in front of large crowds, he said he wasn't nervous.

"You want something to drink, Dylan?" asked Marcus as he entered the room with the rest of us.

"Juice."

He handed me a cup and gestured me to follow him to his room. He closed the door and locked it. "Wow, your brother wasn't lying, this room is clean."

"Yeah, Mom sort of made us clean. It even smells good too."

"Smells better than usual." I walked around then room then spun around to face him. "So, can I get a sample of your grad speech?"

"Nice try but I'm not letting anyone hear it until it's time."

"So —" My mouth got tight until my lips perched open into a giddy smile. "—have you used your powers any this week?"

"Quiet, my parents might hear you," he whispered and gripped my arm, drug me into the corner of the room, and covered my mouth. I smacked his hand off me and smiled.

"Sorry, geesh, calm down."

"My bad. No I haven't. Have you?"

"No, I've been pretty chill. Get it, *chill*?" I laughed harshly and stopped when I realized he wasn't laughing. He stood there with a blank face. "*Man,* you're a real party pooper. You need to lighten up, dude, it's freaking graduation day."

He turned and looked at the window, the rain steadily pouring outside. "Think you could turn the rain into snow?" he inquired, a smile now forming.

"Better! I can turn it into hail," I replied.

He folded his arms across his chest. "Go for it."

We walked over to the window. I placed my hands on the glass and told myself to relax. All sound in the room died except the throbbing beat of my heart. I controlled my breathing to keep a smooth regular pattern. Marcus stood next to me shifting his calm eyes between the window and me. I closed my eyes, exhaled, and then gradually opened them.

"Blue eyes, good sign," said Marcus. "Just relax. Whatever you imagine, you can do it. You control your powers."

"I control my powers." The words rolled off my tongue between each slow and deep breath.

"Whoa. Have your eyes ever glowed?"

Not wanting to break concentration, I didn't reply.

"Come on, Dylan, you got this," Marcus whispered. "Come on."

His raspy voice was soothing to my jittering nerves. In seconds, a thin glaze of ice covered the window.

I grunted as a sharp pain attacked my temples. I stumbled away from the window.

"You OK?" Marcus asked. He put one hand on the window. It defrosted instantly.

"Yeah, just need to relax a little," I said as I took a seat.

"What was that?" Marcus flinched, his body seized in horror.

"What was what?" I said with my hands on my temples like that would somehow ease the pain.

His words shuddered as he spoke. "You didn't see that computer mouse slide across the desk?"

I shook my head and rested on his pillow. After a long pause, completely ignoring the fact that he thought his room was haunted, I asked, "Did you say my eyes glowed?"

"Yeah. Wasn't like a flashlight or anything, but it was breathtaking. I've never seen anything like it."

"Well duh, have you seen anything like what we're doing?"

"I guess you're right."

"OK, Marcus, show me something," I said, my voice barely above a whisper to be sure not to aggravate my migraine.

"No time. We need to get ready."

"You played me, loser."

"Wait, let me check your eyes before we walk out." He gripped my cheeks in his palm and stretched my face. He cleared me.

As we walked into the living room I heard a ring come from my bag.

It was a text from Diana: *Looks like we have ourselves a rainy day.*

Marcus' parents ordered pizza for lunch. I was on all fours, crawling around the house with Katie on my back giggling, while Marcus locked himself in the bathroom to rehearse his speech. He wouldn't even come out for food.

Once Marcus and I finished, we headed up to the school to prep for graduation. We walked inside. The senior class stood around with their blue cap and gowns, trying to grasp the reality we were living in that moment. It all became too real. Cliques were huddled up crying and laughing like they would never see each other again. All of our teachers stood with anxious smiles ready for summer vacation to start.

"This is it, guys, we're out of here after today," Trey said, walking up to Marcus and I.

Trey was moving to Alabama since he received a full athletic scholarship to play football. He was leaving in July to attend camps with his new team. Talk about an adventure and culture shock from New York.

"If it isn't my favorite men of our senior class," Diana said as she jumped on my back. "You and I have a date tonight, Dylan."

"What are you talking about, Diana?" I reached back and cuffed my arms under her legs.

"You told me we could talk on a rainy day. Did you notice the weather today? *It's raining*," she smirked.

"Looks like you have yourself a date tonight, Dylan," Marcus said jokingly.

"You're next, Marcus," she said.

Marcus turned his back to her as Trey and I laughed. As flirty and out there as Diana was, she was one of the coolest chicks I'd ever met.

"Looks like me and you will find some trouble to get into tonight on our own," Trey said to Marcus.

"Don't have too much fun without me, guys," I cried. "Diana and I will try and meet up with you guys after our 'date' I guess."

Mr. Reed came out into the hallway and let out a loud cough. Any other day that would straighten us all up but we ignored him and continued talking.

"Seniors!" he bellowed, silencing us.

He slid his glasses up with one finger. "This is the end of the road for you all. Trust me when I say that four years with some of you was enough." He peered the room, the wrinkles tight in the corners of his eyes. Everyone chuckled. Some seniors really made him earn his paycheck over the past four years.

"Just remember," he continued. "It isn't over until you have your diplomas in your hands and the ceremony is over. I expect *everyone* to be on their best Poughkeepsie Senior High behavior. Here we go." With one thunderous clap of his hands, we were assembled into a straight line.

The stands of the gymnasium were all filled with our families, teachers, and whoever else wanted to attend. Soon as the graduation song blared from the speakers we walked in slowly and in unison. It was the first time our class had accomplished anything together. The crowd now had eyes on us. I didn't want to squint and strain my eyes looking for my folks or the Petersons. I knew they were there and would find us afterward.

Since we were in alpha order, normally, Marcus would sit next to me, but because he was giving his Salutatorian speech, he sat on stage with the Valedictorian. It sucked cause now I had to sit next to Doug — the boy who had a year-round disease. No one ever knew what the problem was but for some reason he was always sick. Because it's raining, I knew he'd be sniffling the whole time.

"Hey, Dylan," he said, running his hand across his nose, collecting drippings of whatever came flowing from his nostrils. He stuck his hand out, expecting me to shake it.

I looked down at his infested hand then waved back at him while trying to disguise the disgusted look on my face.

I think I smiled.

"We better pay attention to Mr. Reed, Doug."

"Greetings, everyone." Mr. Reed called the gymnasium to order and began the ceremony. The moment he began to speak, all the students pulled their cell phones out to text and take pictures. I hoped everyone has their phones on silent because Mr. Reed was the man to hold a diploma if he heard a phone go off during graduation. I unzipped my gown and reached into my breast pocket. I looked down and responded to the message Diana sent me:

> **Diana: Marcus sure is looking scrumptious on stage**
> **Me: Why don't you just ask him out if you like him so much.**
> **Diana: Be serious Dill Pickle. We are leaving for college soon**
> **Me: Well don't try and start something and end it.**
> **Diana: I'm not looking for a relationship ;)**
> **Me: You never are.**
> **Diana: What time are you picking me up tonight??**
> **Me: I'll call you later.**

Some time had passed. A few teachers and the principal had spoken along with the Mayor who was the guest speaker. After the Mayor, Samantha, our class president and Valedictorian, gave her speech. She spoke for about ten minutes and then introduced Marcus as he carefully walked to the podium.

I could feel his nerves.

He tapped the microphone and leaned in. "Hello." It screeched. He stumbled back and fell into the lap of Mr. Reed. A few people in the rows behind me began chuckling. *You got this, brother*, I thought.

We heard what sounded like a wrestling match before he hopped back up and hunched over the podium awkwardly. His hands gripped the sides. He peered around in silence for a moment and then straightened the curve in his back to a line and held his chest proudly. The whole class was now tuned in to what he had to say.

Then, he began…

Hello senior class of Poughkeepsie Senior High,

He started off and the first sentence flowed out. He even managed to slightly fix that raspy voice of his to something more professional and clear.

To the seniors, friends, family, and distinguished guests. My name is Marcus Peterson and I am the Salutatorian for our class. When I was told that I was going to have to give a speech, I have to admit, I was a little bit nervous. I am not the most popular kid in our class, and I've never been known for anything besides becoming prom king, which is still a shocker. My point is, in high school we place a lot of emphasis on social profiles — who's the most popular or the most athletic, rather than getting to know people personally and emotionally. Most of us have been together since elementary school and there is no reason we all shouldn't be best friends. However, rather than befriend each other, we grew apart over the years and split into different cliques. Why can't the student government hang with the basketball players or the chemistry club hang with the football players? Why don't we all know that Emily Stockton was the number one tennis player for the state of New York or that Pedro Santiago speaks three other languages aside from Spanish and English? These are the people who we all have known for years and who are in this crowd of people standing before me.

A few days ago my best friend Dylan Perry told me to not worry about my high school years, because in college, people will not know who I am and that I could be anybody. I told him—

"He said, I just want to be Marcus," I yelled. He smiled, nodded, and finished.

In my head I was thinking that I didn't want to forget my high school years. Even though they weren't the greatest socially, I was one of the few people who remained true to themselves and didn't conform to what society wanted.

Four years ago we entered the doors to Poughkeepsie Senior High with one mission—to graduate. Today we accomplished that mission and I just want to say congrats grads, and stay true to you.

Everyone stood and cheered for Marcus. It was the first time I saw people actually noticing him for the person he really was and giving him what he deserved — respect. I was blown away by his speech and how well he spoke. From the reaction of our peers, they were too. I think he even startled Mr. Reed, who was probably expecting him to go up and fall flat on his face like he did pre-speech. Once he got back to the podium, Mr. Reed began to call our names.

About twenty minutes later, I was finally up and walking in line to the stage. I took a few paces forward and came to the stairs that led to the stage.

This was it.

"Dylan Perry," Mr. Reed called out.

I walked on the stage overwhelmed with joy. There was no way I could hide it, nor did I want to. I walked up to him, shook his hand, grabbed my diploma and threw both hands in the air. The people cheered for me like they did for everyone. I was supposed to walk off the stage after that, but I had to wait for Marcus to receive his. His name was called next. He got up and walked to Mr. Reed to receive his Diploma. Once he got it, he walked over and threw his arms around me.

"We did it, bro," he said, taking his cap that read *Harvard rejected me* and flashed it to the crowd.

Mr. Reed tilted his head and peered over his glasses. Marcus and I both went back to our seats. Once all the names were called we rotated our tassels right to left and when the ceremony was complete, we all threw our caps into the air.

Graduation was over.

We all met our families outside. The rain stopped and the sun was trying to fight its way through the residual storm clouds.

"Nice speech, bro. I knew you had that in you." I hugged him. "I think you might have touched some of the people and don't even realize it."

"Look at my two grown men over there," Mom said. Our parents came over and greeted us. We all took turns exchanging hugs and handshakes. Mom and Dad gave Marcus a graduation card that had two hundred dollars in it. His parents gave me a card with a gift card to *Café Bocca.* We both received some balloons.

"OK, let me get a picture, you two," said Mrs. Peterson. Our moms pulled out their cameras and we struck a pose.

"One more, Mom," I said then called out for Trey to join. We all struck a gangsta pose and captured the everlasting moment.

"Attention, all seniors over here for our last time together," Samantha yelled. We all ran over in a large huddle.

"On the count of three, can we get one last Falcons," she said. We all cheered in excitement. "One — two — three — FALCONS!" We all yelled out.

I spent the next few hours with my and Marcus' family. We celebrated over food before getting ready for the night. I had my date with Diana, while Marcus and Trey were going to ride around and go to different graduation parties. I changed into something a little more comfortable, called Diana, and told her I would pick her up from her house.

Once we met, she had me drive to the same park where Jessica and I used to meet. It wasn't an elaborate park, but it always calmed me when my nerves got the best of me. There was a small pond with a walking trail around it, along with a sand pit, a few swings, and a slide.

Diana never had a bad day. I had on shorts with the back pockets ripped and a black tee that had "I <3 NY" on the front. She, on the other hand, had on slim fit jeans with a pink and purple graphic beater and a black leather jacket. And she wouldn't be Diana if she didn't have on a pair of heels.

"When does school start for you?" she asked.

"The first week of September. I wish it were a little sooner though. I'm ready to get out and be on my own, so to speak."

"I know what you mean. Time to kiss this little town behind and head to the city. So you promised me you would tell me why you and basketball never made it to senior year."

"Ehh…"

"No, you promised me. Talk," she demanded.

"My dad — my dad went to Poughkeepsie Senior High and … well, he was a basketball all-star."

"So what's wrong with that?" She took my hand and guided me to a bench along the trail. She gave me the impression that she was sincerely interested in knowing. She extended her legs and crossed them, signaling her attentiveness.

"My dad placed so much pressure on me when I was younger, he basically *forced* the game on me. I never really wanted to play basketball, well at first I didn't, and when I finally did start to like the game, it was too late."

"Too late for what?"

"I didn't feel I was good enough to go any further. My dad was worshiped at Poughkeepsie. He went on to play college ball and was great there also. When my dad had a son he wanted nothing else but for him to be a basketball star just like him. Anyway, when senior year came around, I wanted to spare my feelings."

"What do you mean?"

"Scouts were going to start coming to the games to look for potential players for their schools. I didn't want to be embarrassed if I didn't get picked by a college."

"Where's the confident Dylan I know who always scored the most points just about every game?"

"That Dylan's a fraud." I couldn't believe I just said that. "The only time I truly feel confident is when I'm around Marc."

"Why Marcus?"

"Most people don't see the strength Marcus has. He's very confident in himself and the things that he does. When I'm around him I feel the same. At times I wish I could be him."

Whoa, I thought. I didn't know why she was so easy to talk to. It was different but comforting. We walked over to the swing and I began to push her on it.

"So when I decided to quit, I thought that I could focus more on classes and try to get into college based on academics as opposed to athletics."

"And how did that play out?"

"Well I got accepted into Stanford," I mumbled. Dirt flickered as her heels dug into the ground. She whipped her head around.

"WHAT! You got into where?"

I whispered again, "Stanford."

"And *why* are you not going there?"

I debated on telling her the whole story. No one knew the reason that I turned down Harvard so I decided to go ahead and vent. "Because I was accepted into Harvard."

Her nose scrunched and her sapphire eyes narrowed onto me like a hawk. "But I thought you were going to NYU? Please explain."

"I got into Stanford, Harvard and a few other big name colleges but Marcus didn't, so I just went with NYU."

"You turned down a school like that so you could play tag with your best friend?"

"I wasn't too sure about going out alone that far. What if something went wrong or I didn't like it or just failed at everything? It would have been nice to have Marcus at Harvard but things just didn't work out like that. I'm not mad at the decision I made, just slightly disappointed at how things played out."

"I don't know each and every detail, but I'm sure Marcus wouldn't have minded if you got into Harvard and he didn't. He seems like he's better than that. I'm not going to judge you on that but you better find some confidence fast before the Big Apple takes a bite out of you."

She was right but I still couldn't bring myself to tell Marcus. Some things you just had to keep to yourself.

We got lost in the time, laughing and talking when my phone rang.

It was Marcus.

He told me to meet him and Trey. He was out of breath and fear lingered in his words. Something told me they weren't out partying like they said they were.

Chapter 10

Trouble!

First stop: Samantha's house. Surprisingly she had a nice crowd.

"Thank you for coming, guys. I think your speech really triggered something Marcus. Look, I even have some jocks and cheerleaders here." Her voice reached soprano as she pointed around to admire the diverse crew at her party.

I smiled and thanked her. I was really hoping that my speech would give our class a deeper understanding of who I was and a look at the way we really treated each other.

Trey and I walked around, chatting with some of the classmates. Samantha's dad was on the grill and the food smelled delicious. He had burgers, sausage, and chicken with a special sauce on it he called "Daddy Jack's make you smack" sauce. I think I may have tried everything twice. I sat down for a moment, or I planned for it to be a moment, because I was too full and it hurt to blink, let alone move.

We walked over to the pool chairs, even though she didn't have a pool, to lie down. There were other people lying around too probably just as full as I was.

"So Alabama? So far, man," I said, patting my stomach and still licking my fingers trying to relive that amazing sauce.

"I couldn't turn down free college money and *what* an adventure that would be for anybody to travel that far and play ball. I'm ready," Trey said.

"What about your family? How are they taking it?"

Trey stood, stretched, and yawned, "They're excited." He sat down and locked his hands behind his back. "They think it would be a good thing for me to get away from here. With my sister gone, they can relax and travel even more and whatever else it is they want to do."

"How *is* Crystal doing these days?"

"She's great last time I checked. She got her first duty station in Germany so I don't get to talk to her very often. How cool is it though that you are moving to the City?"

"Ahh man, I can't wait. I got some scholarships and financial aid to cover most of it. I'm taking out a loan to cover the last of it. Even though I'll be only two hours from home, I still think it'll be quite an adventure for me and Dylan."

"You guys are going to have a great time out there. I've never met anyone who didn't love living in New York City. Just make sure we still hang out during holidays, and maybe in the future you guys can come down and visit the country. *Sweet Home Alabama*," he sung in his Lynard Skynyrd voice.

"Just don't get all *country* on me and start wearing cowboy hats and boots, and please — please — Trey, don't come back with that terrible southern accent they have down there."

"Any more requests?"

"Not at the moment."

Samantha's mom brought out a pole, and started playing limbo with everyone. It was quite entertaining to see the defensive players bend their large bodies backward. The childish limbo music got Trey and I up for a quick game before we left. I grabbed another burger on our way out as we contemplated where to go next.

"Thanks for coming," Samantha waved.

"Where does all that go?" Trey asked, starting the car.

"What? The food?" I gazed at the burger and took a bite. "Umm… I have no clue."

"As much as you eat and you're still a chump. Where to next?"

"Uhhhh I dunno…." He was the popular one. Why was he asking me?

"Well…" He hesitated as he eased on the gas. "I got invited to Jessica's house. Would you care if we stopped by?"

Of course I cared. I didn't want to go to the evil sorceress' house on graduation night. She already ruined prom for my friends and me. I wasn't going to give her another day of mine.

"Sure. I don't mind," I lied.

"OK, whenever you want to leave just let me know."

We got to Jessica's house and the party was everywhere — the front of the house, inside, and the backyard, which is where the majority of the people were. Did the whole high school show up here because this place was packed? We went around the back so we didn't have to fight our way through the door. Jessica was pinned on the wall with one leg kicked back talking with one of the guys from school. I think he was one of Dylan's old teammates. She spotted us and pushed him to the side, leaving him standing clueless and walked over.

"Trey! Glad you could make it," she said. "Macchiato." She snarled not looking in my direction. "You guys are missing one I see. Where's Dylan?"

I didn't bother to look her direction either. "He's on a date," I said just loud enough for her to hear. "With Diana." I added in for laughs and giggles.

"Ooo…" She sneered, curling her lips in anger. I laughed as she stormed off in frustration, adding satisfaction to my night.

"You guys are something else," Trey said. "You know she is going to find some way to get you back, Marcus."

"And you know, I couldn't care less."

We didn't stay that long. The party was packed but lacked real entertainment. I was better off staying at Samantha's house where there was good food and limbo.

"Bonfire?" Trey shrugged, his eyebrows mimicking his shoulders.

"It's still early but we can head over now."

We drove off to the school.

"Turn this up, I love this song," Trey screamed and continued rapping along with the radio. I acted like I didn't know the words so he wouldn't force me to play karaoke, but he pushed around until I joined in.

Keeping his eyes on the road, he handed me a CD. "Here, put this on, dude. I know you'll like this."

I loosened up this time and jumped right into the lyrics. I could have a successful career as a rapper if I knew how to dress and talk to girls. I got into the music, throwing my hands in the air, my body rocking to the hardcore beat.

"Dude, it's *blazing* in here," Trey said, rolling down the windows.

"How bout you close your mouth, bro and maybe it won't be so bad." Although I joked with Trey about the heat, I knew the reason why.

I closed my eyes so that the music could flow through me as I moved.

Trey's attention was elsewhere because he didn't see what was ahead of us. I opened my eyes and my heart instantly punched against my chest.

Palms sweaty, I grabbed the steering wheel and screamed, "TREY LOOK OUT!"

My body tensed as he grabbed the wheel with me.

I braced myself for impact, holding onto anything that wouldn't send me flying. *Mom would freak if she found out I was in a car without my seatbelt on,* I thought. We swerved around the dark object in the street; the tires screeched as Trey slammed on the break, spinning the car out of control down the lonely street. My body jolted against the window, sparks flying from the clashing metal. The car rammed into the guardrail on my side and came to a complete stop.

"You OK, Marcus?" Trey asked, cursing up a storm. Above his eye was a small cut, a thin line of blood coming down. He wiped the blood with his palms.

My chest tightened and the sounds coming from my trembling lips tormented me as I gasped for air. I was fine for the most part. Scared, but fine. My arm felt hot.

"My arm," I said, clenching on to it, "It's bleeding, but I can still move it. Just a few scrapes."

Trey reached over and hauled me out of the car on his side since my door was pushed against the rail. We looked behind us to see what was in the street.

It was a man.

Judging by the distance he was a few inched taller than me.

He was facing away from us not moving.

We walked over slowly, but I had to stop when the pain said so.

Trey walked up alone, glancing back with each step. The man was dressed in all black — hoodie, jeans and boots. He didn't appear to be hurt or scared.

"Sir, are you OK?" Trey yelled, getting closer. You could feel Trey's fear in the dark of the night like needles with each inch of him getting closer to the peculiar stranger.

I stopped on the side of the street and ripped off some of my shirt to use as a tourniquet for my arm that was now steadily bleeding. Trey unsuccessfully got the stranger to say anything.

"Maybe he's in shock," Trey called back to me. His voice was faint as I was concentrating on wrapping my arm. Trey was now close enough to where he could touch the man. As his hand slowly rose to tap his shoulder, I knew something really didn't feel right.

He saw us coming and didn't move or budge and he *still* hasn't moved or said anything to us. This man was not in shock; he had no business being in the middle of the street.

Trey's hand was almost on his shoulder.

My heart was now in my throat, making it hard for me to breath. My hand, still pressed on my arm with a dirty shirt wrapped around it, started to cover in blood. Smoke from the car infiltrated my nostrils and the lack of light had those needles stabbing the side of my neck.

I raised my head after soaking in the accident and the words reacted to fear. "TREY!"

Trey froze, his hand right on the stranger's shoulder, his head twisted my direction. I stole the surprise off of Trey's face.

I gasped.

"Duck!" I yelled.

Trey didn't ask any questions and hit the ground in just the nick of time. The man put his hands together and shot a beam of sparkling blue ice particles that was moving faster than lightning striking to the ground. The ice without a doubt would have killed Trey.

There I was struggling to stand with a half-wrapped bleeding arm and ice racing to my death. I didn't have time to think and in an instant, my hands went from brown to flame. I mimicked what the ice guy did and stuck my arms in front of me and it was like I absorbed the ice. When I took the ice in, the momentum spun me around in a three-sixty and I shot a stream of fire at him.

Trey, still on the ground breathing viciously with one side of his face planted on the asphalt as the battle of fire and ice took place above him, darted his eyes back and forth between the two of us with sweat dripping to the pavement. Right before my attack could hit the stranger, he sprung into the air and disappeared. I ran to Trey, who was now back on his feet.

"I'm fine, how did you — MARCUS LOOK OUT!" he screamed, pointing over my shoulder.

He grabbed me and ran, pushing me to the side as the stranger flew past us so fast the wind whistled in my ear. He left a trail of ice on the ground as he went back into the sky.

"Stay right here, Trey, don't move." I grappled his arms to make sure he understood how serious I was. I figured he wasn't going to leave us alone unless we could escape, but I didn't see that happening.

Paranoid, I walked back into the middle of the abandoned street that only had one dim streetlight, to try and find out who he was and what he wanted with us.

I couldn't stop shaking.

But I knew I had to pull it together.

This was a life or death situation.

And I wanted life.

I looked back at Trey resting on one of the guardrails. As I turned back around I realized I was no longer on the ground and Trey voice calling out for me was becoming more distant.

It happened that fast.

The man grabbed me by the throat and held onto me as we breezed through the air with my feet dangling. I grabbed his arms for comfort; in the event he was to lose his grip, I needed something to hold. I couldn't get a good look at him since his hood cast a large shadow over his face. We sprinted through the winds and into the tree line then — SMACK!

He slammed me into a tree, my body now crippled in pain, his grip still tight on my throat. He rose to stand tall, taking me with him; the bark of the tree scraped the back of my head and neck, tearing through my cheap tee shirt with every movement. I grunted and moaned as he continued to strangle the life out me. My head felt as if I was hit with a baseball — no helmet. I couldn't focus on the pain of everywhere else until I got rid of my energetic headache.

My hands slid off his sweaty wrist as I tried to create a wedge and break the hold of his hands around my neck, but his meaty fingers had dug deep into my throat. The shapes around me were growing dim from the lack of oxygen and all I could think was, *what the hell.* He removed one hand and reached for his hood that draped over his face and slid it off. For the first time ever I witnessed someone African-American with translucent blue eyes.

I was captivated.

"What — do — you — want — with us?" I managed to say with his hand wrapped around my neck.

A menacing smile on his face, he leaned into my face and whispered, "Not us. You."

He examined my body like an experiment — looking over my face and neck.

Something wasn't right and I was losing oxygen by the seconds.

His eyes trailed both my arms. "You. Aren't. Like. The others...." His voice monotone. "What are you?"

I didn't know what he meant by that.

"You are... different," he said.

The feeling of me possibly dying caused images of my family, graduation and Dylan to replay in my head. A boost of energy filled me and my hands sparked back up. I didn't know how to control the bursts, but it seemed to happen at the right times.

Almost instinctual.

My hands released from his wrists and stamped him in the chest, catching him off guard. My fists left a scorched mark in the middle of his hoodie. He released me and I slid down the tree as he stumbled back. I stood up, grabbed his arm, pulled him closer to me and watched as fire took over him. He knelt down and I grabbed his other arm and lit him up.

He cried out for me to stop. His eyes suddenly went from blue to dark brown. I couldn't fathom what I was doing, so I stopped. He was barely alive from what I could tell.

"What the heck am I?" I said, looking at my hands in disbelief. I still couldn't grasp what was going on with my body. I left him there and ran back to check on Trey, constantly looking back to make sure the guy was still alive.

"What the hell is going on?" Trey ranted when I reached him. "That dude tried to kill us."

"Actually," I gasped for air, "he just wanted to kill me. You were just at the wrong place at the wrong time. Think the car can still drive? I need to get cleaned up."

"Yo! You shot *fire* out of your *hands*. How the heck did you do that? And that guy — that guy shot ice from his hands and he *flew*." He continued his rant as he paced down the street. I didn't even care that he knew; I was just happy to be alive.

"Where is that guy? What if he comes back, Marcus? What is going on?"

"Trey, just get me out of here," I said as I fell to my knees. My vision was going in out and I needed to eat to get my chemistry back in order.

We got in the car and drove away from the scene and pulled over in a random alley. Trey pulled some old napkins out from the glove compartment and pressed them to wounds.

"So how long have you known you were — whatever it is you are? *What are you?*" He spoke in an understanding tone. Whatever was going on with me, he wasn't scared. Or at least, he pretended not to be.

"Not that long. It just started happening recently. That was me at your pool party heating the water up and—"

"I know." He smiled; a small chuckled escaped in a breath. "It's not every day you see someone's eyes flash red. I just put two and two together. It freaked me the hell out, you know. So, do you know anybody else with *powers* besides the guy who tried to kill you?"

"No. As far as I knew I was the only one." I pulled out my phone and called Dylan. "Bro, we have an emergency. Meet me and Trey at the restaurant ASAP and come alone."

Trey cranked the banged car up and drove to the restaurant. It didn't run or sound as smooth as it used to. I wondered what his parents were going to say?

"Dylan knows what you can do?"

"Yeah, he *was* the only one."

He caught a glimpse of my playful side-eye. "If you're worried about me telling people, don't be."

"I'm not. I'm just a little bit nervous about what all this means, you know? I have no idea why I have this ability."

When we got to the restaurant, I told Trey to park in the back to be a little more inconspicuous. We went in and I locked the door behind us. We took a seat but kept the lights off and waited in silence. There was a polite knock on the window that caused us to jump.

It was Dylan.

Guess Trey and I were still shaken up from the attack. Trey let him in.

"What happened?" Dylan asked, rushing in past Trey.

He looked at the both of us, analyzing the condition of our clothes and bodies. Trey and I just stood there — him with his ripped-up clothes and scratched up face, and me with half my clothes burnt off and a bloody arm. Not to mention all the other scrapes and bruises I had all over my body.

"We were just driving and in the car goofing around. Some man appeared in the middle of the street, Trey swerved, crashed, and the guy went crazy," I said.

"So I take it that Trey knows everything?" Dylan said.

"Yeah I told him about *my* powers and that you knew. I also told him that I didn't know *anybody* else with powers until our encounter with the crazy guy."

His brown eyes squinted at me then over to Trey. Trey looked at the both of us.

"Okayyy, so what did this crazy guy look like?" Dylan asked.

"That's the thing, he *looked* normal, just like you and I."

"Except he could shoot ice from his hands," Trey added. "Yep, other than that, pretty normal I would say."

"Ice?" Dylan cocked his head to the side. "He could shoot *ice* from his hands?"

"Almost took me out with it. Good thing Marcus was there," Trey boosted.

"And he could fly," I mentioned.

"This is too much for one night. Let's get you guys home. Where's your car, Trey?" Dylan asked.

"It's around back."

"Good. Do you think you'll be fine to drive home alone? I'll give Marc a ride."

"Yeah."

"Be careful, Trey," I said.

I went to Dylan's house to give him all the details. We walked up to his room and I took a seat at his desk. He went to the bathroom and came back with a first-aid kit.

"Now, what really happened?"

"Well, he had the same powers as you but he could fly. He had the whole blue eyes and *everything*. Then, he told me that I'm not like the others."

"Not like the others…" he whispered to himself, looking down at the ground and rubbing his chin. He continued to clean the blood off me. "Damn, Marc, this guy really did a number on you. I always knew you could hold your own."

I grabbed his hand and his attention as he cleaned my chin. "Hey, remember when you said that there would be other people out there with powers and we should find them?"

"Yeah."

"I think they know about me somehow and are coming to hunt me down. And as far as them, I *really* don't think they want to be found."

Chapter 11

Training Day

Since the attack a few weeks ago, nothing else major happened. I've been busy working to save up money for college and spending time with my family. Marcus was also busy working and hitting the gym as much as possible. He was determined to get stronger and gain some weight before we left for college. Trey came around at times but was training and conditioning in preparation for football. I managed to not use my powers or speak about them in front of Marcus due to his encounter with the mystery man. He was suffering from a little PTSD but slowly coming back to his normal self. I'm guessing the weights had been a stress reliever.

Mom spent a huge amount of time with Dalton. Any free time she had away from the hospital was spent doing activities he enjoyed. On Tuesdays she took him to karate class and soccer on Mondays and Wednesdays. I even caught her in his room playing video games. She may act like she didn't like them but was getting competitive lately.

Like Dad.

Speaking of, he was excited that I got my first job. I know that bagging groceries wasn't a real job, but I made an income. Either way, he didn't have to give me any money for the summer. As far as his free time, I'm not sure what he did. I felt like he was never home but that could just be because I never was.

I just got off after working six days straight. The day was blistering hot and my co-workers were all looking like they wanted to fall out every time we pushed a cart out to a car. I quickly realize that my body was impervious to hot and cold temperatures so that wasn't an issue for me. Another cool thing I discovered was that I could sometimes lower the temperature around me similar to Marcus raising his. For the people I liked at work, I would turn the "AC" on for them and if they weren't in my general vicinity I would just give them a gentle blow of fresh air. The ones I didn't like, which were most of them, well … I would just let them suffer. I guess it was because I was the new guy who brought home the most money every other day.

It was the end of my shift and I checked my phone on the way to my car since my boss, Mrs. Lily, hated when we checked our phone on the sales floor. Not sure if she'd ever catch us since she's always on hers texting a mile a minute. I had one missed call from Marcus. He was at work and I wanted a smoothie so it was perfect timing.

"There he is," Mr. Peterson said as I walked into the restaurant. "Strawberry kiwi smoothie coming right up."

"Appreciate it, Mr. Peterson. No rush," I said. The place was swamped with customers and it looked like Mr. Peterson was short staffed. *Maybe I should have taken him up on his offer to help out.* Marcus was running around and tossing orders like a pro. I took a seat at the booth and slurped my smoothie and when it finally calmed down, Marcus galloped over.

"I found a place," he said, taking a seat next to me. "A place for us to train."

"What? Where? When? Let's go."

"Dylan, man you gotta be quiet. No one can know what we're doing."

"Yeah, right, gotcha. Where is it?" I almost spit out my smoothie. He pulled out a balled up receipt from his apron and wrote "10 Hilltop Ross Circle".

"What the hell is this, Marc?"

"Can you get any more stupid, Dylan? It's an address. This is where we'll spend our time away from everyone else and learn to control our powers. And don't talk like that in my father's restaurant."

"Yep yep, power control."

"Take this serious, Dylan. These freakin powers almost got me killed last time, remember?"

"Yeah and *these* powers saved your tail also. See, I didn't say the other word I was really thinking."

His palm smacked his forehead. "OK listen, midnight meet me there and we will develop a plan as to what we'll do. Like a training schedule so to speak."

Marcus had to work until close. He was working another double like he was all week. I, on the other hand, went home to relax and grab a bite to eat until it was time.

My parents didn't like it when I left the house after a certain time. I never knew what time that was, but I knew. Leaving a little before midnight wouldn't fly so I went to Trey's house before it got too late. His parents still haven't figured out how he wrecked his car so he hasn't been driving much these days. Dad would flip if I wrecked my car. The beast would truly unleash. I wasn't sure what lie Trey told, but he was still alive so that was a good sign. We went riding around and visited some friends to pass the time.

"Where to next?" Trey asked.

"Man, I'm super tired. Think I'm gonna call it a night." I fake yawned.

"Come on are you serious, dude? We barely have time to hang out anymore and now you're turning into an old man on me."

"I have work in the morning. How about next week me, you, and Marc drive up to Albany for a day?"

"Sounds like a plan. Don't bail on me." He reached for the handle and opened the door. He paused then closed the door. "What is Marcus?" Trey asked hesitantly. "I mean, is he human?"

He had to be a human. If he wasn't *human* then I wasn't and I know I am. "I'm positive Marcus is human." I assured him. He shrugged, cracked a smile, and then got out the car. From there, I headed to the address Marcus gave me.

I pulled up to a titanic isolated building that sat on a field of withering grass and shrubs. There were other gigantic buildings surrounding it.

Combined they almost formed a small campus. The mix of dead and lively trees surrounding the field secluded it from the rest of the city. Vines crawled from the ground and hugged the walls to provide color to the dull brown bricks and the giant hole on the side provided character. From the outside, it looked like an old nineteenth-century castle. The lot reminded me of an island minus the water that surrounded the place. I got out and began walking to what I assumed was the front entrance.

When I got to the door, I caught myself about to knock before I realized that no one would answer. I grabbed the padded lock and closed my eyes for a few minutes until it froze and cracked. So unlike me, but I felt chills run down my spine when I had to force the old beaten door open. It creaked and scraped the floor from years of not being used. I took a few paces forward and couldn't see much. The only light I had was the moonlight shining through the dust-covered windows and cracks from the boarded ones. I was in a lobby of some sort, but I still couldn't tell what kind of building this used to be. I walked outside to wait for Marcus.

I posted up on the two stairs that led to the front door. A few minutes had passed and that's all it took for me to realize I couldn't sit still. I got up and just wandered around, not really going anywhere.

I just needed to move.

I walked back up to the door and slowly reached down for the doorknob, preparing myself to enter again.

I couldn't do it.

I turned around to go back to my car and gasped. A shadow stood dead in my face, and it took a few moments for my brain to process that it was just Marcus.

"Damn, you scared me," I said. "What on earth is this place?"

"Come to the truck with me and help me get this stuff out."

I followed. "Where are we?"

"It's an abandoned insane asylum." He snuck a quick glance my way. "Scared?"

"Few bugs and dust don't scare me."

"Yeah, they closed it down after a fire or something."

We got to the truck and he pulled out some tiki torches. We carried them inside. We walked around the lobby setting up a perimeter of torches, and Marcus lit them with the touch of his pointer finger. The place became illuminated and we could see how creepy it really was.

We walked the halls to get a feel of where we would be training. Cobwebs infested the corners of every room we entered and the molded walls were decaying. The walls in the hallways had plants growing on them just like the exterior. It was like a nuclear wasteland rainforest. Not to mention that it reeked of mold and dead animals. Wheelchairs, tables, and syringes covered in thick layers of dust consumed the rooms that once belonged to patients. It looked more like a torture chamber than an asylum.

As we walked around, we lost the light from the torches. Marcus ignited one hand and held it in front of him. It took us almost an hour to explore one side of the building and the six stories. After that, we went back to the lobby.

"OK, shall we get started?" Marcus asked.

"What's the first thing you think we should practice," I replied.

"Well I have learned to ignite my hands on command. You should try to cover your hand with ice."

I was ready but still a little nervous about what I would look like to him if I couldn't do it. "OK. Here goes." I flickered my hands in front of me and nothing happened.

"Try again," he said. I tried again and still nothing happened. I tossed my hands into the air as frustration overwhelmed me. "Alright, relax. When I first started setting things on fire, I noticed that it happened whenever I was angry at something. I'm guessing there's an emotional trigger to this thing. The first time your eyes turned blue, what were you feeling?" he asked.

"Don't judge me, but when my eyes first turned blue, it was in class and Diana was trying to seduce me." *Seduction*? I said to myself. Could it really be the trigger to my powers?

"Wow, so a girl tries to seduce you and you freeze things? Hate to see what happens when you have—"

"Marc, Please. Do *not* finish that sentence."

Marc laughed. "OK, so maybe there was another emotion you may have been feeling at the same time. Think back to some other times that you have used your powers or when your eyes turned blue."

Well, I thought to myself, *there was the time that I found out you didn't get into Harvard, or the time that I was walking around with Monica,* but I couldn't tell him those things. I had to think harder, what else? "I got it," I said. "When I tried to turn the rain into hail, your voice was very calming and relaxing. You were encouraging me to do it, so I put myself in a relaxed state of mind and I began to freeze the window."

"So we got it, relaxation. Now relax yourself and give it another try."

I closed my eyes and pictured everything around me as a frosty wonderland. I blocked out all the noises, the annoying bugs buzzing in my ears and creepy sounds of the wind seeping through the cracks of the creaky boarded windows. Instead, I focused on the faint sound of Marcus' voice as he told me I could do anything with my powers that I imagined. When I opened my eyes, both my fists were now covered in rock hard ice. I think that in order for me to use my powers, I may need Marcus around to give me that boost of confidence.

"Good, good," he said. I defrosted my hands, letting the frost smolder from my fingertips up to my forearm. I imagined a ball of ice in my palm and when I did, ice swirled up from the palm of my hands and made the perfect sphere.

"Cool," I said. Next, I took the ball that rested in my palm and flung it in front of me and watched as it went right through the decaying wall.

"How did you…" Marcus asked.

"You try."

He twiddled his fingers into his palm and a swirl of fire formed into the shape of a ball. He tossed it once in the air, caught it, took aim, and with ease launched it forward. He aimed for the window, but it went straight through the ceiling.

"Looks like we can use some target practice," he said.

"We? Mine went right where I told it. You can use some target practice."

We practiced those few moves over and over again and worked on taking control of our emotions so that we could summon our powers whenever we needed them.

"So you said that you shot fire from your hands like a flamethrower?" I asked.

"Yeah, why you ask?"

"Well, I think that could be a useful and powerful attack. We should both learn how to do that."

"Sure. Let's try." His hands lit up and my hands iced.

"Here goes." I stuck my hands out in front of me. There was nothing, not even a snowflake that came out, just the same old cold air coming from my arms.

Marcus laughed mockingly. "Let me give it a try." He did some fancy little spin, the fire in his eyes matching the flames coming from his hands that were shooting fire halfway down the hall. It was clear that Marcus was a natural. It was one more reason to be jealous. I walked over, grabbed him by the wrist and watched as the fire from his hands and tiki torches dwindled until they died.

"Hey," he screamed. "What's that all about?"

"You don't have to show off, Marc," I said as I walked to the window to catch some light. Marcus lit his hand. "See, that's what I mean, you're a natural at this, and I ... well I suck."

"So it's OK for you to be better at everything we do, but me, I can't have just one thing where I'm better? You're selfish, Dylan."

As he was talking, a sharp pain jabbed the right side of my head. This pain wasn't like anything I had ever experienced. It was excruciating, like something was crawling around in my head and poking at my brain. I fell to one knee, screaming in tears.

"What's wrong?" Marcus panicked. I didn't know what was wrong and didn't have the strength to have a full conversation about it either.

"S-stay back," I managed to say. I didn't want to be touched but he didn't listen. He walked up. The pain grew sharper. My body made contact with the dusty floors. I crunched over. My vision went in and out. I lifted my hand to block him from touching me and with one flicker of my hand, my best friend blasted off the floor, spiraling through the boarded window. Everything happened within seconds. The roof then started to crackle and dust trickled down. The ceiling rumbled and caved in a little followed by one of the doors being blasted off its hinges. Black started to fade in and out, and then all I saw was black.

Then I woke up.

"Ugh … my head feels like I was hit with a sledgehammer. What happened?" I said, trying to move. Although my vision was disoriented and blurry I knew where I was. I was in Marcus' bed. I looked down and he was snoring on the floor. I had no clue how I got there. Last thing I remembered was that he flew out of a window. I lay back down and slept some more to ease the pain.

"Dylan, Dylan wake up, Dylan," Marcus said, tapping me gently.

"Ahh…" I moaned.

He backed up like he was scared of me when I finally got my eyes open. He never looked at me like that before. It was the look he gave the football players every time they spotted him in the hallway during freshman year.

Fear.

"What's wrong with you?" I tried to enter his mind and I got nothing.

"You don't remember what you did to me this morning?" he asked.

"No."

"You threw me out a freaking window." He flinched and fidgeted his fingers. He took one more step back as I got up and sat on the edge of the bed.

"How? I remember you falling out the window but that's all I remember. Then I woke up with a headache."

"Fell? You mean you waved your hand and sent me flying out the window."

I tried to remember. "You mean I telepathically threw you out the window, sweet! I'm a telepath."

"Not telepathically, telekinetically. You're a telekinetic you idiot," he said. "Now I'm jealous."

I jumped on the bed to celebrate but then my head pounded. "Where's your brother?" I asked. "He's normally sleeping at this hour." Marcus walked to the window and forced the curtains to the sides. The sun terrified me like a vampire and I ran back under the covers.

"It's three in the afternoon, my brother is long gone," he said. "That headache of yours had you in a coma."

"Well what time did we get into the house?"

"We left the building around four this morning, and if I hadn't gotten up in time that building would have demolished you. Now we have to train on the west wing."

"Oops, sorry."

"It's cool, that's why it's called training."

We both went into the kitchen and grabbed a drink. I was shirtless with the same jeans on from training.

"Can you think of any other times you may have moved something with your mind?" he asked.

"Nope I can't think of a—wait, wait there was that time in school I'd gotten a headache. My eyes turned blue and I think I slammed a locker."

"You think?"

"Yeah, Jess was there and she wondered how the locker slammed by itself."

"Hmmmm … and then it was the time you froze the window and got a headache. Right after that I saw the computer mouse slide by itself. Both times you had a headache, and both times an object moved. Yep, I would classify you as a telekinetic."

"What do you think all this means?"

"Bro, I have no clue but like I said, we have to be careful about what we do and who we talk to."

"It's hard enough keeping this thing a secret now. How do you think it will be once we start school?"

"Guess we can only trust each other."

"Clearly, since somebody wants you dead," I said.

"Don't say that."

Marcus took me back to the asylum to get my car so I could go home. I wasn't feeling up to do much of anything so my plans were to just get in the bed and watch some movies.

When I finally got home and showered, I checked my phone once it charged. I had a missed message from Monica saying that she needed to talk to me.

I slowly drifted away, not paying attention to what was on TV. Couldn't help but think about training and everything going on in my life. Wasn't really sure of how or why I was given these powers or what they even meant, but I was humbled that Marcus was going through this life-changing event with me. He was right. The only ones we could trust from here on out were each other.

Fresh. Meat.

Chapter 12
Fight or Flight

I met with Monica last week. She gave me a quick rundown of what was said and in a nutshell, she never wanted for her and Marcus to stop talking or being friends. And because she *only* wanted to remain friends and nothing more, Marcus distanced himself. Even said she came to graduation to see us but left after we walked across the stage. In the end, she just wanted her best friend back. Honestly, I couldn't blame her. Next time I saw Marcus, I told him what she said. I left it there.

Practice days were Wednesdays and Fridays since they fit best with our work schedules. It also allowed us some relaxation on the weekends. I managed to keep my emotions under control and just accept the fact that Marcus was a natural and I would have to work harder.

On Tuesdays and Thursdays we went to the track together to work on our stamina. Marcus was on the track team, so his time was better during our runs. He finally started to put on some weight. I swear he has been the same size since our freshman year. Despite adapting the busy training schedules, we still managed to go to work and take on the everyday tasks in our personal lives. It's like we became workaholics at seventeen.

I didn't want to break my promise to Trey so today we were all going on a mini road-trip to Albany. Trey told Diana about the plans, and of course, she volunteered herself to come as well.

Marcus and I had been up all morning in an intense training session, so I threw the keys at Trey when I picked him up. Trey drove while I slept in the back seat and Marcus slept in the front. I was a little restless because the short drive didn't leave much time for a good sleep.

We got there around noon. Diana delegated us with the task of carrying all her bags. When we got to about the third store, Marcus somehow managed to escape. When he came back, the bags had doubled. He claimed he went to the restroom, but I'm sure he went to a shoe store.

"Last store, guys," she said, leading us to a lingerie store.

Marcus, Trey and I were all fighting, trying to stop Diana from pushing us in. "But I gotta pee," Trey said, holding his hands between his legs and tipping around on tiptoes.

"Guys," Diana paused and gazed at us. "It's just underwear, get over it." She flipped her hair and rolled her eyes. Trey quit dancing around and held the door open for us. The amount of pink and purple had me thinking we were shopping in a cotton candy store. We all split up and walked around to keep busy until Diana was ready to go.

I walked around looking at all the lace and fluff. While I was walking, a sign for lip-gloss on sale caught my attention. I was so wrapped up in the sign that I didn't pay attention to where I was walking—

"Oh, sorry," I said, bumping into a girl. Wasn't sure why that caught my attention but it did. The girl was dressed in all black — slacks and a button-down. She stumbled a bit, and I held out my hands to catch her before she fell. "I was distracted…" I looked down and caught a glimpse of her name badge. "Imani. So you work here?"

"I do and I can see that you're interested in some gloss. What flavor?" she taunted.

"Nah, it's not even like that. My friend made me come in here," I said.

"So *he* is looking for some lingerie?" Her soft voice lacked any recognizable accents.

"No … oh no, I meant one of my female friends. She may be looking for some."

Imani was short with cinnamon colored hair that came to her shoulders, and a complexion that matched it identically.

"So black is really your color." I don't know what possessed me to say that. Real smooth Dylan.

Her voice hardened. "I look like I'm headed to a funeral."

"What I meant to say is, you probably look good in any color but black really goes good with your smoldering eyes."

"Smoldering?" She grimaced.

Geesh Dylan, get it together, I said to myself. She pushed her hair back and rolled her band off her wrist, putting her hair in a ponytail. "It's been real, Dylan, is it? But I have to get back to slaving over underwear and bras." She turned and started to walk off. In an instant — maybe an act of desperation — I grabbed her wrist before she could leave my sight. She flinched and snapped her wrist from my hand.

I flinched. "Sorry." She glanced at her wrist and pulled her shirt down as if she was trying to hide something. She turned back around and tried to walk off again. "Wait," I said. "I was just going to ask if I could get your number."

"Why?"

"You're cute, I'm handsome. You're nice, I'm charming. You're cool and you have no idea how cool I really am ... c'mon..."

She smiled.

I had her hooked. This cool thing could really score me some points.

"Nobody is cool around me. But you're cute, in a cool-dorky way." She held out her hand, as I fumbled for my phone. I handed it to her and she handed it back with her number saved. She rushed off.

"Imani," I said, looking down at the number on my phone.

"Who was that?" Marcus said from behind.

"I just met this girl. Imani. Damn. Imani."

"Yeah, whatever," Marcus said.

After we left the mall we all grabbed a bite to eat at the food court and went for a walk downtown.

"Two more weeks and I am leaving, you guys," Diana said.

"Well that makes two of us," Trey added.

"We're all grown up now, ready to take on the world," Diana said.

Marcus and I didn't have any sappy words to say since we'd know at least one person in college.

"You guys will be fine, you shouldn't worry about it. Trey, you'll be hanging with the team so much you'll have friends before the semester starts. And Diana, look at you. I'm sure you'll have no trouble making friends or finding a boyfriend," Marcus said.

"Damn right. One lick of these lips followed by a smooch will have any man under my spell. Even you."

Marcus blushed.

As the weeks went on, our training got more intense. By that time Trey had already left for college and Diana had moved to Boston. As far as friends, Marcus and I were limited to each other.

Marcus and I were getting stronger and better with our training. With practice, I was able to shoot a beam of ice from my hands and even create objects out of ice. Even our aim got better with consistent target practice. Marcus bought some little green toy soldiers so we could improve our targeting skills. We'd sit them on the window seal and shoot them down with ice and fire. The goal: try to hit them without freezing or burning anything else but the toy. It worked eventually after Marcus almost burned down the west wing. The migraines still happened when I used my powers so I was constantly popping my migraine pills. It seemed that the more I used my powers, the longer I'd go without the headaches.

Even though today was a power-training day, we went to the track for stamina training before we got started. By the time I got there, Marcus was already at the track warming up. We did a few laps, followed by some push-ups and sit-ups. The conditioning came easy since we were both athletes.

"OK, two laps around the track, full sprint, as fast as you can. Loser buys lunch tomorrow," Marcus said, gasping for breath.

I was pretty sure I had a good shot at winning and if I did, I was going to pick the most expensive place I thought he could afford.

"If that's what you want, let's go for it," I said as we both walked to the start of the track.

"On your mark, get set, go!"

We took off like Olympians, and I was in the lead after lap one. The patting sound of his shoes hitting the ground warned me how far he was without looking. Halfway through the second lap I heard Marcus scream.

Thinking it was some sad attempt to distract me, I ignored him the first time until he screamed again.

I stopped and turned around and Marcus was hovering a few feet off the ground screaming and fighting himself.

His arms ignited.

The more he fought, the higher he went until his feet became flames that rapidly grew to his kneecap, and without warning he took off like a firecracker into the blackness of the night.

It was kind of cool watching him swirl around in the black starry sky like he was trying to spell his name in fire. I knew there was nothing I could do to help him so I sat down on the track and watched the fireworks.

After a few minutes he finally came crashing down and landed in a tree about a quarter of a mile away from me. I ran over to check to see if he was breathing and not bleeding out anywhere. Once I got to him, he was lying on his stomach, moaning. I walked to the tree and put my hand on the bark, putting out the flames that Marcus left.

"That looked like it hurt." I stood over him.

"Urgh ... bro, I can fly," he chuckled. "I'm really like The Human Torch now."

Using our powers led us to learn more about them, growing as we grew.

I was jealous that I couldn't fly, but I guess Marcus could use that ability more than I could since I had a car.

"Still wanna train?" he asked.

"Do I still want to train? You're the one who just fell from the sky into a tree and besides, you burnt up your shoes."

He looked down and noticed he was missing his shoes. I gave him mine and I put on the ones that were in the car. I was a little relieved that my powers didn't destroy my clothes every time I used them. Might get a little wet when the ice went away but that was nothing.

We got to the *safe house* and lit the torches followed by our warm-ups. We called it the safe house because it was a place where we could train alone and be our natural selves.

Whatever it is we are.

Safe house also sounded a whole lot better than the abandoned insane asylum.

I was in one of the rooms trying to form ice all around my body like Bobby Drake while Marcus was walking the halls juggling fireballs.

"What's it feel like?" I asked when he entered the room.

"What's what feel like?"

"When you touch fire? Anybody can touch ice and live to tell about it, but you walk around with half your body torched and you act like it's nothing."

"It, well ... it sort of feels good. It's a sensation I can't explain and don't want to end. Sort of like a massage," he said. "What about you?"

"Relaxing. Just picture last year's brutal summer." I looked at him. He stood there looking back with his dark eyes and darker circles underneath. "Go'head, close your eyes."

He sucked his teeth and closed his eyes.

"Now, last summer's heat blazing down and crisping up your skin. We're at Trey's house and our clothes are flooded in sweat. We strip down to our trunks and jump into the cold water and *that* moment when your body first makes contact. That moment intensified non-stop is what it feels like when I use my powers."

He opened his eyes, cracked out half a smile and nodded.

I continued trying to ice my body while Marcus was looking out the window like he wanted to jump from the fourth story.

"I wonder how I can make myself fly whenever I want?"

"You shouldn't want to fly, Marc. Looks like you'll be spending a lot of money on shoes if you do."

"There you go again, Dylan, won't let me have my shine will you?"

"Ugh! Marc I'm not going to fight with you every time we train, it's starting to get old."

Marcus began to walk slowly in circles around me with this mischievous look on his face. He almost looked possessed with his bulging red eyes and crooked smile. "You want to really train? Well ... let's fight each other," he said still circling around me.

"Marc, for real, you're starting to scare me a little bit," I stuttered.

"The famous Dylan Perry shows fear." He tossed a fireball in the air and caught it.

He quickly threw the ball at me and I iced my fist over and punched it as it came hurling at me. "Quick on your feet. I like that," he said.

"OK, Marc, but just remember, you asked for this." I raised my tension-filled hand and Marcus went straight up for the ceiling but not before he could throw another fireball at me.

I rolled, dodged the ball, then suddenly Marcus hit the floor face first. I was surprised that I somehow summoned my telekinesis without a headache, although I knew the more we fought one would eventually hit me.

I wanted to have the element of surprise so I shot ice at all the torches. I got to the last one and right when I stuck my hand out to freeze it, Marcus shot a stream of fire in my path to intercept my beam.

He walked towards me and I walked back.

The room was almost dark besides the light from the one tiki torch that stood to the right of me.

"Good training today. Let's go," I laughed.

"We've barely done any training today, so quit being scared."

I kept walking back, and he kept getting closer. "What was that?" I said as something moved swiftly in the hallway in front of me. The lighting made it so I could only see a shadow. I didn't even hear whatever it was.

"Stop trying to trick me, Dylan."

Seconds later the flame on the last tiki torch went out. "How did you do that without using your powers?" Marcus turned his head to face the torch.

"T-th-that wasn't me," I whispered. A feeling of uncertainty hit me in the gut.

The lights in the building started to flicker on and off.

Eerie.

"I thought these lights didn't work," Marcus yelled.

The silhouette of a man appeared behind Marcus down the hall facing us. Marcus started to wrinkle up and pain took over him. "Stop … stop, Dylan, turn it off," he struggled.

He shivered. I was sure cold weather didn't affect him.

The lights continued to go on and off and the silhouette got closer with each flicker. Marcus was now on the floor almost lifeless and in pain, struggling to say something. It was too much going on at the moment, and it was all happening way too fast for me to keep track. The silhouette at the end of the hall distracted me and the lights flickering confused me. I had to put all that in the back of my head and tend to Marcus.

"Da-Da-Dyl…" I reached down and picked up Marcus who was starting to turn blue. He managed to get one word out before he passed out.

Run.

I put his arm around my shoulder, turned around and started for the door but there was somebody standing before me. I could only see his face when the light flickered on.

He was African-American with blue eyes.

If I had to bet my money on it I would say that's the guy Marcus fought the day of graduation. Behind him, the shadowy figure walked up with strings of lighting whisking around his body, giving life to the broken lights. The ice guy shoved both hands into my chest and knocked Marcus and me onto the floor. It was two against one with fear beating against my chest.

The ice guy waved his hands around, ice magically appearing between them.

I jumped up.

I grunted, pushing air between my teeth then snapped my hand away. He flew down the hall. I figured it wouldn't hold him down that long so I had to get Marcus up and heated. The lightning guy sprinted down the hall in my direction with electrical currents flashing from his body. He didn't give me much time to think so I dodged left and flicked my hand in the same direction. Marcus' body flew off the floor and crashed right into the chest of the lightning guy.

Marcus pulsated like a defibrillator machine to the chest. Marcus slowly got up but was a little disoriented. He pulled it together and lit his hands on fire but was shot out the window by a bolt of lightning. The lightning guy flew right past me and out the window after him. I turned back around to the ice guy but he was no longer on the floor.

"You are like me," he said from behind me. "You wield the power of ice."

I turned around and he punched me in the face. I instantly felt the blood swish around in my mouth. I fell to my knees and past him flashed fire and lighting through the big hole in the side of the building. It looked like a very expensive light show, but it was more like death and destruction going on out there.

"You don't deserve your power." His hollow voice spooked me.

"What?" I whispered.

He picked me up off the floor and tossed me through across the room.

He stuck his hand out and shot out a beam of ice. I tried to block it back telekinetically. A migraine hit along with blood trickling from my nose. I thought for a split second that it was broken but it wasn't. I couldn't hold on any longer and my force field failed me. I was hit and fell flat on my back.

When I opened my eyes, something was different. It was like I didn't have any control over myself. I pounded my fist twice on the floor, inhaling some of the dust that flew up from it. I stood to my feet, waved my hand, and blasted him out the window. I knew what I was doing but I didn't have any control. It felt like I was watching myself from the outside. I walked over to the window and looked out to see Marcus and the other guy still fighting.

Suddenly, I had control again.

I ran outside and shot an ice beam at the lightning guy to slow him down. The ice guy was on the floor and I kicked him in the face as I walked by to help Marcus who threw a few fireballs at the ice guy to get revenge for almost freezing him to death. We fled the scene before the got up.

When I woke up, I was again in Marcus' room. I'd been asleep for 14 hours this time.

"Marc, what happened this time?" I pulled the blanket off me. He got off the floor and sat on Elias' bed.

"I'm afraid that ice guy is going to keep coming after me, Dylan." His eyes focused on the floor. "And what if he keeps bringing more people until I am dead?"

"That's not going to happen, Marc." I tried to sound as convincing as possible when in reality I had no idea what was going on.

"But you don't know that, Dylan. What if he finds out where I live and tries to hurt my family?"

"Bro, I'm not going to let anybody hurt you. Plus, you're really good at that whole fire thing you got going on. I think you can protect yourself. As long as we stick together, nobody is going to kill us."

So far I have met one other person besides me who can control ice, there's Marcus who can control fire, and now one who can generate electricity. I didn't know what kind of dream this was, but I was ready to wake up now. I didn't want the powers if the price was a death threat.

"Another thing," I said. "That ice guy told me the same thing when I fought him. He told me that I didn't deserve my powers. Marcus…"

"Yeah?"

"Who are we?"

"Not sure yet, bro." he said. "Not sure if I really want to know that answer either."

The remainder of the summer flew right by. We didn't see the two guys again and we never did go back to the safe house — figuring the safe house wasn't too safe these days. We did continue to work out and build our physical strength and Marcus ended the summer finally with a body. He even started to grow a little fuzz on that baby face of his. I continued to talk to Imani through calls and text messages and it was a coincidence that she would be a freshman at NYU with Marcus and me.

Today was the big day. We were moving into our dorms today. Mom and Elias were in one car while the Petersons drove their truck and Marcus rode with me. Dad hugged me and gave me a $50 bill followed by some cheesy advice about being a man before we left. I gave the money to Dalton since mom said she would put money in my account weekly.

The drive to the university was a short drive, which I loved. When we got there we both couldn't believe that we'd be living in New York City. I was ready to be immersed in diversity.

When we pulled up, the streets of the campus were filled with freshmen and their parents moving in. We handled the basic stuff first — making sure our rooms were reserved and classes were paid for. Once we got our keys, we helped each other move in.

First we went over to Goddard dormitories on Washington Square where Marcus was staying. We didn't have much so getting everything up to the fourth floor only took one trip. His roommate was already moving in when we got there. He was a thick guy with a harsh New England accent and when he breathed, it sounded like he was eating a double cheeseburger with the works.

"Sup. Char-Lee," he greeted. He went around and was eager to shake everyone's hand. His father was there with him and just as friendly.

"Marcus. I'll be your roommate this year. Nice to meet you, man," Marcus said smoothly. "This is my friend, Dylan. He goes here too."

"Dill, what's popping, son?" he said while trying to do some fancy handshake with me.

"I'm good. Son," I laughed, attempting the handshake.

We set up Marcus' room before we headed over to my dorm. The walk to Founders on East Twelfth Street was about a mile away from Goddard. Our parents drove the cars and we walked to get a feel for the campus. My room was on the sixteenth floor. The building had a massive twenty-six floors and I would hate to have to walk up there if the elevator ever broke. We took my things up the elevator, which was a drag when hundreds of other kids were moving in. When I got there, half of the room was already set up but no one was there. The spacious room had a huge window with beds on either side. Since I stayed in a suite, I had two suitemates who were already there.

One guy was from Texas, majoring in education. He wore a flannel plaid button-up shirt that was rolled to the elbows and jeans — both fitted to show how buff he was. His get up was topped off with a straw hat tipped to the front and cowboy boots. His roommate was the complete opposite. He was from Vermont and at NYU on a full academic scholarship. His stature was sickly skinny like he was going to die if he didn't eat soon … very soon.

"Howdy, the name is Nathaniel — Nathaniel Gunner but folks call me Nate or Gunner," the buff one said. "And this here is my new friend Chris Fields."

"Uhhh…" I laughed, "I'm Dylan. People normally call me Dylan."

"Well, Dylan, nice ta-meet-ya, I think we'll get along just great this year, don't cha?"

"I think so, Gunner." I shook my head and laughed to myself. "Have you guys by chance met my roommate yet?"

"Nope," they both said.

I hoped that my roommate was as nice as my suitemates.

After everything was set up we walked back to the cars to tell our parents goodbye. I pulled my little brother to the side away from everyone else while Marcus spent his last minutes with his family.

"This is it, little brother, make sure you continue to do what you've been doing, OK."

He nodded. "I will, Dylan."

"Make good grades, take care of Mom and Dad, and if you need anything let me know. I'm only two hours away and I can be there as fast as you need. OK?" I reached into my back pocket and pulled out an old birthday candle from my sixth birthday. It still had dried up frosting crusted on the bottom.

"Here, keep this," I said.

"What's this?"

"When I was younger, I wished for a brother. On my sixth birthday I found out Mom was having a baby. I thanked the candle for delivering what I had always wanted. You."

"Thanks, Dylan." He hugged me. Mom walked over and didn't say anything. She hugged the both of us. She let go and walked to the car, sniffling.

"Stop getting beat by Mom in the video games," I yelled as they drove off.

The rest of the day was spent walking around campus with Gunner, Chris, and Charlie. Gunner met some girls who told him about a frat party and suggested we go. I was all for it. Marcus took some convincing. I basically told him this was part of the college experience. Chris declined and went back to the room.

When we walked in I thought, *Wow the parties really are like this.* Girls were dancing everywhere and red plastic cups floated around the room. A few girls weaved through Marcus, Charlie, and myself and grabbed Gunner and sucked him into the vortex of the party as soon as we walked through the door. I made myself a drink from the punch bowl and downed it. It was like liquid fire against my chest.

I looked at the empty cup in disgust. They were all laughing at me.

"Party punch," Cheered Charlie, pouring himself a cup and downing it.

Once Marcus found out it wasn't "punch" he turned his back to the bowl while I enjoyed one more cup and Charlie relished two. As the party went on we found some other shy freshman and formed one big freshman gang enjoying the night until…

Gunner was near the stairs grinding on some girl when some guy came bulldozing his way towards him yelling, "Get off of my girl, dickface!"

She didn't seem bothered but judging by her inability to stand up on her own, she could have easily mistaken Gunner for her boyfriend.

He pushed Gunner, which didn't seem to do much except piss him off, and another guy ran up to gang up on Gunner. Charlie and I ran over and stood between Gunner and the two clowns. They were dressed in brightly colored polos and khakis with City accents.

"Hey — hey — hey, guys, no need for fighting. We're all just here to have fun," I said over the music as the party continued.

"Well, go have fun somewhere else, freshman, and stay out of *my* frat house," Clown number two yelled, gesturing towards the door.

Gunner was red in the face, fist balled at his sides. He attempted to fight his way around Charlie as the chiseled clowns laughed mockingly at us. Charlie pushed Gunner towards the door and calmed him down.

When I got back to my room it was extremely late and my roommate still wasn't there. It was a good thing that classes didn't start for a few more days so I could sleep in.

The next morning I woke up to the sound of water running in the bathroom. I heard a knock at the door; it was Gunner and Chris. They wanted to grab a bite to eat so I grabbed my things and waited by the bathroom door, and when it opened, "YOU!" we both screamed.

Chapter 13

Birthday Cake

Gunner almost knocked me over in an attempt to attack my roommate once he made eye contact with him. My roommate turned out to be Clown number one. I calmed Gunner down as he cursed at my roommate with his southern accent I couldn't understand.

"So let me get this straight," my roommate said with a towel wrapped around him, "*you* are my roommate and *these* lame guys are my suitemates? You gotta be kidding me," he laughed and strolled towards his bed.

I didn't want to be living in an awkward situation for a whole year nor did I want my suitemates going at each other's throats every time they saw one another, so I introduced myself.

"The name's Dylan," I said, reaching out my hand, which he smacked away. I tried to keep my cool so I wouldn't get mad and turn him into a popsicle.

"Airez." His eye bulged, his lips almost curving in a grin. "Let's make this understood, you stay on your half of the room and I'll stay on mine. We may, just may, get along. Oh, and when you see me in public, act like you don't know me."

I didn't know if Airez was like a code name or if his actual name was Airez. I think that name got to his head because he seemed to think he was a god.

We shall see how long that lasts.

"Come on, Gunner, just drop it and let's go to breakfast," I said.

"What's his deal?" Gunner said as we put our trays onto the table.

"Dude, no clue. But he has *no* idea who he's dealing with," I said. I told myself before I came to school that I wasn't going to use my powers on regular people no matter how badly I wanted to at times.

Gunner was a cool guy. He reminded me a lot of Marcus in some ways. They both had confidence oozing from the pores and yet were both very kind-hearted and humble people.

"Where's your partner?" Gunner asked.

"Marcus? He stays in Goddard," I said.

"So where you guys from?" He shoved a piece of toast topped with butter and jelly in his mouth.

I told him where we grew up and he informed me he was from Grapevine, a city near Dallas, Texas. He said he's always wanted to live in New York so this was his chance.

Airez was on his bed, headphone in ears when I walked back in. I got back in the bed and tried to sleep until Airez got up and plugged his iPhone into his speakers and blasted hard rock. I didn't say anything because actions speak louder than words, so I just changed the temperature in the room to freeze your balls off. The sound of his teeth chattering in his mouth made me smile.

"H-ha-how-did-it-get-s-s-so-cold?" he said.

I was under the covers fake snoring trying to hold in my laugh. I let it go on for a few minutes and called it quits. As long as he was going to keep up the games, I would too and was sure to win every time. A knock at the door broke my *snoring* and I got up to answer it while Airez recovered.

A very tall, good-looking, guy with intimidating eyes stood in the doorway. He barged right in like he lived here and snatched the blanket off the curled up Airez.

"Come on let's go, little brother," he said.

I thought he looked familiar. He was the same guy who threw us out of the party. He was also a member of Xi Beta Kappa fraternity, the same fraternity my father pledged.

He squinted my direction. "Hey, don't I know you, freshman?" His voice was daunting and deeper than the Grand Canyon.

"Umm … I don't think so. I'm Airez's roommate," I said.

"Yeah, I know you. You're the guy from last night." He turned to face his brother. "Wow, brother, this is what you're stuck with as a roommate? And why the hell is it so cold in here?" He grabbed Airez and left out of the room. I rushed over and knocked on Gunner's door.

"Dude, you'll never believe this, not only was Airez the guy from last night but his brother is the other guy," I said.

"Negative, partner. You *gots* to be pulling some kind of leg of mine." Gunner peeped around me. "Where are our buddies now?"

"I don't know. They took off."

"This is fixin' to be one *jacked* up living situation."

I sighed. "Tell me about it. Least you don't have to wake up to 'the god of war'."

"Looks like we made our first enemy, partner."

I went out for a walk and ended up at Washington Square Park. I called Marcus and told him to come down and gave him the roommate update. As we walked, we ran into two female roommates from London who happened to best friends like Marcus and I. Delilah — the exotic looking long haired blonde who had the features and figure of a supermodel. Stacey — the tomboyish girl with the pixie cut and rich chocolate skin with a bit of vitiligo near her eye and forehead.

We walked them back to their dorm; my phone rang right as the girls walked off. It was Imani. After we laughed on the phone for a few minutes, I asked to see her. She couldn't resist my charm and agreed.

"Sorry, my brother, duty calls," I said, brightly.

"Who was that?" Marcus asked, nodding to my phone.

"Remember the girl I met in Albany? I told you she was starting here as well and—"

"No worries, I'll catch you at dinner."

I waited outside until she came out to greet me. I wanted to get to know her better and the day was so ripe that I wanted to enjoy them both. We walked the blocks of Manhattan getting a feel for each other as well as our new home.

"I still think that it's crazy we go to the same school," she said softly, catching my wide smile.

"Are you not hot?" I asked like an idiot. Here I have this beautiful girl who, by faith, goes to the same school as I do, and all I can focus on is the weather and why she's wearing skinny jeans with a denim jacket on.

"Nope. I'm good," she snarled.

Great, Dylan, kill the mood.

We found a spot in the park to chill and laughed for over an hour.

When asked about where she grew up she told me she moved around more than one child ever should due to her parents' divorce and their jobs. She got a little distant after that and seemed to close herself off.

We took a seat on a bench. She pushed her knees to her chest and wrapped her arms around them. She turned away from me and said softly, "I've never been in one place long enough to actually get to know people on a personal level. To be honest, I didn't think I'd ever see you again and that's why it was so easy to give you my number."

"That's completely understandable. I broke up with my girlfriend of three years on prom night and it was sort of a bittersweet moment."

"Why bittersweet?"

"Well, she was my first girlfriend and I loved hanging out when it was the two of us, but the moment my friends were around, she would change into someone I didn't know."

"And the sweet?"

I had no idea where the urge came from, but I leaned over, lightly gripped her chin with my fingers, and pressed my lips onto her dimple. "You're sweet," I said.

She hid her face behind her hair and hands in this cute little shy manner, then laid her head on my arm.

"I'm sorry I shouldn't have." I was feeling light on the inside almost like I was floating away.

"No, it's OK," she whispered.

We stood and continued to walk when it hit me — I was next to a girl and not smelling cherry blossoms. It was weird and different but I guess different was good. We lost track of time and the day hours passed right by us. We stopped and grabbed some drinks on our way back before we caught in the rain.

Once I got back to my room, I quickly threw my drenched clothes off and hopped in the shower. Airez thought it would be a good idea to put rubber snakes in the shower. It scared me for a few seconds but that was it. I had the perfect idea for revenge. I got dressed then Gunner and I headed over to see Marcus.

"How was it with the new girlfriend?" Marcus asked, curiously.

"You had a date with a lassie already?" Gunner chimed in.

Shaking my head, I said, "No, I just went for a walk with a girl I met."

"I hope she is more stable than Jessica," Marcus grunted.

"Who's Jessica?" Gunner asked.

"His craaazzyy ex-girlfriend," Marcus said.

"Mind if I talk, Marc?" I interjected. "Yes, Jessica is my ex and she might have been a little crazy."

"Ha! A little?" Marcus said.

"Yes, just a little bit. And Imani is not my new girlfriend. I don't know if I'm completely ready for that just right now. But she's cool."

We spent the rest of the night hanging out in Founders lobby with Gunner, Delilah, and Stacey. I couldn't tell if Delilah was really into Marcus or if she was just a big flirt. Marcus was so awkward when it came to females. Every time someone would say something funny, she would laugh and throw herself onto him and he would scoot away.

I couldn't take it anymore.

"Marc, mind if I talk to you just for a quick second?" I said.

The girls stopped talking and Marcus jumped out of his seat without question and we walked away. I grabbed his shoulders and wanted to slap the awkwardness out of him.

"Dude, what the hell is wrong with you? Delilah is obviously diggin' you.

You look like a damn kindergarten student over there. Now, do you think she's hot?"

"Yeah," he said, shaking his head up and down.

"So just talk to her. I'm not asking you to marry the girl," I laughed. It shouldn't be this difficult.

"Dylan, man." His head dropped. "You know how I am. I just can't *talk* to her. And besides, what does she want with me? I'm a nobody."

"Bro, look, you can shoot *fire* from your hands and fly. You have every guy on this campus beat by a long shot. You are the *man*, Marc, and Delilah can see that in you."

"Are you saying I should show her that I can fly?"

"That — is — not, what I'm saying. Bottom line, you're Marcus and there is nobody out there like you. Now, go talk to her." I turned his body around so he could admire her in her candid moment.

We walked back over and he finally loosened up and started to relax a little bit. Gunner was a natural with the ladies, and attracted a flock of girls wherever we went. I think it was the country boy thing he had going on. Cowboy hats were not something you saw every day in the City, so ladies were intrigued.

"*Marcus,*" Delilah said. I loved the accent. "I hear you are very smart."

"I'm no smarter than Dylan," he said.

"Well, you graduated with a better GPA than I did," I said.

"Do you think you can be my study partner this semester?" Delilah let down her high ponytail and gently shook her head to let her hair play in the air.

I gestured to him to say yes while she wasn't looking. Marcus was looking at me like I was crazy until he caught on to what I was doing.

"Ugh … I guess I can." The words stuttered slowly out his mouth, his eyes still on me. "I mean yes, yes I can be your study partner." This time the words flowed and he actually glanced at her. His eyes may have looked as if they were about to pop out the socket, but he did look at her.

"Your grades are sure to be top notch. Marc is a whiz-kid," I said.

He looked over to Delilah and smiled with his lips sealed.

"OK, guys, this was fun but it's getting late and I have class first thing in the morning," I said.

Airez was watching TV when I walked in and greeted me immediately with, "Hey loser."

"Sorry, your brother isn't here," I replied.

"You better watch it." He got in my face, nostrils flaring like he wanted to hit me. He didn't scare me, but I didn't want to go through this every time I walked into the room. His brother, on the other hand, for some reason scared me just a little bit.

I pushed past him and flopped on my bed. I put my headphones on and turned the music up to the max. I put on some rap and concentrated my energy onto some of his books he had on his desk. I pictured in my head his books dancing around in the air. It felt like the veins in my neck and head were about to burst so I called it quits.

The next week was the same thing every day: wake up, argue with Airez, go to class, eat, argue with Airez, and sleep.

I was over it already.

When I woke up, I had to rush to class without even brushing my teeth. Somehow my phone had turned itself off in the middle of the night. I had on a pair of basketball shorts that I slept in and a jacket that I threw over a tank when I ran out the room.

When I finally got to class I was a half hour late and the whole class stopped to face me as the door slammed behind me. I was embarrassed and looked like a bum off the streets. The teacher made it known that I shouldn't be late again to his Composition class again.

I had a break around noon before my last class. I went back to my room to grab my phone that I left. I turned it on and had a ton of missed calls from my parents, the Petersons, and some old classmates. All these bad thoughts ran through my head as to why they would all call me today. I called my dad first and I didn't get an answer. I knew Mom was at work, so I didn't think to call her, but then I thought that if there were an emergency she wouldn't be at work. I called her.

"Mom, what is it?" I yelled at the phone as soon as she answered.

"Happy birthday, Dylan," she cried.

I was confused. Did I get so wrapped up and busy already that I forgot my eighteenth birthday? "Wow," I said to myself, "I'm eighteen today."

"Please don't tell me you forgot your own birthday, Dylan?" Mom asked. "You haven't been studying too much already, have you?"

"No, Mom. I told you about my roommate, right? Well, he turned my phone off and I was late for class and my teacher chewed me out in front of everyone."

"Welcome to the college life, son."

"How's Dalton doing?"

"He's doing well. He misses you a lot."

"Yeah, I know. How about Dad, does he miss me?"

"Your dad will be your dad. He did put some money into your account this morning and he told me to tell you to make sure you get an oil change."

"Mom, can I ask you a question?"

"Sure."

"Are you and Dad doing OK?"

"Of course we are," she said, defensively.

"No, I mean is your marriage OK?"

She paused for a second.

"We're fine, Dylan. School should be your only focus at the moment."

School *should* be my only focus, but it wasn't. I had school, my family, and hoping that no one else tried to kill my best friend and I because we had powers we couldn't explain. She didn't want to talk much after that and quickly ended the conversation. I knew from her reaction that something was up with the two of them. If I can spot their troubles, it would only be a matter of time before Dalton started to notice them too. I called everyone else back and received my birthday wishes.

I went to my last class of the day then met up with Marcus. He told the gang that it was my birthday so they decided to take me to an early dinner. We ate at a bite-sized restaurant a few blocks from campus. I really enjoyed the company of my friends — new and old. I invited Imani out but she was swamped with homework.

Once we left dinner we all went back to my suite. Gunner and Marcus got me cake and ice cream so I was happy. The cake was decorated with the X-Men characters *Iceman* and *Pyro*. I laughed when I saw it.

Had to be the best cake I'd ever gotten.

"I'll light the candles," Marcus said.

When I heard him say that I whipped my head around so fast, it almost did a three-sixty spin. I looked over and he had a lighter in his hand, laughing at me.

He smirked. "You OK, Dylan?"

"I'm fine. Light the candles so I can make a wish."

Marcus lit the candles and hit the lights. Everyone followed me as I walked up to the cake. I closed my eyes and made a silent wish after they sang. I never liked the singing portion of birthdays. I thought about my life and everything I was grateful for. I've been blessed since I was born, so I didn't want to be selfish this year. I wished that all my friends and family found inner peace and happiness.

I took in a gulp of air and blew. The candles didn't budge. I tried it again and everyone laughed at me. I knew Marcus was behind the madness.

Everyone clapped and cheered after I got the candles out.

Stacey turned the lights on and blasted the music. I cut the cake and passed out pieces on X-Men plates. It was the perfect eighteenth birthday.

"OK, guys, I have an announcement." I turned the music down and walked over to Marcus. "So today is my eighteenth birthday and I have enjoyed it all *except the waking up late this morning*. So on this day we celebrate but on the eighteenth, in nine short days, it will be my best friend, my brother, Marcus' eighteenth birthday." Just when I'd said that the door flung opened. In walked Airez, his brother, and another guy.

"Looks like we walked in on the loser parade, little brother," Airez's brother said. He walked around the common area of the suite, taunting my friends, then walked up to me.

"I heard you had some words for me?" He pressed his forehead to mine. I didn't want to move because I thought he would kill me if I did. "Looks like it's your birthday, I see." He walked over and picked up a piece of cake off the table and tasted it.

"Taste good," he said. And then smashed it in my face and pushed me down.

"That's it," Gunner yelled.

He and Charlie ran towards Airez and his brother, arms swinging. The girls screamed and Chris ran into his room. My day went from being good to bad in a matter of seconds. I smeared my hands across my eyes, removing frosting. Marcus was oddly silent just staring at Airez and his brother. His body was stiff, his face stale. His cheeks slowly turned red with anger. Anger that would soon turn to fire.

"Marcus, calm down," I whispered over all the commotion.

He balled his fist and his eyes became destructive.

"MARCUS, RELAX!" I yelled.

It was too late. He wasn't listening.

Chapter 14
Truth, Dare, and Lies

I couldn't really focus on all the commotion going on in the room. All I could focus on was trying to stop it. Dylan was faintly calling my name, telling me to calm down and relax but that didn't help the situation. My vision got fuzzy and the sweet scent of the buttercream frosting that brushed my nose hairs was like fuel to the fire. I pictured Airez and the other two guys in flames and before I could flicker my hands, I was pinned against the wall.

"Don't do this," Dylan whispered to me while cooling me down. "Relax."

"Stop." Delilah yelled.

Everyone froze in place. Airez was on Charlie's back. Gunner had the brother in a headlock and the other guy was eating a piece of cake.

"I don't know what the *bloody* problem is but we just want to celebrate our mate's birthday," she said.

Airez got off of Charlie's back and gave him a push. Charlie had to pry Gunner off of the brother, which took a few minutes and Dylan was afraid to let me go.

The room was destroyed.

I couldn't believe the destruction that they caused on my best friend's birthday. There was cake everywhere and everybody's clothes were half undone. Poor Chris wouldn't come out of the room.

Once the three guys left, we cleaned and scraped cake off of the walls.

"Do me a favor, guys," I said. They all stopped and looked at me. "Don't plan anything for my birthday." I gathered my things and went back to my room and called it a night.

I woke up the next morning to missed messages from Dylan and Delilah, checking up on me. I wasn't in the mood to talk so I just got ready for class.

Charlie was already up and getting dressed. He managed not to bring up last night and I appreciated that. I had calculus first then a tutoring session with Delilah later. Calculus was a breeze for me so I knew I was never going to have any problems in that area.

After my first two classes, I met up with Delilah in the library. We went over some math problems as well as some of her biology homework.

"You really don't want to do anything for your birthday?" she asked, breaking the silence.

I looked up from my book, "Yes, really," and went back to reading.

She did the same for a quick second then said, "I mean it's your eighteenth birthday. That only happens once, Marcus."

"My nineteenth birthday only happens once as well, and so does every other birthday. I think I'll survive."

She exhaled. "You know what I meant, Marcus. Everybody looks forward to the day they turn eighteen and you are just going to ignore it like it means nothing."

I closed my book and got up.

"What are you doing?" she asked.

"Our hour is up. I have to get to my next class."

"Ugh! Marcus, don't be like that."

"I really have to go, Delilah. Call you later." I ran off.

I didn't really have a class to get to but I needed to talk to Dylan so I went to his room.

"Hey, how you holding up, bro?" Dylan asked.

"I'm good. Thanks for stopping me last night before I escalated the situation."

"No problem, but you *have* to keep your cool. We can't let people find out about us, remember?"

"I know. This is still taking some getting use to."

"Do you think we should still be training? At least every once in a while, I mean, you never know when we would get attacked again."

"Do you really think those guys would find us all the way in New York City?"

"You're right. How would they know where we are now?"

"So what did you think about your eighteenth birthday?"

"It was one for the books. I can guarantee I will never forget it. Are you sure you don't want to celebrate it?"

"I think I've changed my mind. I want to embrace it and be happy for the eighteen years I've been alive."

"That's the spirit." Dylan patted my back. "Do you remember that movie that came out years ago?"

"Pick one."

"That movie that had the four boy witches with these crazy ass powers."

"Umm…"

"Well anyway, on their eighteenth birthday their powers matured and they got stronger."

"So you think that we're witches and our powers are going to get stronger just because we turn eighteen?"

He shook his head up and down.

"Dylan, I think that's crazy. I highly doubt we're *witches*."

"Please, by all means, tell me who we are then?"

"Dylan, man I gotta go." I gave him a fist bump and headed out.

Later that night while lying in bed, I kept asking myself if I thought we should still be training. I wanted to train but I didn't like the person I turned into when I used my powers. I did and said things that I didn't normally say or do. I became aggressive and feared hurting somebody. But, there was one thing I wanted to practice without Dylan around…

It was about two in the morning and Charlie was snoring louder than a wild pig. I took the books and papers out of my bag and packed a pair of old sneaks, some sweatpants, and an old tee shirt. I snuck out of the room, down the stairs, and out into the streets. I wandered around aimlessly, trying to figure out what I was doing. Then, it caught my attention. I saw a building and remembered why I left my room. I didn't know what kind of building it was nor did I care, but it was perfect. I walked around the side and climbed up the fire escape to the top.

I was out of breath by the time I made it up the thirty-story building. The night was cool and the city looked stunning lit up at night as always.

I juggled a few fireballs while walking around the rooftop to blow some steam. I extinguished the fire and walked over to the ledge. I looked down and didn't think twice, I leaned my body forward and let gravity take over. The air pressed up against my body and free falling had to be the most exhilarating thing I'd ever done. The lights rushed by me and for once, everything around me made sense.

I knew my powers wouldn't let me down. Seconds later my arms and legs were on fire and I was soaring through the air. I felt like a fearless eagle as I flew past the Empire State Building. I tried making shapes in the air but that was an epic fail.

Speeding up seemed easy but slowing down was challenging.

I didn't know how to just stop so I embraced the pain that was to come and crashed shoulder first into a brick wall on top of a building. I didn't really care that I had a bruise on my forehead when I woke up, or that my shoulder was stiff and I was bloody. I was too thrilled that I could fly without wings.

Once I got myself together, I wanted to try my take off. I sprinted like I did the first time I flew and galloped in the air and came right back down disappointed that I wasn't flying. I concentrated on being light as a feather and having complete confidence in my abilities. I bent my knees and told myself that I got this. I sprung up and this time I was in the air. I raced around the city once again, working on my control and speed.

Turning and steering was easy, it was speed control that was challenging. Once I got the controls down, it was like driving a car. I only had to watch out for air traffic and not cars and trucks. I flew around until I found the original building where I started. My landmarks were the two flashing blue lights on top. I told myself I wasn't going to crash this time, so I swooped in and slowed down and dropped myself down vertically. It was a little rough but I was getting the hang of it. I changed my shirt, pants and shoes and went back down the fire escape. I couldn't risk having people see me looking like I just walked out of a burning building.

The remainder of the week was pretty much the same — class and tutoring. My sessions with Delilah were growing once people realized how I was able to simplify things.

During the day, I'd hang with friends and at night, sacrifice sleep in order to fly around the city. I kept *those* sessions private from Dylan, who was still having problems with Airez. If he would just take care of the problem, he wouldn't have to sleep with one eye open.

My birthday was tomorrow and Dylan kept asking me what I wanted and I told him new shoes would be nice. I'd burned every pair I had except two and I didn't have the money to afford new ones just yet. I would be walking around in my shower shoes if I didn't get the flames under control and soon. I told him to spread the word of sneakers if anyone should ask.

Later on, I went to my study session to help Delilah with biology, along with two other classmates in Calculus. Had the brilliant idea to start charging people for my sessions as a way to make money for the semester since I was jobless. After the session was over, Delilah asked me if I wanted to go up to her room and watch TV, but I had to decline. I went to my last class and rushed to my room to get some sleep so that I could fly later.

The next morning I woke up early to make sure I got to class on time. My parents started the birthday calls as I walked to class. I told my friends that I didn't want to be in a dorm room for my birthday, so we caught the subway to Central Park. Delilah and Stacey packed a basket with some sandwiches and snacks for us to indulge. Gunner brought a football and a Frisbee for us to play catch and everyone had a wrapped gift in their hands. The best thing about the day was that there was no Airez in sight.

"OK, everyone, gather 'round," Delilah said, gesturing.

We all circled around her basket. She pulled out some store bought cupcakes and put a candle on one. When I looked around and saw how much time and effort my friends put into making sure I had a great birthday, I felt wanted more than I've ever felt in my whole life. Outside of my adopted parents, Monica, and Dylan, I was never close to anyone.

This was the start of my life.

They all grabbed which gift they brought and began to present them to me.

For the most part all the boxes looked the same. I began to open them all up and I'd gotten what I asked for—sneakers. With each pair I opened up they told me why they picked out that particular pair. Dylan's pair was track shoes. He said he was ready for a rematch and this time I couldn't cheat. I had six pairs of new sneakers.

When we got back to campus I took all my gifts upstairs and thought about going for a flight but found myself just wandering around campus. Something still wasn't right about me turning eighteen. I had a good day with my friends, but I had this feeling something was missing.

I walked over to Dylan's dorm and texted him to come downstairs.

"What is it, bro?" he asked. "This better be groundbreaking news for you to pull me out of bed this late at night."

I hesitated for a moment and finally said what I'd wanted to say my entire life. "I want to find my real parents." I was shocked I even went there and by his face, I could tell he was too.

Flustered, he replied, "Are you sure — I mean how would you even know where to begin?"

"I'm not sure but I was hoping you could help me…"

He was quick with his response. "You know I got your back, but what are you going to tell your parents?"

"I'm *not* going to tell them. I don't want to hurt their feelings, but I need to know."

"So, what do you suggest first?"

"Would you be down for a road trip this weekend to Poughkeepsie?"

"No problem."

After our last class on Friday, we got right on the road and headed home. We both told our parents we wanted to spend time with them for our birthdays.

They bought it.

We spent the car ride talking about how we would find them and what they probably look like. I couldn't picture them since I didn't have a formal racial background. What was definite was that I had color, dark brown eyes and a slim nose. I had so many questions to ask like: *was I exposed to some kind of radiation* or *was I an experimental test subject*? What if they had no clue of what I could do? I wouldn't want to freak them out right away.

The sun was already setting when we made it home. It felt good to be back in my hometown where everything was slower and obnoxious noise didn't hit you when you walked outside. We pulled up to my house and Dylan dropped me off.

"Let's keep a low profile, OK. We don't need any attacks from you-know-who."

I nodded, closed the door, and went inside.

My parents were excited to see me even though it had only been a few weeks since college started. I felt guilty saying that I wanted to spend time with them when in reality I only wanted to look for clues about my identity. Mom already had a meal ready on the counter and we all sat down in front of the TV to enjoy dinner as a family.

By the time I woke up the next morning, Dylan was already on it. He called and said he was setting up a lunch for our families. I sat on the edge of the bed staring at my phone. I picked it back up and sent a message to Monica and told her I was home for the weekend and it would be nice to see her. Figured she wouldn't respond since it was still a little early but she did, and told me to meet her at the *Carrot Cake* later today.

Mrs. Perry called about an hour later right on schedule to ask Mom if we would like to go to lunch. Of course, Mom said yes. I told her I was inviting Monica as well.

"So, how do you like having a room all to yourself now?" I asked Elias.

"I don't have to listen to you snore anymore," he laughed.

I threw a pillow at him and we began to wrestle.

As my family left, I told Mom that I would meet them there. I wasn't sure how Dylan got out of it but within minutes after my family leaving, he pulled up.

"OK, where do we begin?" he asked as soon as he got out of the car.

"I wonder if my parents still have my original birth certificate."

"You have two?"

"Essentially. Once an adoption is finalized, the child is issued a new birth certificate with the updated information. Never seen my original one. Not even sure if they got a copy or if it was sealed away."

We walked inside and went into my parent's room. "They keep a chest of old family things in the closet. Let's look there."

We opened the closet doors and behind some scrubs and dresses was a black chest that had a piece of nude-colored scotch tape with "Peterson" written on it. We opened it, took out the photo albums, the old report cards, a few old doodles Elias and I did as kids, and some other family keepsakes. We still couldn't find anything that lead to an answer or even a start. Next we checked the shed and went through all the boxes and bins and still nothing.

I exhaled and sat on a box.

"Wait — wait…" Dylan repeated to himself while pacing.

"What is it?"

He bolted out of the shed and back into the house.

I called out to him, "Where are you going?"

When I got back in the house, he was on all fours grabbing the photo album from under the coffee table.

"What are you doing?" I asked.

Shuffling through the pages he said, "I remember when I was looking at this book and your mom said — aye, here it is!"

"What are you talking about?"

"Look at this, Marc." He pointed to a picture. "Your mom said that *this* picture was taken outside of your adoption agency."

"Man, you're a genius," I said enthusiastically. "I could hug you right now."

He held a hand out. "That won't be necessary. Now, do you know where you were adopted from?"

"I'm not sure. They don't like to talk about it really. Somewhere in the state is all I know."

Dylan examined the photo intensely then jumped to his feet. "You were adopted from the City."

"How do you know?"

"Look here, the street sign says W 58th Street, that's in the City."

"Dude that not too far from campus. This is amazing."

Dylan reached into his pocket, pulled out his phone and took a picture of the picture. We went around the house and into the shed to make sure everything was set to how it was before we ransacked it.

"We have to get to lunch or our parents are going to kill us," I said.

Everyone was already eating when we walked in. Mom gave me the evil eye because I was late.

"I thought Monica was coming," Mom growled through each chew.

"Well … she decided not to come," I replied, sinking down in my seat.

"So Monica was going to come to lunch?" Dad dropped his fork onto his plate.

"Um … she was, but she said she had errands to run." I hated lying to my parents.

Dad's eyes bulged. "So she didn't go to work today?"

"*She has a job?*"

"She's your replacement. She works for me now and if she's not at —"

"Oh yeah! That must have been what she was talking about then," I interrupted. "She was saying something about me meeting up with her at the restaurant. It was all some misunderstanding. I think I'll order now."

"So how is college going for you guys?" asked Mrs. Perry.

"It's really a good experience. Dylan and I have been enjoying our time in the big city," I said.

"My roommate sucks," Dylan said gloomily.

"Well, next year you and Marcus can room together," Dad said, finally picking up his fork. Mom was still giving me that look like I was about to be in trouble when I got home. Hopefully we put everything back to normal.

"Or, you can get us an apartment off campus, Dad," Dylan said cheerfully.

"Not a chance," said Mr. Perry.

After dinner was over, Dylan and I went over to the *Carrot Cake* to see Monica. She was just as beautiful as she was on prom night, even with the ponytail and ketchup stains everywhere. She looked stressed as she carried orders to the wrong tables and constantly tripping over the hump in the floor that Dad wouldn't pay to get fix.

I just sat in the doorway watching her — laughing because I was the same way when I started off. I wanted to hold her. I wanted to hold her so tight that my handprints would forever be ingrained around her waist. Dylan took a seat and I threw an apron on to lend a hand.

Thank you, she mouthed to me from across the restaurant.

It was only her and another new guy working so I pitched in until the slight rush was over. I removed the apron and we both went to the bar next to Dylan.

"Don't tell me the big city ran you guys away already." She hugged Dylan.

"Never," Dylan laughed. "It's good to see you, Monica."

"We just came home to see the families for our birthdays."

I opened my arms and her eyes gazed up from my waist to my face, a smile forming next. She gave me a warm hug.

"Have you talked to Jessica lately, Dylan?" Monica asked.

"No. And I don't plan on it anytime soon," Dylan said.

"Why didn't you tell me that you were working for my dad?" I asked.

"We ran into each other one day at the grocery store and he asked me if I wanted a job. I needed a way to save some money up for college."

"Well, it's good to know that I'm replaceable."

"Are you kidding me? I suck at this. I don't know how you did it."

I kept catching myself getting lost in her beautiful brown eyes. I got up and made a smoothie for Dylan to distract me from staring.

"Well, I had lots of time to practice, and besides, I practically grew up in this restaurant."

We sat around and played "catch up" while still running orders to tables as needed. Dylan got tired of me leaving the table and taking orders while he sat there eating cake so we left. On our way out the door, Monica stopped me to talk in private.

"I'll be in the car," said Dylan.

"What's up?" I asked her.

"I just miss you that's all." She pushed her loose hairs back into the messy ponytail.

"Well, I miss you too, Monica."

"Can you come over tonight?"

"Yeah, I can make that happen. Dylan is waiting for me so…"

"Oh yeah, and I should probably get back to taking orders or something."

"Cool. I'll catch you later."

I went back to Dylan's house because I didn't want my dad to question me about Monica. I figured if I gave him some time, he would easily forget about it. Dalton wanted to spend some time with his brother so I watched as they played video games.

"Mind if I use your car tonight, Dylan?" I stood up to stretch.

"No problem. I'm in for the night." He put his controller down and stood. Dalton imitated the both of us.

I grabbed the keys and drove to Monica's house. Along the way she texted me, telling me her parents weren't going to be home so we would have the house to ourselves.

"Bring some swimming trunks?" she asked right as she answered the door.

"You never said anything about going for a swim," I said, raising an eyebrow.

"It's a pretty warm night. I figured you wouldn't mind."

She pulled me inside and dragged me through the house until we got to the glass sliding doors around the back. She pulled me through the doorway and guided me across the patio to the edge of the pool. She let me go and unbuttoned her shorts exposing her black bikini, sliding them down her legs and kicking them off when they reached her feet. I turned around. I took my shirt off and her eyes began to flirt with me when I turned back.

"Are you swimming in pants," she asked while removing her shirt now exposing her leopard print top that covered her chest and wrapped around her neck. I took my shoes and pants off and stood there in my boxers.

She sized me up and down.

She never looked at me that way before even when I was her boyfriend. She looked like she really wanted me in ways I've never imagined anybody wanting me.

"Have you gained weight?" she asked.

I smiled — confidently and walked over to the pool. "Are you just going to stand there or are we going to get in?"

We both jumped in the water and when we surfaced, we were on opposite sides of the pool.

"Marcus," she whispered, yet, I still heard her. "I like this. I miss this."

"I miss you too."

"Are the ladies treating you OK in college?"

"The same as they did here." I downplayed it even though I was somewhat interested in Delilah.

"You seeing anybody these days?" I asked her.

She swam towards me and I did the same. She wrapped her arms around my neck once we met halfway.

"Right now," she replied, tickling the back of my hairline, "I'm seeing you."

She reached in for the kiss and I met her halfway. She pulled away from me and her eyes sparkled. I couldn't hide the smile I had nor did I want to. I leaned forward for another kiss. She forced her body closer to mine, our movements creating waves. My hands breached the surface of the water to rest on her lower back. Her kisses went from slow and gentle to fast and forceful. She whispered my name with each breath and break we took.

"It's getting hot in here." She pulled away.

My eyes were still closed wanting to continue to kiss her. I forced her back to me and tried to kiss her again.

"Marcus, stop! The water, it really just warmed up." She turned and walked around, examining the water. Through the water I noticed her back had two red marks where my hands were.

I panicked and rushed out of the pool.

"Where're you going?" she cried.

"I — I — I really have to go, something came up."

"Marcus, are you serious? You just got here!"

I grabbed my clothes and ran through the house and out the front door until I got to the car. It was that moment there I noticed that my powers could hurt the people that I cared about. If I would have held onto her any longer, I could have killed her.

"Marcus, Marcus!" She ran out the house towards the car.

"This was a bad idea, Monica. Let's just accept the fact that we're not meant to be anything more than friends." I didn't really mean that. I just couldn't be with her knowing my powers could possibly hurt her. Her eyes began to water and her hands slowly balled into a fist.

"You know what, Marcus, I don't know what it is you want," she cried.

"*You*, don't know what I want? Monica are you serious?" I got out the car and slammed the door, shirtless and dripping water. "I stood on *this* porch and basically handed you my heart and you tossed it away, not even giving it back to me. So don't tell me you don't know what it is I want. I *wanted* you."

"Wanted?" Her wet eyes squinted as she slowly backed towards the door. "So you don't have feelings for me anymore?"

I hesitated before I answered. "I don't know what it is I feel, honestly."

"Well," she wiped the tears from her eyes, "I guess you'll have plenty of time to sort them out in the City because I don't want to go back to just being your friend, Marcus."

She walked inside and slammed the door. She was making things so complicated.

I was hurt.

I was hurt because I knew I wanted her but me being whatever I am, won't let me be with her — maybe anybody.

I walked back to the car and drove off wiping the tears from my eyes.

Chapter 15
ASAP

Even with the picture and Dylan's assistance I was now second-guessing my decision to search for my birth parents. Went through a whole bunch of "what ifs". *What if* I did find them and they got outraged that I came looking for them. *What If* I show them what I can do and it scares their hair white. The more I thought about it, the clearer my decision became to just leave everything as is.

I went on for weeks ignoring the thought of the picture. Knowing Dylan, I was sure he would have tried to push me into the search but was actually supportive. On the other hand, Monica and I haven't spoken since that night. Why did things have to get so complicated between us?

With the weather changing, Delilah needed to go shopping and dragged Charlie and me along. If it was one thing I hated about living up North it was the snow. I tried to get Dylan to come, but he'd been spending every chance he got with that *Imani* girl. Still can't believe I've never met her. I wondered about her existence. He's probably sitting in his room twiddling his fingers when he says he's with her.

"How about this?" Delilah said, holding a sweater up to her chest.

"I like it … I guess." I didn't know anything about fashion, let alone female fashion. Sweat pants and a jacket were dope to me. She shook her head, her nose scrunching as she giggled. She put the sweater back on the rack.

"You sure can make a lady feel pretty good about herself, yes." She walked by, stroking her finger across my face. She continued around the store commencing her retail damage. Charlie was leaned against one of the racks, huffing and puffing, so I took him outside.

"I can't believe you don't have a jacket on, son. It's freezing out here," Charlie said. He caught a breeze — froze and shivered.

"I know. Don't let me walk out without one next time," I said. We walked across the street to sit down and wait for Delilah.

"She really has a thing for you, son." Charlie nodded in the direction of the boutique.

"Delilah? Nah, I think she's out of my league. We're just cool."

"Yeah, you guys are only friends because *you* won't make a move on her. She's waiting on you, son."

I looked back to catch a glimpse of her shopping through the glass panels. She was such an amazing girl — smart, personable, funny and foreign. Maybe if I asked her out on a date, I could get my mind off of Monica for good.

But I was too nervous.

I obviously didn't have control over my powers, otherwise, I would have never bruised Monica. Still, I had to take charge and pray that I won't hurt anyone. I got up and started back to the store.

"Son, where you going?" Charlie said.

The bell chimed when I opened the door. I walked up behind her at the register. I startled her a bit when I tapped her shoulder.

"Hey, you guys almost ready?" she asked, getting her money from her wallet. I didn't exactly know what I was about to say and the way the lady at the register looked at me made me a bit nervous. "Marcus, you guys ready?" she asked again.

"Um, yeah. So Delilah … next week … I was thinking that after our Friday study session…" I looked over and still the cashier was glaring down at me. I stopped talking and looked down to see if something was wrong. "Next Friday night you and I should … we should … hang out … you know, just the two of us."

She froze for a moment and laughed. My head dropped.

"Are you asking me on a bloody date, Marcus?"

"Yeah. You didn't have to laugh at me."

"Blimey, I laughed because I thought it was cute." She leaned forward and pecked me on the cheek. "You're so adorable."

"So that's a yes?" I stood there with my hands in my pockets.

"That's a *hell* yes," she said. "What did you have in mind?"

"Honestly, I have no idea. I guess we can do whatever you want to do."

"Union Square," the lady from behind the register said.

"What?" Delilah turned around.

"Union Square, it's a cool little hip place where people hang. Shops, food, and entertainment. What more could a young couple ask for?"

"We'll look into that I guess," I said as we walked out.

"Do you think Stacey would go out with me?" Charlie said as we walked back inside our room.

"Dude, I have no clue, just ask her out. Same thing you said about me and Delilah."

"We could be roommates dating roommates."

"Whatever."

He was too excited about that idea.

"What did you even say to her?" He plopped on his bed. I took a seat at the desk and spun my chair to face him.

"Well, I just went for it. I took your advice and didn't worry about what she would say."

"So when you guys get married, son, you can thank your best man for hooking you two up back in your NYU days."

"Who, Dylan?" I laughed.

"Whatever, son. I'm asking Stacey out tomorrow."

Later that night when Charlie was sleep, I packed my bag and went out to my "flight pad" aka the tall double-lit building. I wanted to perfect my flight ability some more and this time, I took my shoes off and went barefoot. I started for a sprint that didn't feel pleasing as my feet ran across pebbles and other debris. I jumped off the ledge and took off like a space shuttle in the night sky. I was good, but still needed to practice speed control. I thought about a fighter jet and how it tears up the sky ripping through clouds, yet remaining in control.

When I would mimic that my speed increased.

Just couldn't slow myself down.

I went faster and faster, tearing through the air catching every bug and dust particle in my face.

Still, I couldn't stop.

I considered the only way I would stop was to crash and I wasn't too fond of smacking my face against the side of a building — again. I saw Central Park Lake from the top of the sky and I didn't think about it.

I splashed down.

I made it to the surface.

My body was sore, aching all over.

At least I wasn't in the sky anymore.

Barefoot and dripping wet, I hobbled until my body slowly lifted back in the air, flying snail speed. When I made it back to get my things, I couldn't find my bag anywhere. *Where did I leave it?* I diligently searched the whole rooftop and couldn't find it. I did another search and felt my heart attempting to escape when nothing turned up.

Did the two guys find me?

My hands wobbled.

Thoughts took a wrong turn.

I didn't want to spend any more time up there.

I took off running down the fire escape and eight blocks until I got to my dorm. When I got in I slammed the door and tried to catch my breath. Charlie was awake staring blankly at me.

"Are you OK? Where are your shoes? And son, why are you so wet?" He was throwing questions at me left and right and I just couldn't concentrate. I was still panicking about my bag inexplicably disappearing.

"Quiet." I said softly to myself while Charlie threw question after question. "Charlie, be quiet." I repeated over and over. I was on edge and he wanted to play twenty-one questions. My emotions quickly got of control.

My head was spinning.

I was nervous.

Anxious.

Overwhelmed.

Tears fell and my vision got blurry. I felt like I was at Dylan's party all over again. I looked up and the trash can set aflame as my head hit the floor.

I jumped out of my bed in panic mode. Charlie sat on his bed looking at me. Out the corner of my eye I caught a glimpse of the burnt trash can.

"I gotta find my backpack," I said.

"Marcus, what are you talking about, son?"

"My backpack. I gotta find my backpack." I was still in the same state—anxious and nervous. My throat was sore and it felt like I couldn't swallow or breath.

"Yo, chill man, ya backpack is right there."

He pointed to the edge of my bed and there it was, sitting on the floor. I didn't know what to think. I knew I wasn't going crazy. I know I took my backpack with me.

But who put it back?

I know I didn't.

I jumped up and ran over to check it. Charlie was right, it was mine. Had the same pair of shoes and shirt I brought with me to change. Reached down through all the mess and couldn't feel it.

"My phone…" I said.

"What about your phone?"

"Nothing. I think I just misplaced it. I'm sure it will turn up."

"You hit the floor pretty hard. Do you want to go get that checked out?"

"No, no I think I'm just going to take a shower and maybe sleep the day away,"

"Hey, one more thing. The strangest thing happened when you fell out, the dang trash can set fire and almost burnt this whole building down."

"Well, umm… guess it's a good thing it didn't. Gonna just hop in the shower. My head is starting to hurt again. Think I just need some peace and quiet."

I took a shower and got back in the bed. I didn't get much sleep. I was too paranoid about my bag. It haunted me the whole day and the next. During class and walking the streets, I looked over my shoulder constantly. The thought of sneaking out and flying didn't even cross my mind again. I didn't tell Dylan about it either. He would've been outraged that I did some kind of training without him, even more so that I put myself in danger.

Over the next few days I tried to be normal. I went to my tutor session after my last class that had grown to about ten freshmen. Each paid me twenty-five dollars every other week so I always had money. When my session was over, Delilah and I went over to Dylan's room to hang before dinner.

"You have to hurry and get a new phone, Marc," Dylan said. "Nobody can survive these days without one. Where did you say you lost it at again?"

"I've been so busy these days, I could have left it anywhere."

"Oh, ok..."

"So how are things between you and Airez?"

"Couldn't be better."

"Thought I heard the gang." Gunner walked out from his room and shook my hand. "Marcus. Howdy there, Delilah."

"Cheers," she said. "Somebody's in a bloody good mood."

"I just completed my darn seven-page *Who Am I* paper for my Composition class. I can finally go back to having a social life."

"That's great, help me write mine then," Delilah said.

"You're the one with the genius boyfriend. I bet'cha he can write some good papers," Gunner said.

"We're just friends, isn't that right, Marcus?" Delilah smiled my direction.

"Just friends," I confirmed.

"Plans for this here weekend?" Gunner said.

"Well, actually, *we* have plans," Delilah smiled. Gunner walked over and took a seat on the bed between Delilah and me.

"Describe this 'we' little lady," Gunner said.

Dylan stopped cleaning and looked at the two of us.

"We have a date." I broke the silence, only to be followed by more awkward silence.

"Oh, that's cool. That's all you had to say the first time. I'm sure we can find something to get into then," Dylan said. Once he finished cleaning his room, we all met up for dinner in the cafe. It was the first time the seven of us had been together since my birthday.

Gunner was going around the table trying to get everyone together for the weekend when Dylan's phone went off.

"Imani just texted me so I'll have to pass," Dylan said.

Everyone stopped eating, looked around, then locked eyes on Dylan.

"When are we gonna meet this bloody girl, Dylan?" Stacey asked.

"She's just shy that's all," he said.

"I'm starting to think she's a ghost," Delilah said.

"So no one believes that she's real?" Dylan said.

"No, they're not saying that. We would just really like to meet the girl that's all," I said.

Dylan rolled his eyes. I knew he didn't have to lie about a girl, but I was starting to have my suspicions with her and why she never wanted to show her face.

"Can I tell you guys a story about something crazy that happened earlier this week?" Charlie said.

"Yeah sure," everyone said.

I choked.

"So I'd just woken up when I heard the door slam. I turned around and it was Marcus looking like he'd just escaped a bar fight or something. I mean, son, you looked pretty rough. He was a complete wreck. Mumbling and ranting and going on and on about some crap and then it happened."

Everyone was into his story and constantly looking at me while he talked, especially Dylan.

"What — happened?" Dylan said, stressing the words.

"Poor Marcus over here passes out and smacks the floor."

"Ouch." Everyone's bodies crunched.

"But that's not the weird part. As soon as he passes out, the trash can goes up in flames and dang near takes the whole room with it."

"Is this true, Marcus?" everyone asked. I couldn't believe he told people that story. I didn't want to answer and I knew Dylan was going to give me a lecture later.

"I don't know about the fire, but I was a little sick that day," I said, wanting to pound my head on the table.

After dinner was over, Dylan asked to speak with me away from everyone else.

"So is it true? Did you set the trash can on fire in front of Charlie?"

"Yeah, but before you get into big brother mode, let me explain."

"Marc, we shouldn't even be having this conversation to begin with. It's already bad enough that Trey knows about you. Last thing we need is Charlie finding out and running around campus screaming that his roommate is a witch, or mutant or *whatever* it is we are."

He didn't let me get a word out. I didn't get to tell my story of how my bag disappeared off the roof and magically ended up in my room. If it were him, I'm sure he would have sent the campus into the ice age. He walked off and left me there covered in guilt.

Charlie flinched and jumped to attention as I slammed the door behind me. I slid my bag off my shoulder and tossed it to my bed. His eyes followed the bag then back to me. I still had the stench of guilt Dylan left on me, only, it escalated to anger on my walk back to the dorm.

"You OK, son?" Charlie asked, finally sitting back on his bed.

"Charlie, are you serious?" I had to hold back to stop my fist from burning. "Why would you tell everybody that embarrassing ass story?"

"Chill, son," he laughed.

"No you chill, Charlie. I passed out and damn near had a psychotic episode. Next time you decided to use my health as the root your entertainment, think it through again." I walked out of the room to catch my cool before things really got heated.

Later on as I got ready for my date with Delilah, I tried on what seemed like a million different shirts just to find the perfect one. I was no more stylish than a gym rat on a Friday evening.

So I called for backup. Luckily Dylan brought over something decent for me to wear. Glad I could always count on him to save the day when clothes and women were involved.

I grabbed my wallet and did a quick once over before leaving. Couldn't believe I was really about to go on a date with Delilah, the girl that had the campus lusting over her. She was actually interested in me... Marcus.

We decided to check out this Union Square place the cashier at the store recommended since it wasn't too far from campus.

Delilah walked out in skinny jeans and boots with a silver scarf and red jacket. We walked with her hands clenched tightly to my arm, conversing about our favorite snack foods. Walking through the area, we were greeted by a mime. He followed Delilah mimicking her actions: her strut, the way she brushed her hair down the left right before flipping it, and even how she put on lipstick. It was hilarious until she caught on.

There were all kinds of street acts and people just enjoying the night. We grabbed a hot chocolate and sat down on a patch of cold grass next to a tree.

"I'm glad you asked me out, Marcus," she said.

"Yeah, me too. I was extremely nervous so when you said yes, I was shocked."

Her tone got serious. "Why? You should give yourself a little more credit."

"What do you mean?"

She repositioned herself to face me, took my hands and placed them into hers. I began to warm them up.

"You walk around like there is something missing. You always seem a little worried about everything."

"This's just me," I replied.

"Come on."

"What?"

"Come."

She stood, still holding my hands, forcing me to stand with her. She ran to the center of the square taking me with her. Music played and she began to dance, never letting go of my hands.

"Dance with me, Marcus," she said.

I joined in and began to move. "I suck at dancing," I said. "Last time I danced was prom."

"You're doing fine, just move to the beat."

We spent the next half hour dancing before we went to grab a bite to eat. We grabbed some hot dogs and talked about her life in the UK. She wondered how I became so smart. I laughed at that part because I've always loved studying.

"Oh, so did I tell you that Charlie is feeling Stacey," I said.

"Fe-el-ing?" she said slightly confused.

"Yeah," I chuckled. "It's a way of saying *he likes her*. Charlie wants to ask her out, so see if you can get some info from Stacey on how she feels about him."

"Hmmm… interesting. I'll see what I can find out."

We finished up and started back towards campus.

"I had an amazing night." She cupped her hand into mine.

Her blonde hair fell down my back as she rested her head on my shoulder. We took the paved trail that cut from the Square to University Place.

"Can you do me a favor?" I asked.

"What is it?"

"Wait for me by that street light over there. I need to go."

"Sure. I'll be over here by the phone booth." She pulled her phone from her purse.

I ran into the trees on the opposite side of the road and almost peed my pants I had to go so bad. I found a tree and let go.

In mid-stream, I heard a noise coming a few yards ahead of me and I peeped around the tree. There was a small glowing light on the ground. I finished up quickly, zipped up my pants, and walked towards it. I glanced back to see if I could see Delilah, but I was too far into the trees. I didn't want to mess this up, but my curiosity got the best of me.

As I walked closer, I recognized the sound as a ringtone. I picked the phone up when I reached it and—

I couldn't believe it.

It was my cell phone.

Ringing with an unknown number showing on the screen.

My hands trembled as I looked at the screen. *How the hell did my phone get out here?*

Again letting my curiosity get to me, I pushed the talk button and put it to my ear.

Hello, I said gently. Before I could say anything else, a force from behind blasted me off the ground. Luckily there was a tree to catch half my face.

Not again. Not now.

Back searing with pain, I rose to my feet only to be greeted by someone covered in sparks bolting at me. In seconds, I sprung up in the air. I looked around to see if I lost him but all I saw was black sky and city lights. I floated, looking around for something, anything.

I started to fly off until thin, heavy fingers choked me from behind. I couldn't shake him off me as my body wiggled to get free. A stinging sensation overcame me. My bones ached. My heart pumped faster. It felt like every vein, artery, and capillary in my body was about to burst.

Then my body vibrated wildly.

Jolts of electricity generating from his body were transferring to mine. Once he stopped, he pushed my body away and kicked me out of the sky like I was nothing but scum.

I almost crashed, but I caught myself.

My hands flared.

I peered up.

And there he was, agilely rushing down from the sky — feet together and hands at his side.

My back and face were soaked in sweat.

Once he got inches from my face, I boosted back up, causing him to crash into a tree. I followed up with two fireballs. I landed behind him and we stood face-to-face once he got up.

I panted.

He panted.

"No way," I huffed, taking a step closer to confirm. "You're a girl."

It turned out that he was really a *she* and she was tough. Her arms had angry strings of lightning racing around them and her eyes were hazardous. She rushed again and let out a Spartan war cry. Our arms locked and eyes connected. I ignited fire from my hands and she released lightning. We separated.

Once I got a closer look and shook away the haze, I realized that I knew her. I'd seen her somewhere but couldn't recall. The more we fought the more it became clear. This was a setup.

Union Square.

The backpack.

The cell phone.

All of it.

It was the girl from the boutique who suggested this place. I pulled my hands back and unleashed a swirl of flames. It knocked her out of her shoes and she tumbled into the dirt. I hurled loads of fireballs; she dodged most by rolling around.

I rushed her and grabbed her off the ground. She grabbed my arm and swung me. We both flew into the air. Then I noticed her attention was no longer on me. She looked down and started to gather energy. Lightning surrounded her body and centralized in her hands. She shot a bolt of lightning down to the ground, but I didn't know what she was aiming for. I raced down to try and block the attacked aimed at a couple walking through the path.

I flew down and tackled them, leaving spots of fire in the grass. "Sorry, guys. Get out of here!" I screamed. I jumped up and shot back into the sky before they could see my face.

She waited in the sky.

My face tensed and anger boiled at my core from the thought of her trying to hurt innocent people. The flames on my arms grew stronger. I bolted at her, grabbed her by the waist and took her all the way down until we crashed into the lake.

I gasped when I made it to the edge coughing and spitting up water.

I lay there.

My body couldn't keep taking these beatings. I'm sure with these powers there was a natural resistance.

But this still hurt.

No way a normal person could survive all of this.

I didn't see her get out of the water.

I wobbled through the razor-like grass as it cut my feet along with all the sticks and wherever else I was walking in. I got to the bench where I told Delilah to stay and to my surprise she was gone.

I felt like crap.

I had no idea how I was going to explain what happened.

I didn't want to fly, nor did I really have the strength, so I walked back to campus. I made it to Dylan's dorm and knocked on his door.

"Whoa, dude you stink. Did you just bathe in a dumpster," Airez said, walking out the front door.

I flipped him the bird as I walked in.

"Damn, Marc, what the hell happened to you?" Dylan asked.

I slid down the wall as I rested on it.

"I was just attacked. Again."

"By who this time?"

"Dylan," I exhaled.

"Yeah, what is it?"

"I *have* to find my real parents. ASAP!"

Marked

Chapter 16

Ferrari

I hadn't talked to Delilah in days. She ignored my calls and didn't show up to study sessions. Dylan went into overprotective mode and had me check-in every twenty minutes. Once again, I had to stop practicing my powers. I wasn't sure where all these super powered people came from or why they wanted me dead. Maybe there was some proverbial sign over my head that said: *he's a flame-throwing freak and must die.*

I sat in class tapping my pencil against the desk, stalking the clock that wouldn't seem to move. The girl who sat behind me kept popping her gum over and over, breaking what little concentration I had. I counted down the final seconds and once the teacher ended his discussion and handed out the homework, I darted out of the building.

Outside, Dylan stood across the street with his graffiti bag slung across his back, his hair pulled back in a ponytail.

I ran over.

"What are you doing, stalking me now?" I said.

He took a sip from the smoothie he had in his hand. "Someone has to keep an eye on you since you can't seem to stay out of trouble. Are you ready?"

Today was the day that I've always dreamt. I knew I wouldn't actually get to meet them today, but it was a start. Dylan had already tracked down the street and building to match what we saw in the picture.

"Are you ready for this, Marc?" he asked.

"Ready as I'll ever be," I replied, hands suddenly clammy.

We got in his car and drove off. The ride was short and long and neither one of us spoke a word. Once we parked, we got out and walked towards the front entrance. I stopped half way while Dylan kept walking.

He turned around. "Marc, what's wrong?"

"Do you mind taking a picture for me?"

"Sure."

He pulled out his phone and I stood in front of the building. It was the same location eighteen years ago where my parents took our first picture. I put my hands in my pockets and he snapped.

"Can you smile this time?" Dylan put the phone to his side and smiled.

I freed my hands and locked them together in front of me. He snapped another. He started walking while I still stood there.

"You sure you're OK? We don't have to do this," he asked.

"Yeah, I'm good. Let's go in."

I was shaking on the inside at the simple thought of just opening the doors. Still I pushed back the nerves and headed down the path to my real life. Walking through the glass double doors, I didn't know what to really say. We approached a circular desk that sat in the center of the lobby and was greeted by a young lady with shoulder length curly brown hair.

"Anything I can help you gentlemen with?" she asked.

"Hi. My name is Marcus, Marcus Peterson," I stuttered.

Dylan reached out for a handshake as he introduced himself. She obliged.

"Marcus and Dylan, what can we help you with here today?"

This was it. My body started to tremble. I was getting cold chills and it wasn't because of Dylan. I was literally scared as to what kind of answers I would get, if any at all. I took a deep breath and exhaled.

"I think I was adopted here eighteen years ago. I was just wondering if you had any kind of records if I was? Maybe some that would lead me to, well… finding my biological parents."

"How brave you are. I just need a bit of information from you. Fill out these forms and give it back to me when you're done," she smiled.

At least the atmosphere was calming. It had four huge decorative pillars and behind the desk were a set of offices and stairs leading somewhere. I started filling out the paperwork but lost control of my hands. Dylan had to finish it.

"Dude, I need you to relax," Dylan whispered, handing me the completed forms. "You know what happens when our emotions are out of whack."

"I'm trying but this is *sort of* an emotional situation I'm in." People were starting to make quick glances at us. Last thing I needed to do was cause a scene.

"Alright, alright," Dylan continued, "just breathe, please."

I took the papers back to the desk and handed it to her with my ID. She took the papers and informed us it could take a moment to locate the files if any, then went to the back. I went back to my seat and waited patiently for my name to be called.

"So how are your classes going?" Dylan broke the silence.

"Ehh, OK."

"A little more than a one-word answer would be OK. Stop being so nervous about everything." He was leaned back in his seat, legs spread widely apart, chewing the end of a pen.

"I got all A's on my mid-terms."

"Smart ass."

We both laughed then he got serious once again.

"I think I blew it with Delilah, bro."

"She'll come around. She's a woman. Just give them a little space and they'll forgive you."

"I left her, on a bench, in the middle of New York City, at night. American or not, no girl wants to have that happen to her."

"In your defense, you had a very valid reason. Like I said, she'll come around. I don't know what kind of lie you're going to tell her, but I can talk to her to see where she stands."

"I'm not sure if I will ever be able to get close to another female, EVER!"

"Quiet and stop being so dramatic."

"Sorry. You're right, but I'm saying… before, I couldn't even pay a girl to look my way, and now I'm not sure if my powers will allow me to get close to anyone."

"Explain."

I sighed. "While we were home, the night I borrowed your car, I went to see Monica. We were in the pool swimming and things got a bit steamy. Right when we kissed, I noticed small burns on Monica's back from me where my hands were. I panicked and hopped out, wet clothes and everything. Things didn't end well that night."

"With a little more control, you'll be OK. I'm sure of it. Oh yeah, I forgot to tell you, I talked to Trey this week. He loves the South. He won't be home for Thanksgiving, but Christmas it will be the three of us again."

"Nice. I can't wait—"

"Marcus Peterson?" The receptionist interrupted.

I got up and began to walk to the front desk but stopped when I noticed Dylan still sitting.

"Are you not coming?"

"Oh no, this is something *you* have to do on your own. I'm just the chauffeur and moral support. Now go find your parents. I'll send you these pics since you got a new phone finally." He flipped through the pages of a magazine.

I walked back to the desk. "Well…"

"I'm sorry, Mr. Peterson, we don't have any files on your adoption." Her words sounded rehearsed like she's practiced her lines multiple times for multiple clients.

I immediately thought I should just give up my short search. My head dropped and I thanked her for her time. I turned around and started for the door until her voice, now whispering, stopped me.

"It seems your adoption was a … sort of a special case. Could you come to the back please?" she asked anxiously.

I forced down the lump in my throat. Was this an answer? Confused, I followed her up the stairs into an office.

Still whispering, she said, "You can have a seat and someone will be in shortly." The door closed behind her.

I sat for a few minutes looking over the office, praying this wasn't a trap. There were two degrees on the wall from Syracuse, and pictures of a group of middle-aged girls on the desk alongside a few snow globes from different states along the west coast. The door creaked. I snapped around.

"Hi," I blurted as if I was doing something wrong seconds prior.

In walked a finely aged woman with pale skin and salt and pepper hair that barely reached her ears. She walked around and sat at her desk across from me and smiled not saying a word.

"My..."—she marveled at my face and body—"have you grown, Marcus."

Now I was really confused. What did she mean by *I have grown? Was this lady my mother?*

"My name is Stephanie Burch," she said then spoke in a whisper like we weren't the only ones in the room. "I knew your father."

"You knew my father?" Both hands tapped the desk as I leaned forward.

She straightened her body, her posture and voice now professional. "I didn't know your father on a personal level, but I did handle your adoption."

I fixed my posture. She took off her glasses.

"I thought there was no record of my adoption?"

"There isn't any. I've been waiting for you."

Her cryptic messages had needles pinning my spine.

I sat back in my seat. "I don't mean to sound rude, Mrs. Burch, but you're really confusing me. What exactly do you mean by: *you've been waiting for me?*" I prepared myself for a fight just in case this lady jumped across the desk and attacked me.

"Let me explain what happened that day. At the time I'd only been working here a few months. I was working late trying to help a family adopt this sweet little girl. It was a real bad storm that night, heavy rains and thunderstorms all throughout the night. The power went out and the room was pitch black. I'm normally fine in the dark, but for some reason I was frightened. So I left my office to find a flashlight and right when I grabbed one, the lights came back on. I looked outside and noticed that the whole street was still in a blackout but for some reason, my building had power. It was eerie nonetheless, but I headed back into my office. I swear I'd almost had a heart attack when I walked in and seen a man in *that* chair you're sitting in right now."

"Who was it?" I asked.

"My first instinct was to scream and hit him upside the head with my flashlight, but he looked so scared, so terrified like his world was about to end. His calm voice kept telling me over and over that he wouldn't hurt me and he needed my help. I believed him once I saw what he was holding."

"What was it?"

"A beautiful baby boy. He looked to be no more than a few weeks old. The baby started to cry. The man held him to his soaked chest and started to rock him saying that it was going to be OK. He soon stopped crying.

"I took the baby from the man and dried him off. It then caught my attention that the man was bleeding from his shoulder. I quickly got him a first-aid kit and helped him get clean and dry. While bandaging him, he went on to tell his story, saying that he had these "powers", and that people were hunting him down, wanting to kill him and his baby. His name, I'll never forget, was Ignazio Ferrari.

"He continued on saying his son would one day come into his powers and people wouldn't stop until he was dead. He asked if I could take his baby and find him a good home. This wasn't the life he wanted for his son. So I agreed.

"He said there were just two things he wanted out of the deal: for me to keep no written record of this and that the boy kept his birth name. His story had me in tears. I just couldn't understand why anyone would want to hurt an innocent child. Knowing the protocols and being new, I agreed anyway and promised to make it hasty. He grabbed me, hugged me, then reached out and took the baby saying his last words of the night."

"What did he say," I asked, shaking, gripping the edges of my seat.

"*I love you, Marcus,* were his last words. He jumped out of the window and flew into the night. Then the power shut off again. At that moment, I knew I was holding a miracle."

I couldn't believe that I had a link to my father. My eyes were filled with tears that were waiting to fall down my face. She handed me a tissue and welcomed me home. I was ecstatic, sad, joyful, and mad. All these emotions were going through my body and yet I felt so calm.

"Did he ever say anything about my mother?" I said, drying the tears from my eyes.

"I'm sorry, but he never mentioned her," she said.

We spent the next hour talking about adopted life, my family, what my father looked like, and everything in between. She described my father as very handsome with a youthful face. He was tall and tan with light brown eyes and jet-black hair that trimmed at the sides with a heavy Italian accent. It all made sense now. I'm sure I'm the spitting image of him.

Right as I got up to walk out of the door, she stopped me. "One more thing before you leave, Mr. Ferrari." She handed me a large brown envelope. "A few days after I got you, this envelope came in the mail. I opened it and it was a thank you note with another envelope enclosed. The note instructed to give this to you *only if* you ever started looking for answers. This belongs to you." She handed me the envelope and her businesses card.

"If you ever need anything, Marcus, I'm here."

When I got to the door, I turned around and she was standing behind her desk with that permanent smile painted on her face. I walked back and hugged her. "Thank you, Mrs. Burch."

"You're welcome, Marcus." She responded with a light embrace. "Be great and protect yourself. Whoever *they* are, they're still looking for you."

I nodded and headed towards the lobby. I was still a little teary-eyed and emotional. Dylan jumped right up when he saw me.

"Did you find them?" he asked.

"My father's name is Ignazio. Ignazio Ferrari and he's Italian," I cried. I sat down, face collapsing into my hands. Dylan bent down and rubbed my back, comforting me as I let my emotions run wild.

Once we left the agency, we headed to Central Park instead of going back to campus. Flashbacks of my previous battle plagued my memories as we walked around.

Maybe I needed a therapist?

I did my best to tell the story exactly the way Mrs. Burch told it.

"My father has the power of lightning," I said.

"Guess we know how you got the powers now. What's that you're holding?"

"It's an eighteen-year-old envelope from my father with the name *Marcus Ferrari* on the front and the numbers 3-1-1-9 on the back."

"Don't you want to open it and read it?"

I was still trying to process everything. I opened the envelope and pulled the note out. Wasn't expecting it to say much since we didn't know each other. I read:

Marcus, I'm sure you now know what you are capable of and probably confused. I'm sorry I couldn't be there to help you with this process. I've done everything I can to help protect you and even in death, I will continue to protect you.

Love, Dad

"He's dead," I said. I parked it on the grass and put the note in my pocket.

"I'm sorry, man," Dylan said.

"I don't get it? He said he could protect me even in death."

"Let me see the note," Dylan said. I handed him the note and envelope.

"Look right here," he said. "How did you miss the address written on the back of this paper?"

"An address to where?" I asked.

"I'm not sure, but I'm guessing it has something to do with this key and this other paper in it."

"Where did that key come from?" I snatched the key from his hand.

"You can be slow sometimes. It was in the envelope, genius. Geesh did you even look to see what was all in it?"

I snatched the paper back. "Are you up for a trip right quick?" I said.

"I'm always down for a trip," Dylan said.

We jumped back in the car and made our way through the nightmarish traffic of New York. Within an hour, a trip across the Brooklyn Bridge, and a pit stop for doughnuts, we were there.

"Your dad seems like he went through a lot to protect you from something. What do you think it could be?" Dylan asked.

I just stared out the window as we sat in the parking garage. I couldn't think straight. "Why did he have die?" I repeated under my breath. The address led us to a bank. We finally got out and walked in.

"Let me handle this," Dylan said. He walked up to one of the tellers and asked to go to safe deposit box 3119. The man told him only if he had proof he was authorized, he could enter.

"OK so that plan didn't work," Dylan said, walking back to me.

"Yeah, you idiot, because you aren't authorized. I am." I walked back to the teller.

"I need to get into safe deposit box 3119."

"I'll tell you like I told that last kid I just saw you chatting with, nobody is getting in without property authority," the teller said. I was almost one hundred percent positive that an employee shouldn't be using that tone of voice with the customers. But what do I know? All I've ever done was sling greasy chicken and smoothies to tables for two years.

I pulled out the power of attorney and my social security card and handed it to him. "Here. That safe deposit box belongs to my father and I need to get in it. Sir."

His fingers mashed at the keyboard. That didn't stop him from taking his sweet time and making sure I caught his eyes rolling whenever we made contact. "I'm sorry, Marcus," he said. "Looks like there is a security question on the box. We can't let you in."

"How about you try asking the question," I said. I needed to talk to this man's supervisor.

He shrugged and let out a long breath.

Rude. He didn't want me to do the same.

"If Mr. Ignazio Ferrari had to choose one superpower, what would it be?" He didn't bother to look at me. His monotonous voice and drawn out words didn't sound like he really wanted to ask the question.

"Lightning," I said. My hands started to get antsy. I just answered the million-dollar question and I knew it was right. I was ready to accept my prize.

"Follow me to the vault, Mr. Peterson," he said. I threw Dylan the deuces and followed the teller.

"Here you go," he said, "box 3119."

I walked up to the box and without hesitation, I put the key in and turned it. I slid the drawer towards me. Although I wasn't sure what to expect, this wasn't it.

Journals. Lots of journals.

Some were old, some ancient, and some newer. Some had these weird shapes and symbols indented on the covers. There was an old brown leather satchel that held a few more journals. I grabbed the satchel and threw it across my shoulder and stuffed as many books in it as possible. I carried the rest.

A total of 13 journals.

When we got back to campus we rushed to my room and dumped all the journals onto my bed.

"What do you think all this means?" Dylan asked.

"Not sure, but I think somewhere in these books lies the mystery of who I am and maybe the story of these powers."

"Well, let's start reading then."

Chapter 17
Shapes and Squiggles

Over the next couple of weeks Marcus and I focused all our attention on school and trying to make sense of the journals he inherited. A few of them were written in some weird hieroglyphic language. There was one symbol in particular that stood out on the cover of all the journals.

"What do you think it means?" Marcus asked, sitting on the floor staring at the journal that rested on his bed.

"I have no clue," I said.

"This isn't helping at all. I've been going through these pages for weeks and I can't seem to get anything out of them."

"That's because they each have like fifteen different languages."

"How about we call it a night and pick up again tomorrow?"

"That's fine." I gathered my things. "No sneaking out and flying around the city and fighting guys or whatever else it is you always seem to get into."

I was exhausted when I made it back to my room. I threw my book bag off my shoulders into the dark room.

"Ouch!" A voice yelped.

I turned the lights on and Airez was on his bed wrapped in his blanket rubbing his head.

"Sorry."

"Yeah, it's nothing. Just, next time watch where you throw your things."
His tone elevated.

"Yeah, whatever."

My phone flashed 12:47 P.M when I woke up to a message from Imani asking
to come over. *Great way to spend my Saturday morning.* I got myself together
and walked over to Imani's dorm. She wanted me to come over and spend
the day watching movies in bed. I brought over a few horror and action flicks
but of course, she wanted to watch the romantic tearjerkers. I convinced her
to watch one of my movies and I'd watch one of hers.

"We should all get-together and do something later this week." I said, not
paying attention to the screen.

"Who is *we all?*" she asked, irritated.

"You, me, and my friends and maybe some of yours. Mine would really
like to meet you because to be honest, they don't even think you exist."

"I don't think that's a good idea, Dylan."

"I don't see what the problem is. What do you do when I'm not around?
Do you have any friends? Do you study? What are your hobbies? I feel like I
know *nothing* about you."

"Fine."

She crossed her arms and rolled her eyes. Even with her hair wrapped in a
scarf and missing a layer of her face, she was still cute.

I smiled inside at her complexity.

"Fine."

"I will meet your friends. I will go out, and whatever you want to do. I
will do it I guess."

"Don't sound so happy about it."

When Monday rolled around I asked all my friends what they were doing
tomorrow night, and if they wanted to catch a movie with Imani and I.
Charlie and Stacey had to study for a big test. Chris' parents were in town so
he and Gunner were going to be with them. Delilah had plans with some of
her other friends which left only Marcus available. I probably should've

planned first so it wouldn't look like my friends bailed out on meeting her.

I walked over to Marcus' room to see if we can have another shot at the journals again.

"What are you guys getting into?" Charlie asked when I entered the room.

"Just about to go over some boring chemistry homework."

"I don't know how you guys understand that crap. I'm going to stick to business."

"Care to stick around and learn something?" I asked.

"No thanks. I'm going to the library to meet up with Stacey." He grabbed some books and left the room.

"Whew. Thanks for getting rid of him," Marcus said.

He walked over to his closet, which had everything but clothes, pulled the journals out of a bin and spread them over the bed. That funny looking symbol was randomly located on each of the books in some fashion. It was triangle-shaped with a fancy looking number seven but the ends looked like hooks that hung through the center of the triangle.

"What do you think it means, Dylan?" Marcus asked.

I looked at it and became drawn to the symbol. It was like time stood still and everything became clear to me. I no longer saw the symbols. I saw English. *Shangaleese* whispered through my lips without me knowing.

"What was that?" Marcus looked at me then the journal.

"It says Shangaleese. Look at it."

He looked back at the cover and looked at me. "No it doesn't. I just see shapes."

I glanced again and the words were no longer clear, just shapes. "That's weird, I could have sworn it said Shangaleese."

We both opened the journals and went through them again. Some of the languages in the book we recognized — French, Spanish, Italian, English, German, the others were still a mystery. We focused on the pages written in English and I began to read:

1106 - The year here is 1106? I'm not sure I know what that means just yet. This is all too much for me. The way these people

write, talk, they even enjoy walking? I want to go back home. I miss my father so much. I hope one day he makes it to this strange planet once the war ends.
-Shina

"What war?" Marcus glanced over and eyed me.
"I have no clue. Let's keep reading."

1107 - It has been two years since I've seen my father. I'm starting to think that I may not ever see him again. Mom is still holding on and so is Shyra.
-Shina

1107- Shyra is starting to come into her abilities finally. She is fire just like father and myself. He would be so proud of her if he were here.
-Shina

1108 - Today I met a man. He is very charming, dressed in black tights and black armor. He had this animal they call a horse. It was so swift and cunning. He even let me go for a ride on him.
-Shina

1110 - Sorry I haven't written to you in 2 years. I want to try and have a normal life here and start over again. I think that is what you would want father. I am with child and married now. I am excited to see what element my child will possess. My husband's name is Alaric and you would approve father. I am ready to pass our family history on and keep our family name alive no matter where we are.
-Shina

1111 - A few weeks ago my baby boy was born into this new world. He is amazing. His name is Craft.
-Shina

1111 - I tried my best to fight them off. I don't know how they found us, but they did. I really wish you were here father. I don't know what to do at this point. I have no more tears to cry and nowhere to go. I took the baby out for a few hours and when I came home the place had been destroyed. Mother was dead and then I found Alaric and Shina also dead. I'm just a young girl and I need you badly Dad. All I have now is the journals and Craft and I will make sure he is safe and an excellent warrior.
-Shyra

"Whoa are you reading all this, Marcus?"

"Bro, I don't know what to make of it."

We kept reading and learned that Shyra raised Craft. She talked about how much she missed her father but that she learned as the years went on, her family history was what was most important. Craft started using his powers at the age of five and together they trained in hand-to-hand combat, weaponry, and the use of their powers. At the age of twenty-five she married and had one son and one daughter. Craft was starting to come into a young man and was a good help with the kids.

1126 - The war here is really starting to pick up again. How did they find us here on Earth is what I'm wondering. Craft is a big asset in leading some of the other Vandakhorian people we have met. We know what we must do, Fight!
-Shyra

1129 - Craft is taking the kids and fleeing. I've decided to stay back and fight. This will be my last entry until I find Craft and the kids again.
-Shyra

1130 - Today I am 19 years of age and something strange is going on with my powers.
—Craft

1130 - Every night I tell the kids of how their mother was a hero. I also tell them the same hero stories of grandpa that I was told growing up. I wish I could have seen the beauty of Vandakhor.
—Craft

In shock, I said his name, "Marc."

"What is it?"

"I believe the people in these journals are your ancestors."

"I think you're right. What do you think happened? What's this war they're speaking of?"

"I have no idea but we will go through the journals and find out what really happened."

The next day I overslept and missed my first class. I was still playing the story of Craft in my head—how he did everything to lay low and keep the kids safe. Marcus must come from a family of ancient super-powered warriors.

If that's the case then where do I come from?

We stayed up half the night reading through as much as we could, but the journals hindered us each time it transitioned into another language.

Later that evening, I headed over to Imani's dorm so we could walk to the movies.

"Where're your friends you wanted me so desperately to meet?" she said, looking at her phone like she was pressed for time.

"Well, they all sort of had plans already. However, my best friend Marcus will be meeting us after the movie since he had some studying to do."

Throughout the movie she seemed distracted. She picked at our popcorn and paid more attention to the people in the theater than she did the movie. She hardly cracked a smile while I had tears from laughing so hard at the movie. Her fingers bounced up and down on the armrest and every time I tried to touch her, she flinched.

"You alright?" I asked at every incident.

"Yeah I'm fine." She would falsely reply, edging on the crazy side.

Reminded me of Jessica.

Ewww.

After the movie was over, we headed back towards campus. She didn't say a word. At that point, I was just ready to drop her off. I'd rather be around Airez than Imani. My phone rang and killed the silence. It was Marcus.

Thank you!

I couldn't wait to talk to somebody normal.

"Where are you guys?" he asked.

"Right at 49th and 8th."

"Cool I'm walking up now."

He had no idea how excited I was to see him.

"Yo, bro," I said as our hands met. "This is Imani. Imani this is Marcus."

Everything about her froze except the up and down movement of her shoulders. She didn't speak. Marcus and I both stared at each other.

Then her.

She was climbing that ladder of psycho-weird.

Marcus stuck his hand out to shake hers. "Haven't I seen you somewhere before," he asked. And in seconds, it was confirmed.

Psycho.

I stumbled as she pushed me to the side, and wrapped her arms around Marcus' waist right as she made contact and took him down.

It wasn't any ordinary tackle.

Her jacket incinerated at the wrist, reaming him down an alley. His head smashed into the brick wall leaving a small smudge of blood.

"Dylan, get your crazy girlfriend off of me," he forced from his teeth.

She jabbed at his torso.

"Imani, what the hell are you doing? Stop it." I demanded.

"It's for, your own, protection, Dylan."

I threw her off and jumped in the middle of them; Marcus struggled to stay on two feet. I iced up and pointed both hands to the two of them.

"You sure can pick 'em," Marcus said, holding his ribs.

"Imani, you have some explaining to do!" I yelled.

"Me? You have some explaining to do as well," she responded. Just then the old rusty pipes on the sides of the building rattled against the walls.

We all froze from the banging. Marcus and I looked up. Imani was still on fire.

"What are you doing, Dylan," Marcus said.

"That's not me," I said.

The shaking got louder and harder until the pipes exploded. Instantly we threw our hands over our heads for protection. Water rained down, soaking us, extinguishing Imani's flames. Water crept towards our feet like it had a mind of its own. I watched as it formed circles around the three of us. I took a step back to escape it. No sooner than I moved, it shot up like a geyser and created cages around us.

"What the hell is going on," Imani cried with soaked hair pressed to her face.

The water rose, reaching up half the building then splashed down with high-pressure. We all fell to our knees and when I looked up, there were two people standing only a few feet from us. They both raised a hand and somehow picked the water up with no cup or apparatus.

"Start talking," the girl said, holding a pillar of water in the palm of her hand.

"And who the hell are you two?" I asked.

Marcus and Imani both flared up and went after the two but were easily shot down with a blast of water.

"Don't try that again," the girl said. "Now, who are you guys?"

"Please, just don't attack us again. My name is Dylan, this is my friend Marcus and this is Imani."

"Tell us who you are," Imani ordered. "Friend or foe?"

The girl glanced at Imani like she was searching for something. "Friend. I'm Hachi. And this is my twin brother, Hudson." They were both lightly tanned with dark hair. Hachi had hers pulled back into a knot at the back of her head. Her figure screamed athlete and her beauty said Pocahontas. The guy was carved and looked like he could lift a car with ease.

"How did you do that with the water?" I asked.

The girl looked at me as if I already knew.

"The same way you can do what you do with ice and they can generate fire from their hands. We're all alike," he said.

"No, *we're* not," Imani sneered, glancing over at Marcus.

"Why don't you shut up or we can finish this fight," Marcus said, igniting his hands.

"Both of you just stop — now — damn," I yelled.

"I'm just saying. I don't get why it's always me getting attacked. People act like you don't even exist. Sure, lets go after Marcus, he won't care. Nooo... forget Dylan, we want Marcus."

"You finished, Marc?"

"I'm sorry about the attack. We were just in the area and heard all the commotion. We have an obligation to our people," Hudson said. "Listen, we will talk more, you all go to NYU correct?"

"How'd you know?" Marcus asked, taking a step past me.

"Look down you idiot," I said. He was wearing an NYU jacket along with the rest of us. They both flew away and left us there soaked.

"Why did you attack me?" Marcus asked Imani.

"Your marking that's why." She snapped back, pushing her hair out her face.

"I don't have a damn mark," he said.

She reached for his left hand and pulled his sleeve up slightly revealing his wrist. She then turned him around and examined the back of his neck.

"It was right here. I saw it. I know I did and it started off the same way." She scanned up and down his left arm and paused.

"He doesn't have a mark, Imani." I walked over and separated her hand from his.

"Now I remember. Did you live in Poughkeepsie?" Marcus stared at her. "You did. I remember you from my Dad's restaurant."

"Is that true," I asked. "Did you live in Poughkeepsie?"

"It's true," she said. "I lived with my Dad's best friend for about a week while he was out on a mission. We were attacked in Jersey and had to flee.

We then moved to Albany and we've been pretty safe there so far. I've had to move around because no matter where we moved to, we were always found. That's why I've kept to myself. I know there are many of them out here in the City and at school I'm sure. Last thing I need is for my father to receive a phone call saying I'm dead."

"I had no idea," I said.

"Sorry, Marcus. I really thought I saw their marking on you," she said. *Their?*

"It's always me." He threw his hands into the air.

The next week Marcus and I met up again to read some more before we went home for Thanksgiving break. I cracked the book open and with this particular one, the pages were practically falling out. This one had to have been the oldest. Marcus read from one journal; I had my eyes glued to another. In the midst of scanning, something caught my attention.

"Marc, read this," I said.

He came over, sat next to me and laughed. "Are you kidding me? I have no idea what this says."

"It's in English. Now read it." I pushed the book to him.

"Bro, I kid you not, all I see is shapes and damn squiggles." He pushed it to me.

"You're funny. Fine, I'll read it."

> *-My name is Aarnadore Shangaleese and we finally made it to Vandakhor. Our neighboring planet Qihar invaded our home planet Xarpore. A number of us fled, but we didn't all make it. We took the ships and set course for Vandakhor but on the way there we passed through a stream of glowing lights that slowed us down. Once we landed, we all realized that something was different about our powers. We all could somehow move things by our thoughts, and my lightning power is now stronger than ever.*
>
> *The people here welcomed us with open arms and called us Shooting Stars, a gift from the galaxy. This place is so beautiful*

and tropical—nothing like the tall skyscrapers and buildings we are use to.

-We used our powers to help these people in return for acceptance. We helped with crops and creatures, built homes for people. It was such an amazing experience.

-I've fallen in love with Princess Thanda of the Shihi Nation and cannot wait for her to bring my unborn into this world.

-We have been asked to protect the planet. They divided the planet into eleven different nations and each of us has been put in charge of a nation. I have been crowned king of the Shihi Nation and one day my son will continue my reign as king.

-I think he may wield the power of ice. I wasn't sure how this would turn out but it seems like if we reproduce, our kids will possess the same powers as all Xarponians.

-The Xarponian/Vandakhorian population is slowly starting to grow. It pleases me to see that our families' heritage will not be forgotten and live on here.

"The symbol that keeps appearing on all the books is the symbol for Shangaleese. Marc, I think — and I know all this sounds crazy — but I think you come from the Shangaleese family and — and… you may be an alien," I said.

"No. What's crazy is that you made all that up off the top of your head." He snarled and stood.

"Marc, I have no reason to make this stuff up," I yelled.

"Fine, read some more. What happens next in the fantasy world?" He picked the book up and handed it back to me. I took the book and opened to the page where I left off and stared. I felt myself about to go crazy from the inside out.

I put the book down.

"What's wrong?"

"I can't read it anymore." I closed the book.

"I think I'm just going to call it a night, Dylan."

"Do you mind if I borrow this book and just skim through it some more?"

"I mind."

He showed me to the door.

The following weekend was spent with Imani. She told me more of the powers and a brief history lesson of the journals. She wasn't too familiar about them but knew that each of the eleven families started keeping the books. So somewhere in this world there are eleven sets, and Marcus has one of them. Her powers manifested at the age of seven and by the age of eight she could fly. Her mother abandoned her and her father once she realized what they were. They have been on the run ever since, defending themselves against anybody who would attack them.

I couldn't believe how many people out there were like us. It did make me wonder a little bit about which one of my parents has been hiding a secret. I made the decision that I wasn't going to ask them about any of this. I'm sure they kept it this way in order to protect the family and I wasn't going to be the one to make them a target.

I met with Hudson and Hachi after hanging with Imani. They both possess the power of water, which is one I haven't seen yet. So far I've only met people like me who could generate ice, Marcus and Imani who could shoot fire from their hands, and that strange guy with the lightning.

Hudson and Hachi were sophomores from Jersey. They shared something interesting to me about their powers which made me want to grab a blood sample and take it to the lab.

They've been practicing their powers with their parents ever since they can remember; however, their powers only work when they are in close proximity. Their theory is that our powers are engraved in our DNA and that their DNA, particularly the strand that activates our powers, is only activated when they are close by otherwise that strand shuts off.

I brought up the journals and asked if they had theirs. They said they heard stories of them and the knowledge they contain but that they haven't seen theirs.

Once we all returned to school from break, Hachi approached me with an idea: that me, Marcus, and Imani link together with her and her brother to train together for protection. Marcus was the first one to agree, since he's the one always getting attacked by random strangers. After careful consideration and some time to sleep on it, I agreed.

When I talked to Imani about it, she went into freak out mode.

Maybe I do know how to pick 'em...

"Dylan, I don't think this is a good idea. My powers have brought me nothing good. They're a curse," she said as I followed her inside her room.

"Seriously, Imani, don't you think you're overreacting just a little? It's not like you're alone. This is for *our* protection."

She slammed her books on the desk. "Did you listen to anything I said?"

I flinched. "Yes but —"

"Good. Then you know my answer is no."

"Imani, our powers aren't gonna go away and neither are the bad guys. We can't keep running from people."

"Speak for yourself. *You're* the reason why Hachi and Hudson know about me now. I haven't used my powers or even had to speak of them until I met you. Sounds like I found the answer to my problem. I think we should see less of each other. Things need to die down before they amp up."

"Seriously?"

She walked to the door and opened it. "Seriously. I'll see you around campus."

I was disappointed but maybe it was for the best. I could use less of psycho women in my life anyway.

Soon after the four of us formed an alliance. Marcus and I were both ready to take our powers to the next level.

Chapter 18

Never

I was pretty banged up, but Dylan was giving Hachi a run for her money. She couldn't have been going full-force. Hudson rushed me while I was down catching my breath; I sprung into the air once I caught a glimpse. He had two water trails flying behind him lashing at me as we both flew into the clear sky. Hachi came to my rescue and attacked her brother from behind, buying me time to go in for the attack. He was strong, but so was she.

I knew Dylan felt left out at this point of the battle since he couldn't fly. The teams were now unevenly matched. It was Hachi and me versus Hudson in an all-out air battle. She gripped her brother from behind choking his throat. Her slim arms barely fit around his husky chest. I was in front preparing a giant fireball. The fire between my hands grew stronger and stronger. I unleashed it at Hudson.

It seemed like it didn't even faze Hachi that I was throwing balls of fire at her brother or that a tear shed with each blow. His eyes transitioned from dark blue to dark brown with every impact. Once I landed my last attack, we both decided the battle was over and we won. She let go of her bruised brother; his body descended, landing on his feet then fell to his knees.

"Nice fighting there." Hachi flew over and gave me a high-five.

"It was sort of an unfair fight," I said.

"Do you honestly think they're going to be fair out there when they want you dead?" she snapped.

"I guess not."

We landed to talk about the scenario.

"Hudson," Hachi called out as she landed. "Hudson? Where'd you go? Where are they?"

"Dylan. Hudson. Let's go, you guys. I want some sleep." I added in. It was late and I was tired of being in the middle of nowhere with nothing in sight but trees and a pond. We scanned the field.

We found nothing.

"OK, I'm getting scared. Where's my brother?" she said.

"They couldn't have gotten too far that fast. Maybe they're just trying to scare us. How far can you be away from your brother before your powers deactivate?"

"Once we go past about a mile they stop working," she panicked.

"OK, no problem, try and use them," I suggested.

She attempted to maneuver some water into her palm but nothing happened. "O-K... so now is the time to panic."

I lifted myself up into the air to perform an air search and she joined me.

"Thought your powers don't work unless your brother is around?"

"My water manipulation won't work but our ability to fly for some reason was never affected."

"Ehh... whatever. How about I do an air search and you do a ground?"

"Fine."

I took off into the sky and counted to sixty. Once I got to a minute I sprinted back down head first only to be greeted by Dylan, standing below me shooting a beam of ice shards right into my face. I crashed, tumbling into the dirt. I got up. Dylan and Hudson had Hachi surrounded.

The blistering sting in my face told me Dylan was getting stronger.

They circled her, teasing about how we fell for their plan. She did a one-sweep motion with her arms that looked like Tai Chi, then two twirling circles of water navigated to each arm.

Dylan inhaled.

Deep.

He let it out.

Seconds later I heard glass shatter as ice hit the ground.

They both didn't hold back as they threw attack after attack at her, most of which she gracefully eluded.

I tried to get up and help but when I did, Hudson created some kind of chains with the water holding me down in place. Hachi was exhausted and wasn't going to be able to fight off Dylan's attacks much longer. Then rain begun to pour.

The rain was a heavy-steady flow to the point it disabled my vision. The rain quickly distracted Dylan. He didn't have the chance to see that Hachi redirected the raindrops towards him.

It was over.

We won.

When they both really admitted to their defeat the rain stopped. We were all muddy and wet and not to mention my clothes were half burnt off my body like always.

"You two are really getting good at this thing, I see." Hudson helped Dylan to his feet.

"Yeah, now all we need is to get Dylan into the air and we'll be even better," Hachi added.

"I don't know why I can't fly," Dylan said, throwing a typical Katie tantrum.

"Hey, it takes time. Our older brother didn't fly for *two* months after he started using his powers," Hachi said.

"Marcus, did it in like a month, and he wasn't even trying," Dylan cried.

"Can't help it. I am a natural." I gloated. I tossed a fireball into the air. It exploded into a cloud of smoke when it landed in my palm.

"Good job tonight, guys. Time for rest and class in the morning," Hudson said.

Once we got to neutral ground, Dylan and I headed back to the dorms together, while Hachi and Hudson headed in the opposite direction.

"You know, we really ought to stop doing stuff like this on school nights,"

I said. "I don't know how much more I can handle all this, Dylan."

"What you mean?"

"My body. I have been beaten and mangled on more than one occasion. I've crashed numerous of times trying to learn how to fly and now training. My body hurts in places I didn't even know existed. I have a permanent scar on my arm from my first fight, frostbite from my second, my third left blisters and scratches everywhere. And should I count your girlfriend as another? Add all this in with school and studying and tutoring. I'm getting a little stressed, Dylan."

He looked to the side of my face, examining with his fingers.

"Well, your scars are healing pretty nicely. You just need to take it easy and stop trying to do too much. If you ever want to quit, I will too. I support whatever decision you make."

"Yeah, I guess you're right. If we were normal, there's no way our bodies would be able to withstand all the abuse we've been putting on it."

We walked into my room. Charlie was nowhere to be found.

"What does Charlie think when you come into the room with scorched clothes?"

"And that's another thing"—my voice broke as I turned around—"I'm running out of sweat pants and socks."

Days later I met up with the gang for a game night organized by Gunner. It had been a while since we gathered. Delilah started talking to me again. I think it was once she got her mid-term grades back that she realized she couldn't live without me.

Go figure.

With the weather shift, we had to limit our outdoor activities. It didn't faze Dylan and I.

Stacey and Charlie seemed to have hit it off which gave me more alone time in the room. Chris studied so much I think all he saw was numbers and words through the lenses of his glasses.

Maybe it's best we kept it that way.

Dylan was still upset that Imani left him high and dry. It sucks that she feels she has to keep to herself as a means of protection. I assured him he would bounce back but next time had to pre-screen his potential girlfriends to make sure they have no prior grudges against me.

Once the night started picking up, Delilah was back to giving me the attention like before. The night was perfect, and looking around for a moment…

Life was perfect.

When I woke that following morning, I found Charlie in his bed shivering, wrapped up like a pig in a blanket. I hovered my hand above his body for a moment before heading out the door to meet with Dylan.

"Ahh, I'm starving," he said, rushing into the café as I trailed behind.

"You're always hungry, what's new?" I replied.

"A growing man has to eat plenty."

"You ready for these finals creeping around the corner?"

He grabbed a bagel, a miniature pack of cream cheese, some cereal and milk off the line. "Yeah, I think so. I mean, classes really aren't *that* difficult this semester."

I got some bacon and toast with a muffin. "I'm sure you will come out with a nice GPA."

"Not better than yours, I can promise you that."

"Actually…" I said, taking a bite. "There's a scholarship that I'm trying to get. If I can pull at least a 3.75 or higher, I may be eligible for a full ride next year."

"That's what's up, Marc-man. I have no doubt you'll get it."

"Thanks, bro."

We chowed down for a bit then he broke the silence.

"Have you read any more from the journals?"

"No, not really. They've been in my closet the whole time."

"Oh OK," he said.

We gathered our scraps and dumped them. "Did you really see the stuff in English," I asked, glancing slyly over at Dylan.

He never walked with his hands in his pockets. They were always busy swinging or helping him talk or just free hanging to the side. I took my hands out of my pocket just to see how it felt.

It was weird.

I put them back.

"I promise, I wouldn't make this kind of stuff up," he said.

"OK, understood." There was something else I was itching to ask him, but I didn't try to predict his reaction. "So are you going to ask them?" I just came out and said it.

"Ask who what?" He halted, his face turning red like he already knew what I was thinking.

"If all this is true, and if what Imani and the twins have been saying is true, your parents have been keeping a huge secret from you," I said.

"Ughh..." he sighed and kicked against the sidewalk. "I have put some thought into it. I'm sure one of my parents has powers, I mean, that's the only way to explain how I got mine, right?"

"Yeah." I paused. "Right."

The next day at school I ran into Imani on the quad between classes.

Literally.

"Hey," I greeted.

"Oh, hi, Marcus. I didn't see you there," she said, still walking. She looked me in the eye, and then put her head down.

"Well, if you walk with your head up, you might have noticed me," I said.

"Look, Marcus I don't have time. It's getting cold out here and I have to get to class."

"Oh let's be real, Imani, you and I both know this puny forty-degree weather doesn't intimidate us."

"Seriously, Marcus, what do you want?"

"Just because you don't want to use your powers and broke it off with Dylan doesn't mean you can't at least still talk to him."

"What's it to you? Why do you care what I do?"

"Psst... let me share a secret, I *don't* care about you after you attacked me. I care about my friend and unfortunately he misses you."

"I just want to be left alone. If you guys can't handle that, I will see to it that you do."

I was embarrassed walking in last to tutoring.

"Hey there, babe." Delilah handed me a steamy hot chocolate.

I kissed her on the cheek, being sure to warm her up. During the session, I went over chain rule for the ones needing help in Calculus and the cell reproduction process for the Bio guys. The guys from my sessions were really taking a liking to me. I got an offer to go to a party, but I had to decline. All the parties I had been to in the past have not always gone well for me. I figured I'd just keep to smaller groups of people where I belonged.

"OK, guys, we will have one more session next week and that will be it before finals."

Delilah approached me after everyone left. "So, plans for the night?"

"I don't know, I guess I was just going to go to the room and just chill out," I said, heart racing as I gathered my things.

She slid her fingers down my arm and whispered in my ear. "So you are coming to my room to keep me company?"

"Er-uh… I guess… I — could." I had a real way with the ladies. Never knew what to say at times like these. We left the student center and walked back to her room, hand-in-hand. The only conversation that took place was the one in my head: *What if she tries to take it there? What do I do?* When we got there, Stacey was nowhere in sight. I'm sure she was somewhere with Charlie.

Delilah threw her bag on the floor and kicked off her shoes. I stood at the door, trying to figure out where this was going, until she walked back to me, gripped the sides of my shirt and pushed me until I was pinned against the door.

She forced her tongue in my mouth.

Her kisses weren't the slow gentle ones I was used to with Monica.

"Delilah," I whispered between my lips and hers, trying to slow it down. She tugged on my shirt pulling me towards the bed. I tried to push her off, but the aggressor in her kept the grip strong. I pushed as she pulled. Our hands began a game of tug of war. I tripped on a snow boot and landed on top of her — on the bed.

"Delilah, I don't think this is a good idea," I whispered, trying to get her attention, but her eyes were closed, tongue concentrated on my neck.

"It's a great idea." She sounded like a sex-fiend.

She ignored me and continued her quest down my neck. I was afraid I'd have another Monica situation, so I tried to ignore the moment and focused my thoughts on advanced calculus equations, while naming as many spider species in my head as quickly as possible.

Just didn't seem to work.

No matter how hard I tried to divert my attention, my body still quivered as she ran her tongue from my neck to earlobe.

My body agreed but my mind said no.

"I don't want to hurt you." Slipped out my mouth.

She stopped, looked at me and smiled. "Oh really?" And then jumped back to kissing my neck.

"No, not like that. I didn't mean... ughh," I sighed.

She sat up and so did I.

"I've never done this before is what I meant." How humiliating. I was in college and never had sex before.

"You mean, never?"

"Never."

She kissed me on the lips, softly this time. "I think that makes you even sexier."

As turned on as I was, I couldn't help but think that if I were to try it out, she'd get hurt and I didn't want to risk it.

But I was DYING to know what it felt like.

"Well since you've never done it before, I think your first time should be a bit more special. And you being untouched makes me want you more," she said flirtatiously.

"Really?"

"Really."

We ended up getting Chinese and talking the rest of the night away. We ordered out so I wouldn't get attacked and leave my date behind like last time.

I was surprised how she responded to me being a virgin. Most girls, I'm sure, would've thought I was a weirdo, being eighteen and never intimate with a girl.

I got back to my room right before midnight. The temperature around me was starting to drop. I knew my body had a slight resistance to cold but not completely like Dylan. I got myself ready for bed and right when I closed my eyes, my phone rang.

"Lo," I answered half sleep. It was Hudson.

"Marcus!" He panicked.

"Umm, yea, what's up?"

"Marcus, get over here now. It's Dylan," he said. I sprung up to attention.

"Where you guys?"

He was breathing hard, his words broken. "We're at my dorm. Get over here now!"

I didn't ask any questions after that. I grabbed a shirt, put on my shoes then ran out the door.

Chapter 19
Not Like the Others

Sweat running from every crack on my body, I sprinted across campus to Hudson's room. My lungs caught fire the whole run there — only thinking the worst. I barged in. He was lucky the door was unlocked because I would have blown it off the hinges. Hudson stood over Dylan who was passed out on the bed.

"What did you do?" I yelled. For all I knew this guy could have killed my best friend. I mean we didn't really know *who* these people were or their intentions.

"I didn't do anything I jus—"

"You better start talking now." My hands flared, burning my shirt at the wrist. I approached him. It didn't bother me that he was a few inches taller and fifty pounds heavier. I guess it was a good thing that he had a single room because I would have just exposed us all right there.

He didn't back down. "Look, I don't know what happened for sure, but I'll tell you once you put the fire out."

I refused. "Talk."

"Fine. We were out training. I was trying to teach Dylan how to fly, but he was holding himself back. We skipped that and went onto some battle drills. I agreed to not fly and we would fight until the other one quit but I — I…"

"I what?" The flames grew burning more of the shirt.

"I didn't realize how strong Dylan was. Anyway, I was throwing punches and I think I may have hit him a little too hard."

"What did you do?" I prepared myself for a fight.

"*I* didn't do anything." He looked at the comatose Dylan, his eyes apologized for even training with him alone. "Once I laid my last attack on him something happened and I went spiraling through the sky with the scars to prove it. He was on the ground when I got back to him. I couldn't take him to the hospital so I just brought him here. That's when I called you."

I exhaled. The flames died to a smoke cloud. I backed down and took a seat on the floor next to the bed. It wasn't the first time he had passed out. I wondered if passing out came with the powers? But if so, this wouldn't be a surprise to Hudson.

"I don't know how to explain it, but Dylan isn't like the rest of us. To be honest I'm not even sure if he is whatever *it* is we are. Right when Dylan first started using his powers, things around him would move without anybody touching them."

"How so?"

"We were out training, just like you guys were doing. I think we were pushing ourselves too hard that day and just like you, I was at the wrong place at the wrong time. I found myself being thrown out a window and when I went back to check on Dylan, he was on the floor passed out. Can I ask where did you hit him before you went flying?"

"It was on the head, but it was an accident I promise."

"Dylan has chronic migraines, and when he gets migraines his telekinesis unleashes. I've had migraines maybe once or twice but not as often and as severe as Dylan. I've also passed out once. Is this normal for our kind?"

"Wait, so Dylan has telekinesis?"

"Yeah. I don't know how or why but I was thinking, maybe Dylan isn't like us. He can't fly and he is the only person who I've met who has the ability to move objects with his mind. It could also explain his parents, I'm sure they don't have powers. Perhaps he's in a classification of his own."

"I've never heard of headaches or blackouts with these powers. So what do you think he is? I mean, he does have a Xarponian power."

I got myself comfortable. "I'm not sure, but maybe our kind isn't the only ones invading this earth. Grab a pillow and a blanket. He might be out for awhile."

"How long is a while?"

I laughed. I made a pallet on the floor and rested my head.

When we woke up, Dylan was sound out of it.

I anticipated that.

I went back to my room to get dressed and Hudson stayed to watch him. In between classes we switched out so we could make it to as many classes as possible. I talked with Dylan's professors and let them know he had the flu and wouldn't be in class until he got over it.

I spent the whole night there hoping he would wake up. I passed the hours doing my homework and his so he wouldn't fall behind. Day two went by and so did day three, with no sign until day four.

"Argh," he wailed, feeling around his head.

I was on the floor with my legs crossed, studying the two textbooks in front of me. Hudson was wheezing at his desk that overflowed with multi-colored notebook paper. I called his name once Dylan started to wake. He jumped up knocking over his homework.

Dylan didn't move, but his hand cradled his head. "I feel like I've been run over with a truck. How ... did ... I end up — awe man, did I? Not again," he sighed. "What fun is having telekinesis if I can never really enjoy it?"

"Dylan." I stood up and Hudson and I walked over to the bed. "You were out for almost four whole days this time."

"No wonder I'm so hungry." he joked. He got up and turned his body to face us. His feet dangled off the edge of the twin bed that was clearly too small for Hudson.

"I don't think you understand how serious this is. I think it's best if you don't use your telekinesis anymore." I took his hands off his head and looked him in the eyes.

"How am I supposed to control it? It just happens."

"You just have to find the trigger like you did for your ice powers. Now just relax and lay down."

He took his hands back. "Lay down? I been out of it for four days. I want some food."

It was starting to annoy me slightly. He was making joke after joke. It was clear I was more concerned about his health than he was.

So…

We took a trip to grab some burgers.

Just the two of us.

"Geesh, Dylan, can you fit anymore food into your mouth at one time?"

"Yup," he said with a mouthful. He washed it all down with a soda and began stuffing garlic fries at his face.

"How you feeling, bro?" I enjoyed seeing him eat, even if it was like a child eating cake on their first birthday.

He was alive.

"The hunger is almost gone and I don't even have a headache anymore. So I would say I am better."

"Dylan, we need to talk."

I waved my hand in front of his face to grab his attention. He didn't respond.

"Dylan."

"Shoot."

"We have to find out what exactly it is you are."

"What do you mean?"

"I don't think you're the same species as the rest of us."

"What do you mean by that?"

"You can't fly and you're nowhere close to learning. You have telekinesis and no one else does. You get migraines and pass out when you use too much power. Hudson said these things are not associated with being Xarponian."

"Well, what are you thinking?"

"I don't know, but we'll find out, promise. But first we need to focus on finals and making sure we don't flunk our first semester of college."

"SCHOOL!" he yelled, dropping his fries onto the table right before it could reach his mouth. His chair screeched as he backed away from the table.

"Don't worry, I talked to your professors. They think you have the flu. I also did all your homework. Your Mom called and wanted to know when we were coming home and I told Gunner you would be staying in a friend's room to prevent the guys in the suite from catching your germs."

"Thanks, bro. Where would I be without you?"

"Lost for sure."

Chapter 20

Holiday Blues

Marcus and I headed home for the break after finals. My house didn't really feel like the holidays this year. Mom was working major overtime at the hospital so I've been spending my days trying to find ways to entertain Dalton. Yesterday I took him to the mall to do some Christmas shopping. Today I tried to get him out of the house so we could go do something with Marcus and his brother, but he declined. He wanted to lie around, play video games and eat pop-tarts all day.

So, we did.

Christmas was just a few days away. My aunt and two cousins were coming down on Christmas Eve to spend the holiday with us. I hadn't seen my cousins in two years, so it would be nice to see some family to bring some cheer into our household. I really haven't been spending time with my dad. For some reason his attitude was always turned on when I was around. Wasn't sure if it was because I decided to go to NYU or what, but I thought he would be over that by now.

Guess not.

When Thursday morning came around, I was awakened by a loud bang on the door and the repetitive ringing of the doorbell. I rolled over because I thought my mom or dad would've gotten up to answer it.

Of course not.

The knocks only got louder and the rings picked up the pace. I pitched a fit in bed, kicked around, and threw a few pillows before I finally got up to get the door. If the knocks were loud enough to wake up Dalton, then I knew my parents heard it. He and I got to the door and opened it.

A parade hit us in the face.

"OHHMYYGOSHHH! DALTON AND DYLAN!" she screamed.

Totally forgot my aunt was a little eccentric. She dropped her bags at the door and rushed us, nearly taking Dalton and me to the floor as she wrapped her short stubby arms around the both of us. We were like ants, compared to her in size. Probably why my parents refused to answer the door — to avoid the dramatic greeting. Her two sons grabbed her bags and walked in behind her as calm as can be.

"Dylan, how's it going, little cousin?" Cory said. We shook hands.

Cory was Aunt Chloe's eldest son. He was twenty and a junior at Florida State. I remembered always wanting to be around him and the cool kids.

Now I'm the cool kid.

"Haven't seen you in forever," Chad, the youngest son, said to Dalton. Chad and I were closer in age. He was just a year behind me. They're both pretty cool but Chad was occasionally a bit hyperactive.

Think he inherited that from his mother.

We all spent a few moments catching up before Mom and Dad finally decided to wake up and come downstairs.

"If it isn't my wonderful big sister." Aunt Chloe hugged Mom, while Dad took a seat on the couch next to Chad and Cory. "Christine you look fab-u-luss," she screamed, admiring Mom's hard-earned figure. She took full advantage of that free gym membership the hospital offered. Mom walked over and hugged her two nephews and we all sat around the coffee table sharing stories.

Later that day, all the adults went out and did whatever it was adults do when they got together. We dropped Dalton off at Marcus' house and picked him up. We all met up with Trey to catch the new action flick. After the movie was over, we still needed to do some last-minute shopping. Of course the mall was packed on Christmas Eve, so trying to find a parking spot was a hassle. We split up once we got inside. Chad and Cory went their separate ways and we went ours.

Once we finished shopping, we met up with Cory and Chad. They had multiple bags full of gifts.

"Who's going to wrap all these gifts for us?" Marcus asked as we headed back to the car.

"I suck at gift wrapping," Cory said.

"If we have a place to go and wrap all these up, I'm sure I can find someone to come help us," Trey said.

"Who," I asked.

"Don't worry about that. Just know I can get us help," he said.

"Ok, I'll get us the place. Trey you get the help," Marcus said.

Marcus unlocked the door to his restaurant and let us all in. Between the five of us, we had a ton of presents to wrap. Marcus turned on the lights and we set up some tables to get started.

"Where is the help you promised us Trey?" I punched his arm.

"Well, aren't we just demanding," an unknown yet familiar female voice yelled out. I turned around; Diana stood in the doorway — straight and tall with a red designer bag at her side.

"Diana!" I walked towards her with open arms. We met each other halfway and greeted with a tight hug. "It's good to see you," I whispered.

She kissed me on the cheek. Something about Boston and college boosted her sex appeal and ironically she was wearing tennis shoes. I could count on one hand how many times I've witnessed that. Her hair was in a high ponytail, natural nails nicely manicured with pink polish.

"Good to see you too, Dill Pickle." She spotted Marcus and went to give him a hug.

"Why didn't you tell us she was home?" I punched Trey on the arm again.

"She told me it was a surprise." Trey gave me a sneaky smirk as he lightly rubbed his arm.

Diana walked up to Cory and greeted him. "I don't think I've had the pleasure," she said. Marcus, Trey and I laughed.

"These are my cousins Cory and Chad. They're here for the holidays," I said. "OK, so you're going to help us wrap all these gifts right?" I had to keep her busy before she tried to get busy.

"Geesh, don't rush me," Diana said.

She walked over and started wrapping the gifts one by one. She never took a seat. She leaned over the table making sure Cory had a nice view of her astonishing frame. I stepped back and stood next to Marcus.

"You know, I could help make this process go a whole lot faster," I whispered.

"You mean you could use your telekinesis for a few minutes and then I'll be nursing you back to health over the next week? Yeah … not the best idea." He shut the idea down.

"Relax. I think my body's really getting used to it," I reassured him.

"I'd rather not take that chance today and risk exposing us." He ended the conversation and gave me a look that said *quit asking*.

After all of the gifts were done, I was worn out like I did something. Diana wanted to finish the night with a movie in her basement. I had to decline. Marcus and Trey both went with her while my cousins and I went back home after picking up Dalton. It was subtle, but I think she really just wanted Cory to come over.

It was late — an hour before midnight when we made it back to the house. I expected everyone to be knocked out but they were wide-awake. Freshly baked oatmeal and sugar cookies hit us when we walked in.

"Well hello there," Aunt Chloe said. Our arms were full of wrapped gifts. We place them underneath the tree. Photo albums and wine bottles covered the living room table.

"Seems like you all went overboard," Mom said.

It may have appeared that way. Between the three of us and all the gifts we had to get for everyone it really wasn't. I walked to the kitchen table and grabbed two cookies—one of each. Dalton and Chad did the same.

"Come, take a seat, have a glass," Aunt Chloe said. Mom's eyes sharpened as they cut a glance over to Aunt Chloe. Dad busted out laughing.

"I'm trying to cut back. I get enough of that in college," I said.

"Dylan," Mom panted. She knew I was playing. Dad continued to laugh and Cory tried to hold it in.

"Mom, you know I don't drink."

"He's grown, he can have a drink if he wants, Christine. Have a drink if you want one, Dylan." Dad instigated, waving his glass towards me.

"I'll take one," Cory said.

He walked over to the table and sat down next to Dad. Dad poured him a glass. Mom put her hand to her head.

"Listen, guys, I'm pooped. I think I'm going to call it a night." I yawned, my arms naturally stretched.

My room was a mess when I walked inside. I wished Mom would stop opening the window. I picked up the papers that fell from the desk then looked up at the window. I walked over and stuck my head out. This eerie, tingly sensation crawled up my skin, stabbing my spine. I started to pull my head back when a bird whistled past scaring the crap out of me.

I fell back.

Laughed a little to mask the nerves.

I stared at the window, did a slight tilt with my head causing the window to close.

It was morning.

Dark.

But morning nonetheless.

Before I could open my eyes, the decadent scent of french toast and maple cream cheese with bacon awakened my senses. It was the same scent every Christmas. Couldn't figure out why anyone was cooking this early. I rushed downstairs even though I was still tired.

Didn't even wash up.

When I got to the bottom of the stairway, I was at peace.

It was just what I wanted for the holidays…

My family.

Everyone was gathered in the kitchen pitching in for breakfast. The lights from the tree bounced off the white walls like a disco ball.

Postcard perfect.

"It all smells so good," I said, walking into the kitchen. "Did you guys even sleep?"

"Sleep, what's that?" Aunt Chloe turned around with a pan full of blueberry muffins hot out of the oven. "We've been up having such a hoot, we lost track of time and just went ahead and started the festivities."

I walked around wishing everyone a Merry Christmas, then joined Dad and Chad on the couch for holiday cartoons.

"You don't want to help your mother out in the kitchen, Dylan?" Dad asked.

"Dad, you know I have just about as much cooking skills as you do. I like the house, don't wanna burn it down."

"Can we go ahead and start opening presents, Dad?" Dalton asked.

"Have you eaten yet?" Dad replied.

Dalton knew Dad never allowed us to open presents before breakfast. We tried that once when we were kids, and we skipped every meal. From that day on Dad's rule was eat first, presents second.

We gathered at the table covered in the foods Mom only cooked during the holidays.

Dalton was the first to dig in. After he made his plate disappear, he rushed over and slid on his knees to the tree, grabbing all the boxes with his name on it, clawing the paper and bows right off of them. Everyone else took their time enjoying all the wonderful food, then walked over to the tree and began opening their gifts. Seeing everyone else smile made me smile.

Later on I headed out to Marcus' house to drop off his gift. I ran back up to my room to grab my phone and noticed I received a text. It was from Imani and read: *Merry Christmas.*

I smiled.

I turned around and ran right out the room, crashing into Chad.

"Whoa, cuz, why the rush?" he asked.

He gave me weird looks as I bent down to pick up my phone.

"Yo, Dylan, when did you get contacts?"

"Crap." I huffed.

"What was that?"

"Nothing. I'm just blind as a bat and normally don't like wearing them."

"Most people just go with the clear so it won't be so obvious."

"I'll keep that in mind."

"So where you headed?"

"Marcus' house. I'll be back soon. I won't be too long, and you don't want to be around his crazy family." I responded, pushing him aside and dashing down the stairs. I got right to the door when Mom yelled from the kitchen—

"Where're you headed to in such a hurry, Dylan?"

"I'm just going to the Peterson's house." I walked out the door thinking I was all in the clear.

"You're not going anywhere in that snow," Mom said.

I walked back inside.

"I'm walking. I'll be fine." I stepped out the front door again.

"It's freezing out there. You won't be fine," she said.

I walked back in. "Mommmm!" I was having a serious *WTF* moment. It was like the universe or something was stopping me from leaving. All I wanted to do was get to Marcus.

"If you get sick, it's on you then, Dylan." She taunted. She finally showed her face and walked up holding an envelope. "Here, drop this off to them then."

I finally made it to the house.

"Merry Christmas, everyone," I said, shaking the snow off my coat once I walked in. I made my way around the room greeting everyone then handed Mr. Peterson the envelope Mom gave me.

"I got you something, bro," I nodded to Marcus.

"Oh, *you* got *me* something?" Marcus laughed.

"Of course, dude, I wasn't going to forget you."

"Well, what is it?" he asked, trying to snatch the package from me as I tossed it between my hands.

"Let's go in the room right quick."

We walked into his room and the door closed behind us.

"Dylan, really?" Marcus said.

I laughed and handed him the gift. He tore the paper off with one swipe and looked at it awkwardly. "It's an antique journal," I said, admiring him admire the journal. "Thought the look would at least fit the rest of them. I know how bad your family, your *other* family, wants you to keep the tradition of telling the future generations the family history. Now you have your own book for whenever you decide to start telling your story."

"Wow, Dylan." He kept his eyes on the journal, rubbing his fingers on the leather cover. I thought it was only right to have his family symbol indented on the cover. "This ... this is really something. I think I'll start right away and write what's been happening so far."

"I think that's what your father would really want. Oh yeah I almost forgot, turn it over." He turned it over and engraved on the top corner read: *Marcus Ferrari.*

New Year's Eve came around and it just meant one thing: school was right around the corner. I spent the day with a few of the guys I used to ball with, and the evening with my family and the Petersons over dinner. Evening became late night, and we all waited in front of the screen until midnight struck, cheering and toasting, champagne-filled glasses clinking.

Marcus and I climbed onto the roof and went over the past events of the year, reflecting on how much our lives have changed. We knew that this year was just the beginning and whoever was after Marcus was still out there.

"Ready to set off some fireworks?" I asked.

"I thought Dalton and Elias set 'em all off?"

"Marcus, I'm sure we can make our own fireworks."

With just a thought, blue lights of ice swirled in my palm taking the shape of a ball. I threw the ball of ice into the air. Marcus grinned, stood, and flickered a mini fireball at it, causing it to explode into colorful ice particles that resembled fireworks. We laughed and threw more, seeing how the size of the balls made each particle unique.

I did most of my packing before I went to bed so I spent my morning cleaning my room since it was used as an extra guest room or if Dalton needed extra space to kick his soccer ball around. After having all this fun, I wasn't ready to go back to the fast-paced environment, filthy streets, or the stench of public transportation in the City.

Once I got everything ready I went downstairs to get some food. Mom and Dad were sitting at the table.

"Can I join you?" I asked.

"Sure, son, have a seat. We've been waiting for you anyway," Mom said in a low tone.

"What's this about?" I sat.

"Can I start?" Dad asked.

"Sure, Jackson." Mom agreed.

"Your mom and I are getting a divorce." Dad blurted as if he was excited to let the words leave his mouth. Mom elbowed him. He was never the one to sugarcoat anything. I got up from my seat, my fingers tightly gripping the edge of the table.

"Please sit," Mom said.

"I'd rather stand," I said dismissively.

"Things between your father and I just haven't been the same for a while. We still love each other very much and—"

"Have you told Dalton yet?" The tone in my voice darkened. I fought hard to keep my tears inside. I was furious they made a huge decision like this that affected the whole family alone.

"Not yet. We're just waiting for the perfect time," Mom said, tears forming in her eyes, her voice cracking.

"You two are selfish. When do you think is the *perfect* time? There is no perfect time. You guys are going to crush him from the inside out and I don't even think you care."

"Dylan, calm down," Dad roared.

"No! How can you do this to us? I just pray that Dalton doesn't hurt as bad as I am right now."

As soon as I turned around and fixed myself to walk off, Dad jumped up and gripped my arm, pressing firmly into my skin.

"Watch it, son. We're still your parents and you *will* respect us."

I pushed him with my free hand. My powers kicked in and Dad tripped, hitting his head on the wall. Mom flinched, tears a constant stream down her cheeks. I ran upstairs, grabbed my luggage, and rushed back down.

"Where are you going, Dylan?" Mom said, trying to help Dad to his feet, but he waved her away.

"Back to school. You need to have this talk with your son. I can't do this right now."

I called Marcus and told him to be ready. I got to his house and of course he wasn't finished packing yet. I didn't have time for his great ability of procrastination so I went in and helped.

"Dude what's gotten into you?" he asked as I tossed his things haphazardly into random bags.

"We'll chat on the way back. Let's just hurry up and get on the road. I'm over Poughkeepsie."

My mind wasn't focused on the road; I had no idea how I managed to not hit anything. I told him what happened and we talked about it the whole time on the road.

It felt good to be back on campus and in my room. I was the first one back from the suite back and was pleased to not see Airez's face first. I put my luggage down and sat on the bed. Wasn't sure if I was ready for school or anything else this semester but I was going to take it head on no matter what the challenges were.

The Revealing

Chapter 21
Genocide

It was the first day of classes and my mind was scattered. I desperately wanted to call my parents and apologize for the way that I acted, but at the same time I was still furious. My heart ached for Dalton. I wasn't sure what life was going to be like for any of us when the divorce finalized.

I had so many questions that needed answers.

Always thought that I had the perfect family.

Guess you can never judge a book by its cover.

I was ambitious this semester taking seventeen credit hours. I had the dull subject History II bright and early on Mondays and Wednesdays.

My professor sounded like the guy from Clear Eyes commercial — monotone. I don't even think it really bothered him that half his class was asleep.

Next on the snooze list: Dylan.

I woke up as class was ending. It was a good thing I wasn't snoring or woke up to a crowd of people staring at me. I walked outside and headed towards my next class. A thick layer of snow covered the ground and everyone walking around in their colorful winter gear looked like Skittles on white paper. I smirked as I walked by. That was me pre-abilities. Still, I wore a light jacket to fake it.

As I walked into my next class, Imani walked up beside me. "Seems we have this class together," I said, voice charming as ever. Her face instantly turned red as her eyes gazed past me and she hurried into the classroom.

"So how was your break?" I took a seat next to her. "I was happy to get a text from you on Christmas."

She rolled her eyes and pulled her books out. I put my finger on her pencil and watched as it instantly covered itself in ice. She snatched the pencil, threw it on the floor, and grabbed my shirt pulling me in closer to her so that our foreheads connected.

Lips practically sealed, she said, "Are you trying to get us caught by every Qihar in the city?"

I snatched myself back. I heard that term before in one of the journals. "What's ... a... Qihar?" I asked.

"UGH! Just forget about it. You're so blind to everything. You have no clue who you really are."

"What's that supposed to mean?"

I couldn't understand how a girl so pretty and petite could have so much hostility built up inside. When class was over she gathered her things, and raced for the door. I raced after her, grabbed her by the arm, and pulled her away from everyone.

"Talk to me," I demanded.

"Dylan, do you think we were given these powers to go around and have fun with? We're in the middle of some *intergalactic war* and *these* powers are a curse to everyone like us. They bring nothing but death."

She began to walk off but stopped abruptly. She turned around, walked back towards me then took my hand, raising the sleeve on my right arm and looked stunned.

"I don't get it," she said.

"Get what?" I asked. She just kept looking but I couldn't see what she was looking for.

"You're not even marked."

What mark was she talking about? "What do you mean?"

"You're not even like us.... Who are you?" She looked at me like I was a complete stranger then walked off.

I met up with Hudson in his room where Marcus was. I walked into Hudson telling the story of how he and his sister were attacked back home over the break. It must really suck that they have to always be around each other just in case danger pops up. I didn't want to tell them about what Imani said, but I did wonder if he was *marked*.

While he was talking, I closed my eyes and channeled my energy on Hudson's sleeve. I pictured it slowly, inch by inch, the sleeve of Hudson's thermal lifting. I opened my eyes and noticed black ink tattooed on his wrist. His mark had me in a trance. It was beautiful, like artwork, the way it twisted and coiled up past where I could see. As I continued to stare, my gaze met his. His narrowed eyes and wrinkled nose said one thing: Disgust.

"What are you doing?" His left hand jumped to his right arm, lowering his sleeve.

"Dylan!" Marcus screamed. They both jumped up like they were ready for a fight.

"OK... OK ... OK, guys, I'm sorry." I threw my hands up.

"Why are you trying to look at my mark?" Hudson asked.

"I was trying to see if people with abilities really are marked," I said.

"Of course we are, just look at your own if you're *that* obsessed with it."

"I ... I don't have one."

Hudson cocked his head sideways and took a step towards me. "What? What do you mean you don't have one? Gimmie your arm." He raised my sleeve. "How is that even possible?" He looked over at Marcus and raised his sleeve. There was nothing but the color of his skin. His eyes jumped back and forth between the both of us holding our sleeves up.

"How could I have missed this?" Hudson whispered to himself.

"Are people born with these markings?" I asked.

"No, but we normally have them by puberty."

"Maybe we're just late bloomers," Marcus said.

"Yeah ... maybe." He stared at us like he'd never seen us a day in his life. He went on to finish telling the story of their attack.

Everything was going in one ear and out the other as he talked. I was curious as to why Marcus and I didn't have a marking. I wasn't in a rush or anything for a tattoo but it was kind of odd. Marcus should at least have one if anything.

I wanted to know more about Qihar so I asked Marcus if I could borrow the books for the night. Although he said no, he offered for us to read them together. I understood. He didn't want the books leaving his sight. Charlie was watching TV in the room so we went to the library, found an empty corner and collapsed on the floor.

I looked for the book that I read from the last time that had all the shapes and squiggles. Once I found it, I opened it to the first page.

I looked at the page and all of a sudden the symbols moved around until English words appeared on the pages.

There was a loud explosion outside. It wasn't just a normal explosion we hear when the warriors are out training in the battlegrounds. This one felt different, it felt dark—real. I got out of bed, walked into the hallway, and saw my parents gearing up for a battle. I asked what was going on but they told me to get my sister and seek shelter. I offered my assistance but I was told getting my sister out was more important.

I grabbed her, activated A.N.T and the three of us headed outside and what I saw was a sight I will never forget. Dozens of massive ships covered the murky purple sky and thousands of warriors flying out of them.

Without hesitation they started attacking my people and destroying the planet with their abilities. I knew who it was the second they started attacking. It was the Qihar, a race of people from our neighboring planet. There are four planets in the Mocra galaxy: Qihar, Xarpore, Vandakhor and Xioh. Nobody knows why or even where they come from but for some reason the people of my planet and the people of Qihar all have unique abilities. We all possess one of five abilities: fire, air, water, ice, and lightning.

Even though our two planets are so close that it's visible with the naked eye, contact of any form between the two races have been forbidden far before time itself—prophesizing the ultimate destruction. Everything happened so fast. I hugged my parents and they told me to head to town but to be sure to stay out of the sky. They promised they would meet up with us when they could. That was the last time I ever saw them.

A sinister chill froze my bones. It now made a little more sense as to what has been going on and what Imani was saying.

"Is there more?" Marcus asked.

I kept going.

We were both exhausted when we finally made it to King's Square. There were a bunch of other kids both younger and closer to my age, meeting there as well. I saw a few friends, which eased the anxiety. When we got inside, the King and teams of his best warriors were all leaving to aid in the war. He told all of us to go into the caves and wait for his assistants to come give us further instructions.

We all followed the King's order and went to the cave alongside his daughter, the Princess of Xarpore. There were hundreds of escape pods used for emergency evacuation. We were there for days as the battle above ground took place. I felt cowardly just sitting there when I could have been helping my people, but the Princess assured me that our people were doing fine.

We were starting to run out of food so one of the guys decided, on his own, to go out and get more. The Princess ordered him to stay and that we shouldn't disobey her father's orders but he didn't listen. It was like he unleashed the gateway to all evil when he opened the door. A rush of Qihar swarmed in and attacked all of us.

We fought back. I did everything I could before the princess grabbed me and shoved me into one of the pods. I yelled to her that I couldn't find my little sister or A.N.T and that I had to go find them. She told me that she would go back and find her but that we had to start evacuating. She set the destination to Vandakhor and closed the door. There were a good number of us that made it into the pods but most were shot out of the sky by the Qihar ships. I now wait in my pod until landing. I hope to see my family again one day.

. ~Shangaleese

"Bro," Marcus said, hovering over me, "this is some intense stuff."

He grabbed the book from my hands, and I could feel the waves of envy released from him. It had to be painful knowing I could read his family history and he couldn't. It was still a mystery to me, but it wasn't one I was going to question. I took the book back and ran my fingers against the raised symbol on the front that read *Shangaleese*. If the princess had never forced him into that pod, Marcus wouldn't even exist today.

Shangaleese sacrificed everything he had and all he ever wanted was to help his people in the war. Instead, his family was killed and he was forced to start his life over on another planet. I didn't know who this guy was, but he was brave. Reading this really had me thinking about my own family and what I would do if the same situation happened to me. It didn't feel right knowing how I acted, so I knew I had to apologize.

"Don't you want to know more, Marc?" I asked.

"Nah, that was enough. We should head back and get some sleep."

By the end of the week I finally gained the courage face my parents and call home. I spoke with Dad first and let him know I was sorry for raising my voice and putting my hands on him. *"Someone's been in the weight room,"* he responded.

Typical Dad.

I mean he had to know by now that I have powers just like him. He did have the markings like Hudson.

I ruled out Mom because I figured I would have caught her slipping by now. Then there was that chance I was something completely different and just born this way. When I spoke with Mom, she explained the living situation. Dad was moving out and getting his own place and Dalton was staying with her. She gave me the option as to where I would like to stay when home for breaks.

The following week when class got out, I approached Imani and semi-apologized for not knowing the whole truth.

"Look, I know now," I said. She stopped and turned around before she could make it out the door. "The Qihar. I know who they are." She walked back and grabbed my arm pulling me with her. We both took a seat in the empty classroom.

I raised the sleeve of her jacket and there it was. It looked like one of those tribal tattoos—abstract and ritualistic. She held her arm out to me like she wanted me to examine it. I gently rested her arm into my hand and studied it. The design started at the wrist on her right arm and stopped at the forearm.

"So I will get one of these?" I asked her.

"I'm not sure, Dylan. I'm not sure you are even one of us. I've never met anyone your age with these powers that didn't have a marking."

What if I was an experimental test subject injected with some kind of serum at birth? I wanted to know everything she knew so I asked. I asked about the stories she knew to see if it matched with the one Marcus and I had.

She began by saying all she knew was stuff told to her, how today less than a small percentage of the world's population is both Qihar and Xarpore and how the mission of the Qihar is to annihilate the population of Xarponians, liked they originally planned before the Xarponians fled.

"So the markings … that's how they spot—us?" I asked, sounding unsure if I was considered in the "us".

"That and their natural sensors. But I guess you and Marcus are safe since you blend in with the humans."

Blend in? If she only knew. "Answer this. Why did Qihar attack Xarpore anyways?"

"How did you know it was the Qihar that attacked first?" She smiled for the first time in a long time.

I smiled back. "I've been studying."

"Well, allegedly the Qihar wanted to be the superior race and rule the galaxy, but since Xarpore also had abilities that mimicked their own, they had to take out everyone on the planet."

"Genocide…"

"Exactly. It would have worked if it weren't for a few kids no older than you and I rebuilding the population of the Xarponians."

Everything she said matched up with what was written in Marcus' book. I knew she was telling the truth. We both got hot sitting in the room with our jackets on, so we finished our conversation as we walked around campus.

"And Earth comes into play how?" I asked.

"You see, after spending about two-thousand Vandakhorian years on Vandakhor, Qihar invaded them. Once they had complete control over Xarpore, they wanted to finish what they started by taking out everyone on the planet since the Xarponians reproduced with the Vandakhorians. No one knew whether or not if the offspring of both races would have powers, but they did. Now, with another planet in the galaxy with powers the Qihar felt threatened."

I was in shock over all the knowledge I gained over the year. Most people my age were learning networking and business skills. I, on the other hand, was learning that life on other planets in a distant galaxy really did exist. I almost wanted to change my major to astronomy and prove some professors wrong with all this newfound knowledge.

"They say history repeats itself," she said, turning around and walking backward, facing me. "Once the attacks started, the Kings and Queens already had a plan in mind. They each had a section in their regions packed full of escape pods. They loaded as many as they could and set a course for a place they thought they would never be found."

"Earth," I said.

"Correct. But they were wrong, they were found … *we* were found. Fast forward to the present. Hundreds maybe even thousands made it to Earth. Once again, each started their lives, this time as Earthlings. Soon they noticed that the Qihar were also on Earth doing what they promised — killing anyone with the blood of Xarpore running through their veins." Her voice took a more serious tone. "That's us, Dylan. We're the descendants of the people of Xarpore and *that's* why we are being hunted."

"So the people of Qihar, are they marked as well?"

"The people of Qihar have tribal markings just like us, but harder to see."

"Why is that?"

"Their tribal marking starts at the bottom of the neck and goes down the spine. Since everyone wears a shirt, we can never look and tell."

"I don't get it."

"What don't you get?"

"If the markings of the Qihar start at the bottom of neck why did you attack Marcus when you saw him? You said you thought you saw a marking on his arm."

"I thought I saw the marking of Qihar on his left arm," she corrected. "Everyone with the blood of Xarpore is marked on the right arm, never the left. All of our markings start the same. You see how it starts off as a solid black ring approximately half an inch thick around the wrist?"

"OK. I get it now." I examined her marking. It started the same way as Hudson's.

"Once they appear, the tribal markings start to grow as your powers grow. They take you on a journey so no one marking is ever the same. The Qihar start with a black line and grow down."

"Well it's a good thing that he has the blood of Xarpore in him then."

"Are you positive?"

"Hundred and ten percent." I said, confident. He had the books to prove them.

We stopped and took a seat near Silver. It was the most we've talked since she tried to kill Marcus.

"So when did you know?" I asked.

"Know what?" she said, picking at the ends of her jacket as she stared down.

"About your heritage." Whenever I asked a questioned that was deemed too personal, her shield came up. "I mean, you don't have to talk about it if you don't want to."

"No, it's OK. I just, lied earlier." She moved her attention to her fingers, rubbing them against her palm. "I was about seven and life was great as far as I can remember. I lived in Chicago. It was a better than normal life actually with everything we needed and wanted, and loving parents who did whatever they could for their children. I was the social kid, popular. Everyone wanted to befriend me and I the same. I was well aware my parents had powers. They would use them around the house and told us bedtime stories of our ancient family history. All was well until this one Saturday when Dad had to make a run to the store to get some ingredients Mom needed for dinner. She kept telling him to hurry because she was ready for the food to be done and I was hungry. I remember clearly like it happened yesterday, the back door being blasted off the hinges while I was in the kitchen.

"Mom reacted fast. She gave me one look and I knew. I ran and hid behind the couch and peeped out to see what was going on. This short and muscular guy wearing black jeans and a sleeveless shirt walked in right after the door flew off. He shot a bolt of lightning so powerful it went right through Mom's shoulder. She flew across the kitchen, knocking over everything on the stove. Blood splattered everywhere and just that fast, the kitchen was unrecognizable. He walked in closer to her and Mom tried to fight back but she was too weak to use her powers. I remember the look he gave her — his smile haunts me even to this day. He struck her with one more bolt of lightning, ending her life.

"He went on to search the house. He started to make his way back to the bedrooms and I ran out to check on Mom, but she was no longer moving. No child wants to see their mother lying lifeless in a pool of blood. I didn't have time to cry because I heard another door being blasted away. I walked into the back room and I never thought I would see this in my life."

She started crying. I slid my fingers across her jeans and slipped my fingers into her hands.

"You don't have to finish if you don't want," I assured her.

She nodded. "It's OK. I've never told anyone my story. I walked into the room," she said, trying to wipe and talk through the tears, "and saw the same guy take no mercy on my little sister. I couldn't hold back anymore and I stood there crying. I guess he didn't know I was there and my crying startled him. I felt my hands getting warmer and warmer by the seconds. Moments later, they were on fire. It was the first time I ever powered up. He extended his hand in my direction, and I saw the lightning sparking around his palm as he was about to attack. Right when the bolt started to form, Dad busted in and shot him down. The guy tried to escape but Dad … Dad wasn't going to let that happen."

"Imani, I-ugh, I had no idea." I scooted over as she cried and pulled her closer to me, taking her hands down from her face and wrapping them around me. She buried her face so deep into my chest the sound of her crying was mute. I now understood why she thought her powers were a curse and brought nothing but destruction. She pressed away from my chest and wiped her eyes.

"Ever since then, my dad and I have been on the run trying to avoid being spotted. I trained heavily as a teen, but I hope and pray I never have to use my powers unless absolutely necessary."

Her tough and isolated exterior faded away like leaves changing with the seasons. We talked for a little while longer, shifting the conversation to our favorite cookies before calling it a night. I walked her to her dorm and held her in silence. I let her know I was here for her and she walked inside.

The next day, I caught up with Marcus and shared some of the information I learned from Imani. It sucked the Qihar were still trying to become the superior race after thousands of years. They've destroyed two planets already and planned on another. It's up to our generation to put a stop to it and end this war.

Over the next few weeks, Hudson, Hachi, Marcus and I took the training up a notch. The three of them went over flight fighting while I covered ground attacks. Even though I still couldn't fly, I knew my ability to think on my feet as well as telekinesis was an asset to the team. We all knew the war here on Earth would pick up soon and we wanted to be ready.

Chapter 22
Typical College Student

Focus ... focus ... focus, I repeated to myself, staring at my history test, tapping my pencil constantly on the desk. I wanted to blame the teacher for not going over the material, but I had to take the fault. I'd been staying out all night training with the others. The teacher gave the ten-minute warning and that time flew by. Everyone had their test turned in and I was the last one still penciling when he called time.

There was no way I could bring any bad grades home to my parents. I had to find the balance between school, friends, training and figuring out who *I* really was. Marcus was doing well for himself. His grades were nothing less than perfect, his girlfriend was hot, and he was making money from tutoring people and making new friends.

I walked back to my room and opened the door to Airez and his brother talking. His eyes looked me up and down and I froze. "What?" I asked, checking myself for something out of place. They both got up and took their conversation into the common area.

You would think that after a semester, we could at least stand to be in the same room together. Guess we'll just never get along. I waved my hands, opening the closet door. I threw my book bag in and plopped on the bed.

When I woke up, the night was just starting its shift. I had dinner plans with the clan off campus. I knocked on Chris and Gunner's door and we met the others at the bus stop.

When dinner was over, Gunner, Chris, and I went back to the room. Gunner heard about a party that was going on and wanted to check it out. That was one thing I liked about Gunner, he was fearless and always down for a good time. Chris wanted to study, what I should have been doing, but I couldn't leave Gunner high and dry. We got dressed and headed out.

The party was in Queens. It was crazy how many people greeted Gunner as we walked in. I hadn't been to as many parties as Gunner, so I was limited to the amount of people I knew.

Girls were walking up hugging him and giggling as they walked off while guys shook his hand as they passed him.

"You're too popular for me," I said.

"I get out often," he said.

I was nothing how I was in high school. I was so used to being the popular guy all my life and people wanting to be around me, but now it was like people had no clue I even exist around here.

"I think you may be right," I said. When we finally made it past the crowd of people that wanted to greet Gunner, I felt something lay across my left shoulder. I turned and Airez was right in the middle of Gunner and me with his arms rested on the both of us.

"Well if it isn't my lame-o roommate and my steroid infested suitemate. What brings you two out?" It was obvious why he was so friendly as you could smell the whiskey on his words.

"Daggonit, is there no escaping you?" Gunner pushed Airez's arm off his shoulder.

"Boys, I'm just here to have a good time," said Airez politely as he walked off. "See you two around."

"That was awkward." I shrugged as he left us there, confused. "Was it me or was he actually … well … pretty tolerable for once."

"Yeah, I think he may have something itching up his sleeve," Gunner said. "We may need to keep an eye on him."

Gunner grabbed two cups of punch and handed me one.

"Come on, let's go have some fun." He gestured for me to follow him. He walked up behind a random girl, took his cowboy hat off, and put it on her head. She turned around, grabbing the hat.

"Gunner." She hugged him.

"Howdy, Emily. This is my friend Dylan. Dylan, this is my friend Emily," he said.

"Howdy, Dylan." Her accent matched his.

"Emily's also a Texan," he joked.

She grabbed her friend, who if I had to guess was almost intoxicated, and pulled her over to me.

"Dance with Dylan," she said to her friend.

She didn't ask any questions. She threw her hands in the air and danced circles around me. Emily and Gunner chuckled as they looked over our way and began to dance. I wanted to have a good time so I danced along with the drunken girl.

I looked down at my watched as Gunner and I left the house, realizing that it was past three in the morning.

"What is it?" Gunner asked.

"I told myself I would start getting more sleep so I can make it to class on time and study more."

"You'll be fine. Every college kid goes through this."

I was completely drained, eyes burning and body heavy, when we finally made it back to the room. Airez walked in right when I got the lights off and crawled into bed.

"What's up, punk?" He turned on the light and took off his liquor-covered clothes. I pulled the blanket over my body and tried to force myself to sleep.

I could hear him shuffling through his clothes when he said, "You need to lighten up. You're so uptight and way too easy to piss off."

I pulled the blanket back off and glared coldly.

"So that's why you walk around like you're better than me? Because you think I'm easy to get to?"

"To be honest, yeah. You need to grab your man-sack and stick up for yourself."

Was I a pushover? I didn't think I was, I mean, I could easily take him out. "You got it all wrong. Just never understood why you never liked us."

"Well besides the fact that you and your little posse are lame, your friend tried to get at my girlfriend. But, a little birdie told me I should learn to be nice to people, so I thought I'd start with you, punk."

I couldn't tell if he was joking or if he was actually being serious. "So you're telling me you want to be friends?" I felt my face twisting up as I said that.

He held back a laugh.

"*Friend* is pushing it. I'll just start by stopping the rumors I started about my roommate who wets the bed."

"WHAT!" I freaked.

"Night." He turned the lights off.

Surprisingly, I woke up on time the rest of the week. Hachi called Sunday evening asking if I wanted to train and run drills after going the week without. I couldn't resist.

She had me meet her at an old paper factory. Rusted paper-making machines, pipes, and chains, were the first thing I noticed followed by Hachi, standing in the center with matching gray sweatpants and jacket, her hair pulled back like always.

"Is your brother coming?" I asked, eagerly walking towards her.

"Yes. He's currently doing independent exercises with Marcus like I'm doing with you. Shall we get started?"

"Sure. I just don't understand what exactly *it* is we're doing," I said as she walked up and took my hands.

"Well, Dylan, you're special. You have something the Qihar wouldn't expect, telekinesis as well as the ability of ice generation."

"Yeah, but my telekinesis is very dangerous to myself and others."

She released my hands, grinned playfully, and walked around me. "Correct. *But*, don't you want to gain control over it?"

"Hell yeah! I — wait, is that why you guys separated me and Marc?"

"Understand, he doesn't want you to use this ability. We're here to help you reach your full potential."

I was pumped. It didn't bother me that they split us up and didn't tell Marcus the plan. "I'm all for it, let's go."

"OK, so I'm thinking the reason you may be blacking out is your telekinesis requires a lot of your physical, mental, and emotional energy, and when you use it, you use up more than what your body is producing. What may help is if you can use it in stages. I think you can train your body to start producing massive amounts of energy so it can keep up with your ability over ice and telekinesis. Maybe it's a good thing you can't fly. I'm not sure your body would be able to handle that much power usage."

"I think I'm following you."

"Good. Now, if you use your telekinesis every day in small doses instead of once in a while in one big burst, that may stop you from passing out."

"I'll give it a try."

"OK let's get started. Move this from my hand to yours." There was a quarter in her hand. I reached out and it flew right into mine.

"Too easy."

"Good. Now try stopping these from touching the ground."

"Stop what?" Instantly she pulled out a bunch of change from her pocket and threw it in the air. I raised my hand above my head and focused on the coins not hitting the ground. The coins in the center stayed floating above us but the ones on the outside ended up hitting the floor.

I flinched as her tone sharpened, voice stern. "You *have* to learn to keep your concentration and to be able to use your ability on command."

We ran a few more tests like moving pieces of scrap metal from one side of the building to the other and blocking chairs she threw at me all while making sure not to overexert me. She wanted to run one more test on me. Hachi steadied herself and hover in the air.

"I'm going to rush you, and I want you to stop me," she nodded, her eyes confident like she believed in me more than I believed in myself. Raising her body higher and higher, she quickly rushed me without warning.

I squared my center. As she got closer, I staggered both shaky hands in front of me. Her face was fierce like an eagle going in for the kill. I pictured an imaginary barrier in front of me that would block her, but it didn't work.

I found it difficult to breathe as my feet dangled; she shook her head with a smile. I glanced back, noticing she was flying towards the wall, and sealed my eyes shut. But she stopped, sparing me the pain.

"Not too shabby," she said, landing. "We'll work on it more. Hudson and Marcus are on their way in."

"Whoa, do you two have some freaky little twin telepathy thing going on?"

"Yeah. It's called a cell phone," she laughed as the both of them walked in.

"Didn't know you were going to be here." Marcus walked up and shook my hand.

"Just waiting on you two to show up," I said.

"One-on-one training with Hudson."

"Yeah, how'd that go?"

"Pretty awesome," he said, juggling fireballs. I stuck my hands out and the fireballs iced over. We shared a laugh.

Hudson coughed. "OK, time to get serious, guys."

The night was intense and before we called it quits for the session, I warned them about keeping me out too late.

I took Hachi's advice to try and build up my energy. In the mornings, I brushed my teeth and dried off after my showers with just my thoughts. I stayed up for the most part in my History class but when I got to my next one, Imani wouldn't let me go to sleep. She did nothing in particular to keep me awake, but her presence just seemed to give me the boost of energy I needed to get through the day.

"You look like death," Imani whispered.

My straight face made her giggle and I responded with, "Late nights. Training."

"I'm sure your parents will be proud to know where their hard-earned money's going to."

I folded my arms on the desk and laid my head down. "Trust me, I'm done for a while." I yawned. The teacher's lecture was going in one ear and out the other.

"Listen, you know what tomorrow is right?"

"Yep, I think it's Tuesday, but I could be wrong. All the days seem to just fly by now."

She chuckled and caught herself; she focused back on the instructor. Couldn't figure out why she was being all extra friendly towards me, but I wasn't going to complain.

"Yes, I know, but tomorrow is Valentine's Day."

I looked up and my head followed. She now had my full attention. "I guess I didn't realize that."

"I was thinking maybe you could be my valentine and we could get out and just enjoy each other's company?"

I laughed.

She exhaled. "Or maybe not."

"No, no, no, I wasn't laughing at you. I just wasn't expecting a *girl* to ask another guy to be her Valentine." I straightened my posture up. "I would be humbled to be your date for the evening, Miss Gordon."

"Great. How about a fun, steamy, greasy night at *Artichoke Pizzeria?*"

"You want to spend Valentine's Day at a pizzeria?"

"Hell yeah," she whispered. I instantly fell in love with her. What guy doesn't want a girl who wants to sit around and laugh over some cheesy pizza? Add that in with her ability to throw fireballs and her tough personality, she was almost perfect.

"I think you're reading my mind, little lady."

She toyed with the ends of her hair, her smirk teasing from her profile.

I passed out when I made it back to my room. That seemed to be the routine lately: stay up all night, go to class, and sleep when I got to my room. While I slept into the night hours, Marcus and the twins went out for a flight. That was my excuse to get more hours in dreamland.

Marcus was a natural at school. He could go the whole semester without opening a book and still pass all his classes with flying colors. The twins, well I've never heard them talk about school, so I don't know what their grades look like.

I woke up anxious the following day. It took me almost thirty minutes to pick out a pair of shoes to wear to class. I was just ready to spend my night with Imani and hope we could start over. I'd say we were off to a good start. Everyone was walking around campus holding teddy bears and boxes of chocolate. It made me realize: I didn't get anything for her.

When class was over I went to a local floral shop and got some flowers and a bear holding a heart with *Be Mine* stitched on it. We agreed on a relaxed dressed code — NYU sweatshirts and jeans. I mean it was only pizza.

When we got there the line was nearly wrapped around the corner. I couldn't believe the amount of people that wanted pizza on Valentine's Day and were willing to stand in the cold over it.

"This is one of *the* best places in New York for pizza. This is the short line, honestly," she said.

We got our box and took a seat.

She grabbed a slice first. "I've been waiting all day for this pizza," she said, taking the first bite. "H-H-Hot." She dropped her pizza and immediately fanned her mouth with cheese dripping from her lips.

"What? Hot?" I chuckled. "You can throw fire from your hands. I'd never thought I'd hear you ever say the word '*hot*'."

"Yeah, well, that has no effect on my taste buds."

I blew on my pizza to lower the temperature a little and stuffed it into my mouth.

"No fair, cheater."

"It's not cheating. I'm just using my natural born gifts to my advantage."

Ignoring the pizza, she crossed her arms and leaned across the table. "So now that I have told you a little about my past, tell me more about yours."

There wasn't really much to tell about my life. It's always been pretty normal except this last year. "Well what do you want to know?"

"Whatever, just, how was your childhood I guess?"

"Well I lived in Poughkeepsie the majority of my life. My parents were always loving and supportive of whatever my brother and I wanted to do."

She looked down and whispered to herself, "Spoiled." She snapped back up to giving me her attention. "How old is your brother?"

"He's twelve and like my other best friend." I laughed simply at the thought of my kid brother being my best friend but he was special to me. "I loved living in Poughkeepsie. It's the perfect town. My dad's a college professor and my mom is a doctor, so we lived a somewhat lavish lifestyle I guess."

"I knew you were a rich boy?"

"No, not really rich, just well off. My parents didn't just give us money. We still had to earn our funds. I had lots of friends, played basketball and dated the hottest girl in school. The end."

"So everything was just perfect like that?" I put my pizza down and pushed it away from me.

"Everything *was* perfect. I found out not too long ago that my parents are in the process of getting a divorce. My perfect family apparently had some hidden flaws no one saw. Now I'll go from having one room to two rooms next time I'm home. I'm not sure how I'll cope with this. I'd never thought I would have to go through this kind of situation. I think I'm more worried about my brother since he has to be there directly, you know?"

"That's a very common thing people have to deal with on a daily basis. Every situation is different. I'm sure your family will get through this." She rubbed my hand.

"Can we get back to this pizza? It's getting cold."

She placed one finger on the box, and it was warm again. We both took a slice and finished eating.

"It's getting late and I need to get you back to your room. You need to be well rested for class in the morning," she said.

She walked me back to my dorm holding my hand the entire time. Touching her felt right. The cooling sensation of my hands and the fiery ember she let off worked together. I sometimes doodled "icy hot" on my notebooks when I thought about her in classes.

"Thanks for the teddy and the flowers. This night was perfect." She stood on her tippy toes and wrapped her arms around my neck. I bent down to meet her halfway.

She kissed me on the cheek leaving a warm sensation at the site.

The night was still pretty early, so I called Marcus to see how he was doing on his Valentine's Day. I felt as if we were growing apart. He was spending more and more time with Delilah and his new friends while I on the other hand was trying to keep up with school so I wouldn't be put on academic probation.

He had a double date with Charlie and Stacey. He asked if I wanted to go do some training tonight but I told him I was going to call it a night and we should hang out this weekend, power free.

When I finally entered my room, Airez was crying on the couch while his brother consoled him. I didn't want to intrude on their moment so I climbed into bed, waved my hands and the lights went out.

Chapter 23

Life of Dylan

I woke up to the sound of zippers and bags being tossed on the bed.

It was Airez.

Again.

His puffy red eyes and constant snorting had me thinking he was up all night crying. He looked over at me as I got up, and I saw nothing but pain in his eyes. He went back to packing.

"Good morning." I stretched and yawned.

"Morning," he said before I could finish, not even acknowledging me.

I started getting dressed when somebody knocked on the door. Airez and I glanced at each other, then the door. Airez answer it. It was his brother.

"Hey, freshman." He walked in right towards Airez. "You ready, Air?"

Airez grabbed his bags and they walked towards the door.

"Is everything OK, Airez?"

"Don't be late for class," he said, closing the door behind him. I felt really bad for him and I didn't even know why. Neither he nor his brother tried to pick a fight or have some belittling comment for me. I didn't have too much time to think about it. I got ready and headed out the door.

I couldn't wait until history was over. Hearing my teacher's voice twice a week was torture. The real reason was that Imani was in my next class and I felt as if things were looking up for us. The more time we spent together, the more I fell for her.

"Someone looks well rested," she said. She was already in class with her book filled with post-it notes. "I see you took my advice."

"I didn't need to take your advice. I've just been telling myself to stop staying out late and focus more on school."

"Don't get smart." She smiled and her eyes flashed red for a second. I didn't want to get her upset knowing she could incinerate me with one touch. But if getting under her skin fired her up, I'd be the annoying pest she'd loved to hate.

When class was over, we went out and got some milkshakes from the café.

"So I don't think I ever asked you what you're studying?" I asked.

"Journalism," she said. "I want to be a photographer as well as an editor."

"That's different. My major is chemical engineering."

"And … what do you plan on doing with that?"

"I've always been fascinated with chemistry and matter. I've been leaning towards a career in research."

"Wow, you don't hear that on a daily basis."

"Nah, but you know, I've been in love with chemistry ever since I got my first kit for Christmas when I was eight."

"So what made you choose NYU?" I took one more sip and put my cup down.

"Marcus."

She rolled her eyes. "That makes a lot of sense." I couldn't tell if she was confused or read right through me.

"So you know Marc and I are best friends, right?"

"Yeah, I can tell. He's all you ever talk about."

"Whatever. Anyway, so Marc always had this dream way before I met him that he was going to go to Harvard on a full scholarship and his life would somehow make sense. Everyone knew that's the school he wanted to go to and that's what he was working towards. Since he was adopted, he always had a hard time not knowing where he came from or who his parents were. When Harvard rejected him, it left me with one tough decision.

"Which was?" She gestured her hand and if I was taking to long to hit my point.

"Do I tell him I was accepted and once again live his dream, or settle for NYU?"

"So in order to protect your best friend's feelings, you didn't go to the school?"

"Correct."

"Honorable."

"Thanks."

"And stupid."

I grimaced. "What do you mean?" I folded my arms and crossed my legs leaning back in my chair.

"Sometimes you have to let people down in order for you to live your own dreams. Best friends don't always last no matter how long you guys have known each other."

"But Marc and I are different. Have you ever had a best friend?"

She looked away from me for a moment and turned back around.

"Sort of. When my family was attacked my childhood sort of ended and I had to grow up pretty fast. Dad always said that having friends would only put them in danger."

I felt bad for Imani in a way. Living life on the run, never having fun or making friends was a sad life.

We left the café then headed back to my dorm.

"We have to stop having these serious conversations," I said. "I get too mushy when I'm around you."

"So I bring out your soft side, Dylan?" She held out her hands asking for mine. I gave them to her.

They fit perfectly.

"Dylan Perry doesn't have a soft side." My macho voice activated and my chest puffed out as we walked into my room.

"Where's your roommate?"

"I'm not sure. I think he may have moved out." I knew he didn't move out for good. He still had his things in the room. I honestly didn't know what his situation was. Maybe he was staying at his brother's place for a little while.

We kicked our shoes off and climbed onto the bed.

"Up for a romantic comedy?" she asked.

She knew how much I despised romantic anything when it came to movies.

"I thought we were studying. Midterms are coming up really soon and I haven't been on my A-game this semester. My parents are going to kill me if my grades don't turn out decent." I pulled my books out, went to the desk and slammed them down. "Come on over and tutor me, woman."

She sat on my lap and read something about Chinese Civilization. None of it made any sense, but I acted like it did.

Hours passed and we got more serious about studying. Snack wrappers and empty water bottles consumed the room. We went through all of our subjects that were giving us trouble. It was a good thing that the ones I needed help in, she knew enough about to help me and vice versa.

Our minds were getting exhausted as the night hours hit. I knew I had to keep pushing on to make sure I understood everything for the following week. She went to lie down on the bed then slithered under the covers.

"I know you're not cold," I said, looking back to catch a quick glimpse at her snuggled against my pillow.

"Hey, just because my body temperature is warmer than the average human, doesn't mean I don't like snuggling up under a blanket and besides, you have the AC cranked up in here."

I guess I still had some work to do on controlling my powers.

"Come, lay with me," she said in the sweetest voice. It was so seductive I don't even remember getting out of the chair and into the bed. I lay there looking at the ceiling when she rested her head on my arm and pressed her body to mine.

"Your eyes are blue," she said.

"I bet."

I waved my hands and the lights went out.

The moonlight of the early night shined into the room casting a silhouette of a building on the floor. I kissed her on her forehead and wrapped my other arm around her stomach. She slowly tickled my chin then pressed her smoking hot lips onto mine.

It was like when she kissed me her warmth negated the effect of my icy chills. For the first time in a long time my body felt genuinely warm.

She climbed on top of me and I rose up still holding onto her. I ran my fingers up her spine. She hissed when my lips made contact with her earlobe.

She worked her lips on my neck, whispering my name between each warm and pleasing peck.

I wanted her to stop and keep going all at the same time. I pushed her off me, making sure to do it gently and smoothly. I climbed on top of her to gain control. She moaned and tried to resist as I pushed my body onto hers. Her flirtatious brown eyes said she liked it when I took control.

I rose up, taking a break from kissing her to remove my shirt. She lay there looking vulnerable. I slowly went back for another kiss.

The next morning when I woke up, I reached my hand over to touch Imani. The spot was empty and I snapped up. She was gone like a thief in the night. I didn't have time to call her. I was running late for class. During the day I caught up with her on campus.

"What happened? You made me feel like a two-dollar John when I woke up this morning."

She chuckled at the comment. "I had to get to class in the morning and I didn't want to be caught sneaking out your room early in the morning."

"So you just decided to jump out the window?"

She smirked boldly. "You were sleeping so peacefully. I couldn't wake you." She locked onto my arm. "Where you headed to now?"

"I'm going to meet up with Marc in the café. You coming?"

"I guess I could come along."

We got to the café and Marcus was already there. I was surprised that Delilah wasn't there. Not that I had a problem with Delilah or anything, it just seemed like lately those two were joined at the hip.

"Hey, bro," he said, walking up to me. He shook my hand and followed with a pat on the back.

"How you been," I said.

"No complaints over this way."

Imani peeked out from behind me and waved to him. "Hi, Marcus," she waved. He grimaced. "Umm … sorry about the whole *me trying to kill you last semester.*"

"No worries, I'm used to Dylan's girlfriends trying to make my life a living hell. You two seem perfect for one another."

His attitude was getting out of control. "Marc, man, you don't have to be rude." I held on to Imani. I wouldn't want to piss either one of them off. Their fiery personalities cautioned me just knowing what they were capable of.

"Shall we eat, boys?" Imani suggested.

I like that nothing scared her, but I needed for her and Marcus to get along. I liked her but I couldn't go through another Jessica situation. We all got some food and took a seat. I sat in the middle just in case any fireballs went flying across the table, I could freeze them before anyone got hurt.

To my surprise, they both got along and even tried to engage each other in conversation.

"So, Marcus, Dylan tells me you have your family's books." Imani said.

Marcus' eyes pierced me.

"Don't worry, I don't want them. He tells me you have a lot."

"I have quite a few," he said.

"That's really rare honestly. Your family did a very good job protecting them. Most books are spread throughout the family or even lost. They hold valuable information to our planet's heritage. They could potentially be dangerous if they fall into the wrong hands. Guard them with your life and be sure to write in them."

"I've already started," he said.

"Good. The more the better."

"So do you have your family books?"

"No, I wish. I just heard stories about the books. That was some inheritance your family left you."

"Yeah, I guess."

The following week was midterms so the campus was empty and the parties came to a halt. Hudson and Hachi gave Marcus a mid-term also and not the kind that required a pen and paper. Airez came back to the room in time for test week. He seemed different almost absent. I didn't question it.

Skin flushed and slamming drawers, Airez asked, "Mind if I borrow your Calculus book? I think I misplaced mine."

"Sure, just grab it off my desk." I think we were in the process of forming some kind of weird and unusual bond. If I weren't so good at math, I'd have him as my tutor.

When it came to my history mid-term, I wasn't sure if I got an A, but I felt really confident taking it. I knew that coming in on time and actually reading a book would help me in the long run.

My bags were already packed and ready to go when my last test ended. I needed this week away from classes. Imani blew up my phone threatening me if I didn't see her before I got on the road.

I decided to just go pay her a visit since I had to pass her dorm on the way to mine. I walked up to her room smiling from ear to ear. I knocked once and before my knuckles could strike her door again, it flung open. I stepped into clothes, books and magazines thrown around haphazardly.

"What happened here?" I asked. She breathed heavily past me and continued stuffing clothes into a small duffle. I walked up to her after repeatedly calling her name and being ignored. "Imani," I yelled from behind her.

"Dylan, I have to go. Now!"

"Relax."

I crept up behind her, rubbing her arms up and down. She inhaled then exhaled.

"Tell me what's wrong," I asked. She fixed herself to speak but stopped. "You can trust me," I whispered in her ear.

"My dad," she said. "He-h-h."

"Just tell me," I said calmly.

"He's been attacked. He barely survived this one. I'm headed home now to see if I can help find out who did this."

"You mean *kill*?" I took a step back.

"Dylan," she cried. "You're new to this. You've never lost anyone to Qihar. It's either kill or be killed with them and I'm sorry, but I refuse to lose anyone else close to me."

I understood everything she said, but I had to ask myself, if it came to it, could I really kill another person?

Deep down I knew I couldn't.

"I know I can't stop you from doing what you want to do. All I ask is that you be safe and watch yourself." I nodded my head and the window opened.

She looked up and I looked down as her fingertips touched mine, sending waves of solidarity under my skin. She gave me a quick hug and I managed to say, "Come back to me," before she grabbed her bag and flew out of the window.

Chapter 24
Sleeping With the Enemy

Gunner refused to go back to Texas for spring break. So with the help of his parents, we had a beach house for the week. When all the girls and Charlie bailed out on us, it was only Marcus, me, and with a little convincing from Gunner, Chris. The drive was seven hours. Growing up my family flew everywhere that was over a five-hour drive. I appreciated all the laughs, stories, and memories made from the time the guys and I spent in the car and on our trip.

When we weren't partying or swimming, I had horrid images of Imani fighting men twice her size. I still couldn't believe all this existed. She was tough for her size but for all I knew it could have been a trap. Trying to talk her out of it would have been foolish on my part. She seemed to be the type that when her mind was made, it was final. I called and messaged every day but never got one response.

During the last few days of our trip, Chris started to open up and have some fun. The first few days, well, it was an act all in itself to get him to socialize with other people on the beach. The last night consisted of lots of beer, sand, and music.

I sat in the passenger's seat on the way back, calling Imani every twenty minutes. Her lack of communication terrified me.

"Something on that mind of yours, cowboy?" Gunner looked over from the driver's seat, reading the expression off my face.

I clinched the phone and tried to relax my face. "Oh … yeah." I looked up for a second to acknowledge him with a smile. "I'm fine."

My phone beeped, relieving me for a split second. It was only a message from Marcus seeing if I was fine. He didn't know the situation, so I held off until we got to campus to fill him in.

It was right around dusk when we returned. We all went up to the suite. Gunner and Chris went into their room and passed out I'm sure. Marcus came over to mine. Airez wasn't back yet because the room was just how I left it. Marcus sat at the desk and started browsing the web. As I put my things away I told him how Imani went on some hunt to find out who attacked her dad.

"So you haven't heard from her since we left?" Marcus asked.

"No, and I'm starting to get real worried. She was so emotional when she left."

He spun around in the chair and stood. "The way she tried to rip *my* head off, I'm sure she can handle herself."

"What if she just got in way over her head and she really can't?"

"Trust me, Dylan, she will be fine."

"And we still need to try and figure out who wants you dead," I said.

"Trust me, Dylan, I'll be fine."

It was a struggle to get up the next morning for class. History took longer than usual to get through only because I was anxious to get to my next class to see if Imani was there. When class finally let out, I rushed to the door and ran across campus to get to my next class. Normally she was there before I was but since I got there so fast, I doubt I gave her any time. I took a seat and kept my eyes focused on the door.

People started to enter and my eyes shuffled through the crowd without a sign of Imani. I rubbed my sweaty palms down my pants. The instructor started talking but my attention was focused on the door. I got about halfway through class when I contemplated walking out, but I weighed the outcomes and stayed. I knew finals would be creeping up on me soon and I still had to look out for myself.

As soon as I got to my dorm, Imani sent me a message saying to come to her room. I called Marcus and told him to meet me there.

Marcus was outside her dorm when I got there. We went up and knocked on her door. She answered, standing there looking emotionless with a big nasty bruise on the side of her face that changed her caramel skin purple.

"What happened?" I rushed her with a hug.

She hissed and pushed away from me.

"You OK?" I said.

"I'm still a little sore," she said, her hands up defensively towards me.

"Well, now that we know she's alive, you can finally let her have it for not answering your calls," Marcus said.

I went with it. "I've been worried all week long. Why haven't you answered any of my calls or texts?"

She looked around her body. "As you can see, I've been busy."

"Did you do what you said you were going to do?"

"I did."

"I can't believe you went at this alone."

She spoke coldly. "I had help."

"Who?"

"One of my father's friends. He's the one who let me know what happened."

"Well I'm glad that all three of you guys are OK," I said, quickly reaching in for her hand. She let me have it this time.

"How was your vacation?" she asked, staring down at her hand in mine like she was questioning it.

"It was awesome," Marcus said.

"I'm mad at you," I whispered.

"Get over it," she whispered back.

"Listen, guys, I just came over to make sure Imani was alive and to make sure I didn't need to toast any bad guys," Marcus said, flaring his palms up.

"OK, Marc. Put that out before you burn the building down," I said.

"I'm out of here," Marcus said.

"OK, bro. Thanks for coming with me."

"Thanks for checking on me, Marcus," Imani said softly. He walked out the door.

"You look extra tough now with that bruise on the side of your face." I joked, stroking her face.

"I'm hungry. I haven't eaten all day."

"Want me to go get you something to eat?"

"Please?"

I left and came back with a pizza. When I got back to her room she was just about knocked out. Her eyes lit up when she opened them to a box of pizza. It took us most of the day to eat because every time she opened her mouth, she hissed from the jaw pain.

I wanted to hold her all night and take the pain away, but I knew she wouldn't let me. Seeing her like this only made me not to want to use my powers or to fight Qihar, but I knew I had to learn to protect my loved ones and myself.

I got back to my room right before midnight. Airez was already there asleep. I still wondered what his deal was these days.

I stopped by the picnic on the quad when class was over to meet up with Hudson. The winter boots and jackets faded away as the temperature shifted with the seasons. Since I found out I could shoot ice from my hands, I fell completely in love with the winter weather.

Hudson had a burger in one hand and a soda in the other when I walked up on him. I'm sure if he had more hands he would be holding more food. Hachi slinked from behind him like a silent killer and snatched the soda right out his hand. She cracked it open and took a sip.

"Thanks, brother." She handed it back to him.

"I *swear* you two have some kind of twin tracking system," I said. It freaked me out how incredibly close they were. I guess the fact that they literally need each other caused them to spend more time with each other than they probably planned.

"Go get your own," he yelled at her.

Hachi rolled her eyes then placed a hand on my shoulder. "Let's go get some food, Dylan." Hachi ran off, dancing her way to the front of the line. She walked back with two plates of food.

As I ate my burger, Marcus walked up, books in hand, pencil in ear.

He shrugged. "No call? He grabbed the half-eaten burger from my hand right as I was going in for a bite and took one for himself before handing it back to me.

My eyes widened.

"And you talk about *us* having twin telepathy." Hachi gave us a blank stare. Marcus and I shared a blank stare then cracked in laughter.

Hudson and Hachi introduced us to some of their human friends as we walked around. They said we're the first ones on campus they've met that are like them, or somewhat like them since we don't have the markings of their kind.

"You two have really progressed since we met you," Hudson said.

"All thanks to the two of you for showing us what we can really do," Marcus said.

"You guys are quick learners," Hachi said.

"Everyone but Dylan," Hudson said. I got used to the jokes although I did want to experience it for myself. Marcus said it was the perfect stress reliever.

"One day I *will* fly, guys, just watch and see," I said.

"That's the spirit, Dylan." Hachi hit her brother's bicep.

When I left the picnic, I dropped off a plate to Imani. She was still sore in some places, but she was a fighter. I had faith she'd be fully recovered in a few days.

I went back to my room after I left Imani's. Airez was on the bed staring at the ceiling throwing a baseball in the air and catching.

"Everything OK?" I put my things down.

"Yep," he replied, still throwing the ball.

"Well if you ever need to talk," I hesitated, "I'll be here to listen."

"Yep."

The vibe was too awkward so I went to Gunner's room to play some video games.

The weeks progressed on and before I knew it, finals were approaching. This semester was one big test itself. Last weekend I went home to help Dad move his things and get his house set up.

My dad was never the most affectionate when it came to Dalton and me, but he apologized for his lack of expressing himself the way he felt he should have. My dad was an amazing father. He made sure to be at all our games and most practices when we were kids. He always pushed us, but he felt like a coach more than my parent when it came to my actual life.

His house was small compared to the one we grew up in. I guess he really didn't need to spend much money on a home no one was going to be in. I expressed my gratitude to my parents for their maturity in the situation. I've heard plenty of nasty divorce stories and that's what frightened me the most. I told Dad I would stay with him on the weekends so he wouldn't get lonely on his off days and he can get his rematch every Saturday in basketball. He cracked his knuckles and grinned at the gesture.

It was the day before finals and I was mentally exhausted. Marcus had his bags packed, ready to go. His instructors exempted him from finals due to his impressive grades. He was driving my car back home and coming to get me at the end of finals. I didn't get a chance to study since we all spent the weekend partying. Well, everyone but Imani of course, so she and Marcus came over to help me pass my finals.

"Thanks for helping me study, guys," I said, opening the door for Imani.

She grimaced and walked past me as I tried to hug her. "You look like the walking dead, Dylan."

"Yeah, *you* knew you should have been in the books this weekend, bro," Marcus added.

"OK, guys we've established the fact that I should have not gone out, but it was our last chance to all be together. And if you were so worried about me studying, Marcus, why didn't you say anything then?" I argued.

"Just pull your books out and let's get to it," Imani snarled, slapping the desk.

I turned the TV off and cracked open the books. Marcus was explaining things in one ear and Imani was spitting out information in the other. I couldn't keep up.

"Ughh…" I exhaled.

Marcus stopped reading and glanced up. "What's wrong, Dylan?"

"Just a little fed up with this history class. Why can't we just trade places and you take my finals for me?"

"Because I didn't sit in *your* classes all semester long." Sarcasm was really becoming his second language.

"Oh you two bicker like a married couple," Imani interrupted. We both glared at her. She had no idea what it was like to have a best friend and the type of relationship we had.

Marcus went out to grab us some food. When he made it back, we quickly closed the books and began to chow. Neither one of us had eaten much all day. Marcus yawned and kicked his feet up on the bed. I jumped back into the books and Imani came over and took a seat on my lap.

I was reading and she was writing helpful notes in my books when a buzzing noise broke the silence. I reached for my phone to check it but it was nothing. I turned around and Marcus was waking up, pulling his phone out of his pocket.

I went back to studying. Imani got up. I turned around when I heard her speak.

"Is everything OK, Marcus?" Imani said, looking at him intently. He didn't answer.

Marcus was holding his phone in front of him with two hands like he was cradling a baby, his eyes slowly getting wet.

"Marc, what is it?" I asked, standing to my feet.

He squinted his eyes at the screen and whispered, "Monica."

"Who is Monica?" Imani asked.

"Is everything OK, Marc?" I walked next to him.

"My dad," he said, standing to his feet. "My dad just sent me a text saying Monica hasn't shown up for work in the past two days and can't get a hold of her."

My hand trembled. "Wait, that doesn't sound like Monica."

"Is somebody going to tell me who this Monica person is?" Imani said.

"I'm going to give her parents a call." Marcus said, stepping out into the hallway.

"Who is she?" Imani demanded.

"Monica is an old friend of ours, and also Marcus' ex-girlfriend," I said.

"Maybe she quit." Imani shrugged.

"No, she isn't like that. She would have let Mr. Peterson know if she did. Something isn't right."

Marcus ran back inside and slammed the door behind him startling the both of us.

"What happened?" I asked.

"Her parents said she ran away. They haven't seen her in a couple of days," he said as he dialed numbers on his phone.

"Who are you calling, Marc?" I asked. He put his finger to his lips and turned around.

"Dangit!" he screamed. "She's not answering. I'm supposed to be meeting up with Delilah, but I think I need to get home ASAP and help look for Monica."

"I'll let her know you had an emergency and had to leave a few hours early."

"Thanks, bro."

He headed for the door but stopped to look down when his phone rang. "It's a message from Monica," he said. His shoulders tightened, his breaths short and choppy. He turned back around with red eyes and tears running down his cheeks as he stared at his screen. His hands dropped to his sides, his chin falling to his chest.

"What did she say?" I rushed over and took the phone from his hands. He slowly backed up until his backed pressed against the door and he slid down. Imani rushed over and looked at the phone with me.

"Who would …" Imani covered her mouth and her eyes enlarged.

There was a picture of Monica with a scratched, bruised, and bloody face, gagged and tied to a chair. I was mortified and couldn't think of a soul who would want to hurt one of the sweetest girls I'd ever met. Frost from my free hand started to fill the room.

"I have to go, Dylan." Marcus stood, ripped the phone from my hand, and reached for the doorknob.

"Where do you think you're going?" I ran in front of the door. He needed a moment to calm down before he got himself killed.

"Move, Dylan! I'm going to save her."

"This could be a trap," Imani said.

"I don't care!" His hands incinerated as he screamed.

"Marcus, just think, *they* sent *you* a picture of her like this to *your* phone from hers. Whoever it is behind this wants you to rush in unguarded," I said.

Eyes still on fire, he took a deep breath in and slowly let it out, punching the air.

"Listen, Dylan, if it was you in my shoes and Imani was the one in the photo, what would you do?"

I couldn't answer. I just stood there in silence. Imani stepped over and took my hand.

"Exactly." he said.

"Marc, I've been trying to tell you, I really think somebody wants you dead. This just proves my case."

"I'm going."

I exhaled, grabbed my keys and handed them to him. "Take my car. Just come back and get me when you're done."

"I know a faster way," he said. He walked to the window. "I'll scope it out and see what I can find. I promise I won't do this without you."

"Be careful and I'll be home soon."

He nodded and jumped out the window. Imani and I watched as an orange glow took off into the sky.

"What are you doing?" Airez said, standing at the door. "And what was that light?"

We both snapped around.

"Airez," I stammered.

"What light?" Imani said on top of my words.

"You guys are weird," he said.

It was the first day of finals and with the incident last night, there was no way I could concentrate. The whole time I was taking tests, I just kept thinking about Marcus and his safety. When I turned in my last final for the day, I didn't feel too confident. I talked to my instructors and begged to take the remainder of my finals on Tuesday since I had a family emergency. They agreed with some forged doctor notes the twins managed to muster up for me.

Imani and I spent the remainder of the day studying. I called Marcus every chance I got with no answers. He should already know about my panic attacks from Imani's little journey when the people I care about are out fighting and not giving me updates. There was nothing more I could do but study and hope he was OK.

The next day of finals was a little better but still no Marcus. I rushed to my dorm after my last test; Imani was waiting outside my door. We walked inside and I immediately finished packing.

"So maybe I can help you pick out some lingerie this summer if you come visit me at work," Imani joked.

"So not funny." I wrapped my arms around her waist and spun her around. She giggled and fought me to stop. I stopped spinning and landed a kiss on her cheek.

"I'm going to miss you this summer," I said.

"You're just one flight away from me."

"And you're just one car ride from me." I continued to throw the rest of my things into my bags. I zipped up my book bag and threw it across my back right as my phone rung. It was Marcus and I answered quickly.

"Hello."

"What time do you think you can get here," he responded.

"I should get back to Poughkeepsie a little after eight."

"I got another message from Monica's phone saying to meet at 10 Hilltop Ross Circle tonight at 9," Marcus said.

"10 Hilltop Ross Circle? Isn't that the—"

"The Safe House, yes."

"I'll be there as fast as I can."

"Oh and, Dylan, don't forget to bring my stuff."

I exhaled. "Be there in a jiff."

"What's going on?" Imani asked. I grabbed her arms and pulled her into me as I sat on the bed.

"Something's going down tonight. More than ever, we could use you."

"Dylan, you know how I feel about these types of things. I don't think I can get involved."

"Imani, please, just this one time," I begged. She bit her lips and fidgeted her fingers. I pouted.

"Fine. What's the address?"

I sent her the address.

"I will meet you there after my dad comes. I'll just tell him to take my things back and I'll fly right there. Promise."

"Thank you. This means a lot." I hugged her and walked out the door.

I didn't have time to stop and tell my parents I was home. I texted Marcus and went straight to the Safe House and carefully entered through a window on the first floor. It was dark, quiet, and eerie, and for a second, wished I had Marcus' powers for some comforting light.

The building still had the broken walls and windows from our last battle here. I stayed low and close to the walls as I duck-walked down the freezing hallways and up the stairs. I walked into a corner room that was fairly larger than the others. There was something in the corner. I walked a little closer.

"Is that her?" a voice said, alarming me.

I turned around and iced my hands up. A fire lit revealing Marcus.

"Marc," I whispered.

We both eased closer to the figure sitting in the corner. It was Monica. Marcus rushed forward. She fell into his arms when he burnt the rope holding her to the chair.

"It's OK, I'm here," he kept whispering to her, even though she was passed out. He stood with her in his arms and I took the lead as we dashed out of the room and down the stairs. We made it to the lobby when the front door covered itself in a glossy coat of ice.

"Put her down, Marcus," a toneless voice demanded as it echoed the room. We looked around to try and catch where the voice came from.

"Who said that?" I breathed. No one answered.

Marcus walked over with Monica in his arms and placed a hand on the door to thaw it. Monica slowly started to wake.

"Are you OK?" he calmly said.

She gripped his shirt when her eyes opened. "No. Where am I?" she cried.

"Shhh … can you walk?"

Her voice was brittle. "Yes."

"Good. Take my hand."

I opened the door to a murky-green sky and heavy winds. I tried walking but a burst of wind prevented that. An even stronger gust came through the door, knocking us all on our backs. The door slammed shut.

"No one told you to leave." The voice echoed again.

"Yeah, the party has *just* started," a different voice joked. A man walked out from the shadows and guarded the door. Next, the lights flickered.

"What's going on?" Monica cried. She held Marcus' hand tight. His thumb massaged her hand.

"I wasn't expecting you, but I should have known you two *are* joined at the hip." I almost recognized the first voice.

The three of us regrouped and walked to the center of the room. Three bodies walked in front of us blocking the door. The lights continued to flicker.

"Jessica?" I said. It was Jessica and the two goons that attacked us here the last time.

"You know, it's a good thing we broke up, Dill Pickle. It just wouldn't have worked out with you now that I'm positive you have the blood of Xarpore running through your veins."

I knew Jessica was crazy but this was on another level. I iced my hands up. If it was a fight she was looking for, it was a fight she was going to get. Mind full of hateful thoughts, I rushed her and with one swirl of her hands, a miniature tornado formed between us that grew as it rushed me and tossed me head first into a wall.

Chapter 25

Jessica's Revenge

Dylan was out cold and my life literally flashed in front of my eyes. Jessica was standing in front of me and the other two guys split a corner behind me. I knew I should have killed them when I had the chance. Monica's sweaty palms gripped my arm so tight I felt the bruises start to form under my skin.

"What do you want with her, Jessica?" I screamed, keeping one hand on Monica, the other free for attacks.

She snickered. "It was never *her* I wanted."

It clicked.

They were right.

It was a trap.

She knew that Monica was the perfect way to draw me out.

"Why me?" I asked.

Monica's fingernails pierced my arm as her grip got tighter. The two guys standing behind me started to pace, boosting my anxiety.

"I won't let them hurt you," I whispered to Monica.

"Relax, Mr. Ferrari," she said.

I flinched. "How do you know that name?" I lost focus on Monica and shifted it to Jessica.

"I've been keeping an eye on you for longer than you know, Macchiato. I just had to make sure you were really who I thought you were," she said, admiring her fingernails. "But there was something different about you that made me wonder."

"Yeah, what's that?"

"You had no markings, that is, until now."

I looked down and through the flickers, caught a glimpse of ink magically etching itself into my skin around my right wrist and up my arm.

"What the heck?" I gasped then focused back to her. "You still didn't answer my question?"

"See, my father and your father go way back — your biological father that is. My dad was hunting your dad for the longest time, but your father was a pretty powerful Xarponian from what I heard. They'd been fighting for months and once word got out that he had a son on the way, the hunt was taken up a notch. My dad wanted you dead, Marcus, lots of people wanted you dead I heard. But your father didn't want anybody coming after his precious boy. He gave you up and hunted my father down. Your father murdered my father before I even got the chance to know him, and now, I will finish where he left off."

"How did you even find me?" That part still didn't make sense.

"You see, my father wasn't the only one hunting your father at the time."

"Then who else?"

"I was only a few months old when Mother got the news."

"Your mom is Qihar?"

"*Both* of my parents are Qihar."

"And what about Dylan?"

"Dylan … he's a bonus. I had to do a little snooping to find out who he really was which was shocking to say the least."

"It was you who broke into his room, and *you* all this time sending maniacs to kill me!"

"There's more to this story than you know."

I needed a plan to get the three of us out of here. But Dylan was still out and Monica was too terrified to move.

"Count to three and duck," I whispered, never taking my eyes off Jessica. I counted to three in my head.

Monica ducked.

I extended both hands, releasing fire at the guys. One blocked it with an ice wall while the other took one to the chest. Monica stood back up and so did the guy. The three of them taunted me as they circled us.

"There's no way you're walking away alive from this, Marcus," Jessica said, creating two funnels in her palms. Iceman powered up and the one who controlled lightning sparked.

"We're gonna die." Monica sobbed and clawed down my arm like an animal.

"I won't let that happen to you," I said.

Jessica unleashed both cyclones at us, sending us crashing through the door. Monica was no longer next to me when I opened my eyes.

I crawled to her.

The three of them walked outside.

I didn't stand a chance.

"Marcus, we're here now." I turned over on my back and Hudson and Hachi landed next to me with water swirling around their bodies.

"Who are they?" the lightning guy said.

"It doesn't matter, kill them all!" Jessica screamed followed by a gust of wind.

The intensity in the air grew thick.

"Get Monica out of here!" I shouted.

Hudson grabbed Monica and Hachi stood right in the middle of both the goons, ready to take them both.

I jumped to my feet and flew past the two goons, right into Jessica. With her in my grip, we flew back into the house, crashing into a moldy wall. When I stood up, a force of wind knocked me back down.

"I'm not done with you, Marcus," she grunted, standing to her feet. Her pupils and irises faded white. Five miniature tornadoes formed on the floor and circle around her creating an earthquake effect. Old hospital equipment, bricks and wood crashed around us. Dust consumed the room, yet she remained grounded. I flamed my hands; my feet flamed on their own.

"Let's just end this now, Jessica. Nobody has to get hurt."

She groaned like it was her way of communicating with her abilities and all five cyclones raced me, spiraling me into the air and through a wall. Dylan's lifeless body swirled into the darkness. Jessica was the first I've encountered with this ability. It was dangerously impressive.

I struggled back to my feet and stepped through the wall I was wearing. I launched a beam of fire at her. She stuck her arms out, creating a vortex that ate my fire.

Two fireballs formed in my hands. I threw them at the ceiling over her creating more balls as I threw them. She crouched and held her arm over her head to block the debris.

She screeched as the roof collapsed on her. I threw the wood off of Dylan's body and staggered towards the door with Dylan at my side.

Hudson was in a defensive stance next to Monica near a tree. Hachi was dodging attacks from the ice guy; the lightning one was nowhere in sight.

I rested Dylan's body on the side of the building. When I turned around to get in on the fight, Hudson was struck from the back by a bolt. The strike barely missed Monica's body. She rolled over and hugged the tree with her face planted on the bark. I conjured two fireballs and ran to the lightning guy. He threw bolts towards me when he noticed me coming for him, but I jumped, flew and rolled to evade them.

I released one fireball and quickly released the other. They each hit a leg knocking him to his stomach. He lay there, grunting and pounding the dirt.

A bolt of lightning crashed from the clouds to the ground with each pound until there was a total of four bolts circling around him.

My knees knocked against one another; the frantic rise and fall of my chest distracted me from the situation at hand.

The lightning guy waved a hand, commanding a bolt to zip past me. The static air brought life to the hairs on my arms. My eyes followed the bolt, wondering why when he could have easily taken me out. I turned around and two massive bolts were gliding across the ground, ripping into the earth towards Hachi.

I screamed out for Hachi, distracting her from battle. Mouth agape, she threw her hands up in a defensive stance before being whisked away by the two bolts.

These guys were strong; they've been training just like we have. A feeling of hopelessness came over me as I looked around — the twins mangled bodies in the mud, Monica clawing the tree in tears, and Dylan's unconscious body resting near the building. Legs stinging in pain, I forced myself up to continue the fight. I looked down at the marking on my arm and remembered everything I learned from the twins, the journals, and my dad. The marking on my arm was a symbol of hope and strength.

I swished the bloody residue around in my mouth before I spat it out. My bones and muscled ached as I held myself up. The two guys began walking towards me with darkness in their eyes. After a few failed attempts, a small spark of fire combusted in my hand.

Iceman held his hand and shot me down with a flurry. I grabbed my arm where I was hit, hissed, and quickly removed it from the bruise that was so cold it burned.

I turned over on my back and realized something with my body didn't feel right — something somewhere was broken. As I twisted my body in pain, I noticed water form a small puddle. I tilted my head back to see the feet of both guys getting closer to me.

I forced myself up again but was too weak to hold steady. The two guys powered up and I failed to light a fire. Behind the two goons was Hudson. His eyes were sealed tight, his teeth clenched, his face a circus of wrinkles. The shirt on his body was shredded, exposing his godly physique; his hand was forced into a fist, his knuckles white.

Hudson whispered something to himself before he howled, unleashing a water attack at Iceman's chest. The attack encased his body in water then entered his nose and mouth, causing his stomach, arms, and legs to swell. He fell to his knees, a stream of fluid coming out of his eyes like tears before his face hit the dirt.

Storm clouds moved in. Lighting sparkled in the sky. Thunder crashed in the distance. A small funnel raced down where Jessica was buried and freed her.

As she climbed from the debris, the lightning guy stood over me laughing mockingly. I looked up to his menacing smile as he held a sparky hand over my face.

As the energy in his hand sparked a few times before collecting to kill me, water spurted up around his hands; his body seized and blood leaked from his ears before he collapsed. Hudson stood behind him.

"No more games, Marcus. This ends now!" Jessica yelled. Her walk shifted to a run that ended with her flying towards me. Hazardous winds protected her. I shuffled back. I caught glimpse of Monica, who was still holding on to the tree, and told her goodbye with my eyes.

Jessica held a hand out, summoning winds that gently tossed me around. She held another hand out that conjured a twister that followed her, then, she froze. She looked around in confusion, the twister faded into thin air.

"Hurry, Marc! I can't hold her much longer," Dylan's tight voice cried out.

He was using the side of the building to hold himself up, his free hand aimed at Jessica.

I ignored the pain and found the strength to stand. Fire grew in my palm and I punched her across the jaw, knocking her out of the sky.

She stood and went after Dylan. The first two fireballs I hurled missed but the third one hit her shoulder; she slid across the mud. She flipped over, looked into the sky, and then shot up into the air. I looked to Dylan then went after her.

"Time to die, Macchiato," she said from behind.

My body got warm and flames sprouted through my jeans and shirt. We rushed each other and our hands locked to the other's forearms. A gust of wind came from behind her. A flame burst from my arms and traveled down to my hands. Her screams were a beautiful symphony.

"It's Marcus," I said and tossed her back down.

I landed and the flames died, leaving me almost naked.

I checked on Monica first. I had some explaining to do. Hachi was the closest to Monica. I helped her to her feet and positioned her next to Monica. I wobbled over to Dylan next.

"You saved the day, bro," I said to him, putting his arm around my shoulder as I moved him towards Hachi and Monica.

"It was all you, Marc. You never quit." He spoke with his eyes close almost like he was sleep talking.

"It was all of us." I looked around. "We're a team. Look down, bro."

Dylan opened one eye and looked down at his arm. "Finally."

"We finally fit in. I guess you're Xarponian after all."

Hachi walked off. "You guys go home before this place gets flooded with police and reporters."

I staggered over to the goons. Hudson really did a number on them.

I wasn't sure where Jessica landed, but I'm sure she didn't survive that.

"Guess we have some explaining to do," Dylan said to Monica.

"Save it for a rainy day," she said. "Marcus, you're my hero."

It was that moment when she wrapped her arms around me that everything I've ever felt for her came rushing back in a giant wave, and the physical pain temporary evaporated.

Chapter 26
Eighteen Years of Lies

The minor injuries were easy to bounce back from. It was the broken bones and nasty bruises that would take longer. On second thought, I wasn't too sure since I was still figuring out what our bodies could do. Hudson and Hachi rested at a nearby hotel in Poughkeepsie for a few days before returning to Jersey. It must be nice to have a family of Xarponians and not have to lie about battle wounds and not coming home for days. Marcus and I's lie: football. They believed me, Marcus, not so much.

Dalton was being a good little helper by making me peanut butter and jelly sandwiches in bed. Mom pried on the fact I wore long sleeve shirts around the house all day. Not that heat really affected me, but I wasn't going to show her my cool new tattoo that I wasn't used to yet. It started at my wrist and spiked angelically up the forearm approximately three inches. Marcus' went up just a bit higher.

Ten days passed since the battle. After my forth sandwich for the day before noon, I left the house for the first time to meet Monica and Marcus at the park.

"Hey, Dylan." She sounded calm like she saw people move objects with their mind and shoot fire from their hands on a daily basis.

Marcus was next to her on the bench and it was obvious I interrupted something.

"Hey, bro," Marcus said smoothly. His right arm was in a sling, wearing a cut-off shirt, his brand glistening from the sun and body lotion.

"Nice tattoo," I said. He smiled and took a second to admire it. I exhaled as I took a seat next to Monica. "So I guess you figured out our big dark secret."

"Yeah … I'm not afraid or anything, but at the same time, you don't see this everyday. I'm honestly just relieved to be alive. But, you guys *do* have some explaining to do." Her head shifted between the two of us as she spoke. Marcus and I both looked past her to each other.

"Do you want to tell her or should I?" I asked. Marcus nodded his head and began talking.

"About a year ago, Dylan and I started to go through, well … changes."

"What kind of changes?" Monica gripped the bench between her legs like she didn't know where the story was going to lead.

"Things would get hot and sometimes set on fire around me."

"And my eyes were turning blue," I added.

"I knew I saw you with blue eyes that day in the hallway." She bumped me with a smile of certainty on her face. My ribs ached slightly.

"So basically, Dylan has these ice powers, and I have these fire powers," Marcus continued.

"But why — how?" Monica asked.

"That's what we wanted to find out. A little after my eighteenth birthday I decided to find my birth parents but instead, I found the family secret. A secret that revealed to us the story of our powers and the reason why we were being attacked."

I jumped to my feet and cut Marcus off. I knew he was going to talk all day if we let him. "So what he's *trying* to say is that we're descendants of some ancient alien race of people who are *still* fighting some thousands of years old war here on Earth." I bounced around, waving my hands wildly as I spoke.

"I was trying to put it in a way that wouldn't scare her off, Dylan," Marcus said, his eyes telling me to be seated.

I took a seat. "Oops."

Monica laughed at our stupidity. "I'm not scared, guys, don't worry. I still see you two as the same old Marcus and Dylan. Now, can you explain to me the psychopathic Jessica and her henchmen?"

"Well—" Marcus started before I jumped in again.

"Jessica's dad was killed by Marcus' dad and she wanted revenge by taking his head off," I said.

He sucked his teeth and shook his head. "I thought we agreed that I would talk?"

"Go ahead." I waved the floor to him.

"My dad killed her dad and she was looking for revenge."

"Eh, same thing I just said, Marc."

She giggled then asked, "Does anybody else know about you guys?"

"Trey," Marcus said.

"Correction, Trey knows about *your* powers. Mine are still a secret," I said.

"Well, if you guys are worried about me telling, don't be," Monica said.

"Thanks, Monica," Marcus said, reaching for her hand. I don't think he really noticed how tight he was holding on to her. She looked up at him and smiled, but he didn't notice that either.

"Well, guys, let's hope this is all over." Monica stood up; Marcus followed. "I need to get back home and get some rest."

Monica walked off and Marcus and I headed to his house.

"Hey, Elias," I said as we walked into the house.

"Hey. Sup." He walked right past us and out the front door. My eyes followed him in disbelief.

"Ignore him," Marcus said. "Elias thinks he's cool now that he's in high school."

"He's not cooler than me, eh, eh?" I smiled, hoping to get a reaction out of Marcus.

It was a fail.

"Funny." His stoic tone and raspy voice were a bad blend. He grabbed us some sodas and we headed out for a seat in the backyard.

"So can you answer me this question?" I asked, slowly stroking my chin.

"Riddle me," Marcus replied, looking off into the sky.

"I still can't seem to put together why *I* can do this." The soda floated from his hand to mine.

He looked at me, and I handed him the soda back.

"I don't know, Dylan. Maybe we'll find the answers for that later in the years to come. It was smart of you to call Hudson and Hachi to meet us there. Pretty sure we'd be dead without them."

"Well, we were *supposed* to have more help. Imani promised me she would be there."

"You know you can't rely on her when it comes to battles that aren't hers."

"Yeah, well, we could have really used her help out there."

"What did she say when you asked her about it?"

"I haven't talked to her since that day. She won't answer my phone calls or text messages. But moving on, how's Delilah doing?"

"She's doing good. Back in London. We've been communicating by E-mail mostly."

I fought the grin that slowly formed.

"Why are you looking at me like that?" he said.

"Nothing." I flung my head up.

He sighed. "Let's hear it."

"Sparks flaring back up between you and Monica?"

"Mind your business."

"Dude, you're my bro, you can tell me. You know *all* my secrets."

Not really all…

"I think I want to be … I know I want to be with Monica, but I also want to be with Delilah. I've never had so much fun with anyone like I have with Delilah. She's so spontaneous and witty and that accent is…"

"Sexy." I finished.

"Sexy. And Monica, well she just has the biggest, purest heart. I've never met anyone so caring, and the feeling I get when I'm around her is indescribable."

"Sounds like you need to make a choice, and fast, or feelings will get hurt."

His head dropped. "Someone's feelings are already going to be hurt."

"That's why you have the summer to figure this all out." I stood. "I'm going home to spend some time with my family." I started for the back door when he called out—

"Hey, bro," I turned around to him smiling. "Remember how we wished for a college adventure?"

"Yeah."

"We gotta be more careful what we wish for."

When I got home, there were still a few things I needed to move out of my car. I popped the trunk and grabbed the duffels, book bag, and a small box. I sat everything down and turned around to close the trunk when I noticed something stuck under the jumper cables. I reached in and pulled out one of Marcus' journals. It must have fallen out his satchel when I dropped his things off.

I pulled my phone out, scrolled for his number, but stopped before I made the call. I stared curiously at the screen with his name on it. I shoved the phone back into my pocket, picked my things up, and walked into the house.

"Need some help with that?" Dalton asked when I walked inside.

"No, I got it." I went straight to my room, dropped everything, and closed the door.

My fingers brushed the smooth edges of the leather journal that Marcus would never let me read alone. The condition was neat which led me to believe it was one of the newer ones.

I cracked it open and flipped through the pages one good time. It had the woodsy scent of Marcus' dorm room. The book was about half full and the beginning was in another language. I stopped on one the pages towards the end that was written in English.

> *This will be my last entry. The world is after me so I know what I am doing is the right thing. I still can't believe myself for this situation. I didn't have a choice to do what I did but it was the only way. Katiana would kill me if she knew what I did but it's already done. Not a soul on Earth knows but her, him, the nun, and me. I wish I had time to get to know him but I had to let him*

go. My sweet innocent first born, take care Dylan. Daddy loves you move than you will EVER know. ~Ferrari~

I inhaled, shut the book, and threw it away from me. This couldn't be right. That couldn't be me he was talking about. *No way.* Mixed emotions were going on inside and I was sick to my stomach at the thought of all the lies I've potentially been told.

If this was correct. If what was in that book was correct. If I'm that same Dylan on the pages, then Marcus was really…

My brother.

www.ingramcontent.com/pod-product-compliance
Lightning Source LLC
Chambersburg PA
CBHW021224250626
47155CB00008B/2919